THE LEGEND OF SPEEDY

Joe Dale said: "You know how it is. This here Speedy, he's a streak of greased lightning with his hands and he can talk seven languages with them. Plain boxing, plain catch-as-catch-can wrestling, that's all right with me. I take 'em on, big or small. I don't much care. I handle myself pretty good, and I've had some experience even if I ain't Methuselah. But you know. He starts a lot of stuff that I never heard of. By the way, how come that he got the guns of yourself and Buck Masters, all in one day? Was that an accident?"

"The way it happened...," began One-Eyed Mike. Then he paused and looked dourly at his companion.

"Yeah, I can guess how it happened," said Joe Dale.

"All right, you guess and maybe you won't be so far wrong," admitted Mike Doloroso. "He kind of has an extra set of brains in each hand, I guess."

—From "Seven-Day Lawman"

MAX BRAND®

FLAMING FORTUNE

LEISURE BOOKS NEW YORK CITY

A LEISURE BOOK®

January 2006

Published by special arrangement with Golden West Literary Agency.

Dorchester Publishing Co., Inc.
200 Madison Avenue
New York, NY 10016

ISBN 0-8439-5444-2

Visit us on the web at www.dorchesterpub.com.

FLAMING FORTUNE

TABLE OF CONTENTS

THE CAÑON COWARD

I
Another Big Man

How I first met with Harry Clonnell was like this. There was seven of us from the Y Bar, counting in Phil Raeburn himself, that was riding the range not for cows, but for The Doctor. That was right after the time when The Doctor had robbed the Oregon Express and got away with something like a quarter of a cold million, and gents was wild to nail him. The express company was weeping, it was so mad, and every day it boosted the reward a little. In all the cow towns—because I was pretty sure that The Doctor was hiding somewhere on the range—the boys got together and swore that they wouldn't go to work again until they'd cleared up The Doctor and saved the honor of the range. So here was the seven of us from the Y Bar burning up a lot of miles and horseflesh and getting nowhere in particular on the day that I rode into Harry Clonnell, and all the awful trouble that he pulled down on us.

I was riding Billy McGee, my best cutting horse. Billy worked his way through the underbrush of a gully like he was soft-footing it through a night herd, not making no

3

more noise than a cat, you might say. I was watching sharp, or I never would have seen Clonnell.

Not that I really expected that I would find The Doctor, you understand, but partly because, in a time like that, the hunting gets to be a game and you keep your eyes open because you're playing pretend like a kid. Partly, too, because, when a gent was hunting for The Doctor, even if the chances were a million to one against finding him, you had to look sharp. You wouldn't ride through brush after a grizzly without all your eyes open, before and behind. So I sneaked Billy McGee along, him hardly breathing, and all the while I was raking the shadows from side to side looking for the picture of The Doctor that was before all our eyes—a biggish man with a pair of horn-rimmed spectacles that gave him an owlish look like a medical man, you understand, and a little, pointed gray beard that finished off the picture. All at once I come out into an open patch, and there I seen a gent lying on his face, with his head in his arms, and the speckles of sunshine falling yellow all over him through the trees.

It gave me a start, I can tell you. Because, by the look of the big, powerful shoulders and the big head of that gent, I sort of figured that I *had* bumped into The Doctor, after all. I unlimbered my Winchester, and I tucked the butt of it into the hollow of my shoulder. I was ready to make trouble, you had better believe.

"Stand up!" I said to him, real mean.

He lifted his head. There was no big spectacles, and there was no pointed, gray beard. I felt myself fifteen thousand dollars poorer and a lot less famous than I had hoped to be. This was just a smooth-faced young gent about twenty-five, say, good-looking and lazy-looking.

"Hello!" I said, meaner than ever, I was so disappointed.

He got up and stretched himself. And there was a good deal of him to stretch.

"What are you doing down here in the brush?" I asked. His answer dazed me a little.

"Hunting for The Doctor," he said. "What are you doing?"

I mean his answer staggered me because he wasn't the sort of a gent that you would have picked out for hard or dangerous work. Over in the corner of the clearing, there was a run-down, skinny horse with a funny neck and a dull eye, picking at the grass. There was a ragged saddle lying not far off, but, high and low, there wasn't any sign of a gun about this guy.

"Are you going to catch him like a mosquito, on the fly, and with your bare hands?" I asked him.

"Me? Catch the Doctor?" he said. "And how could I do that when I don't pack a gun?"

"You said you was hunting him?" I suggested, getting a little more puzzled every minute.

He stretched and yawned again. He was a biggish man, as I've said before, but still he didn't look like much. I mean he didn't look a bit hard. He was wearing what had once been a pretty natty-looking suit of clothes—smart but cheap, you know. Now all of the smartness was wore off of them, so they was just plain cheap, and not very clean. All the same, he had a dash of smartness about him, too. He had on a green necktie, and he wore a dirty gray felt hat pushed back on his head. He had a careless, shiftless, lazy sort of a smile when he looked at you. Brush him up a bit, and I would have said that he was the sort of a man that would have pleased the ladies a good deal. But hunt for The Doctor? No, not in a million years!

"Yes, I'm hunting for The Doctor," he repeated. "I'm hunting for him, but I don't intend to do the fighting. If I

5

can locate his trail . . . why, then I'll just call in some of the real fighting men, like you, to finish him off."

I narrowed my eyes to consider his face as he said that. For a quarter of a minute, I thought that maybe the loafer was trying to see if he couldn't string me a little.

"What's your name?" I snapped at him.

"Harry Clonnell," he said.

"Clonnell, I'm Joe Riggs," I informed him.

I waited for that name to sink in because I was pretty well known to the boys in these parts at that time. I had done my share of gun work in the days when guns was of frequent assistance in making your living and saving what you made.

"Joe Riggs?" said the big gent. "Joe Riggs? Oh, you're the man of Chihuahua?"

It pleased me a good deal. Like when a hotel clerk in a strange town recognizes you. I dunno why it is that being recognized is so nice. Not that I ever done anything really famous, but, after all, that scrap down in Chihuahua and the way that I got out of town afterward was not so bad. Well, it let down most of my suspicions, when he said that.

"I thought maybe that you was kidding me, Clonnell," I said.

"Kidding you?" Clonnell repeated. "You?" As if he would as soon have kidded a cannon ball.

That pleased me, too, and I begun to feel right friendly to this stranger. "But tell me," I said, "what clue you're following that brought you down here on The Doctor's trail?"

"It's a long story," he stated.

"I'm patient," I responded.

"Well," he began, "I was always rather good at finding things. So when they ran the reward for The Doctor up to

6

near twenty thousand dollars . . . why, I had to take the trail. Because, even if I couldn't find his trail, I'd get my share of the money, wouldn't I?"

I had to agree, and I had to smile, too. He didn't seem to mind the smile, although it would have made most men on the range start right in fighting.

He only said: "It's been a pretty hard job. My horse wasn't up to much."

"You talk like you'd actually found something," I said.

He smiled. "I think I have," he said.

"Heavens, man!" I snapped at him. "Found something about The Doctor . . . and then go to sleep?"

"Speed would never beat him," said Clonnell. "Only brains. I lay down to think . . . and I went to sleep, instead."

He was sort of like a child, in a way. But he was always as willing to smile at himself, as he was to let others smile at him.

"You went to sleep!" I shouted at him. "But . . . well, what did you think that you found?"

He pointed to a sandy strip in the clearing. "You see where the fire was built?" he asked.

As a matter of fact, I didn't see at all.

But he was interested in what he was saying, and he didn't wait for an answer. "When I saw that part of that sand was a little darker than the rest, I guessed that a fire had been built there," he went on. "And when I saw how the fire had been put out and moved away, I suspected that it might have been made by The Doctor. It's just his style. Brains enough to deceive everyone except a fellow who really has a clear eye in his head, you know. I happen to see as straight as any man in the world."

He said it so easy and natural that you couldn't help believing him. I looked at him again. Well, he didn't seem much of a man, according to the standards that I had set up for myself all of my life, but, all the same, there is a need for different kinds of everything in this world. You want a bulldog for fighting, but you want a hound for a trail. The same with men. Some good for one thing, and some for another.

I said: "You seen that a fire was built there, and what of that?"

"I guessed that The Doctor might have made that fire, because as I say, it was put out pretty cleverly . . . and unless your attention was called to it, you would hardly know that a fire had been there," he remarked.

I had to admit that was right. As a matter of fact, I still could hardly be sure that one patch of the sand was any darker than the rest. Just then Clonnell stirred up some sand with his toe, and, leaning, he picked up a bit of something dark, crumbled it between his thumb and forefinger, and then blew it away in a little black puff of smoke. Charcoal! That was proof enough that he was right. A fire *had* been built on this sand.

From that moment I was ready to take off my hat to Clonnell—in a certain way.

II
A Born Trailer

I remember that just then there was a streak of something bright above, and I looked up at a blue jay flashing across the clearing, fast and low. When I looked back, it seemed to me that Clonnell was watching me pretty close and curious—or had been while my eyes was turned away. It gave me a rather queer feeling. I mean, if a fellow has a power or sight that can see so much about a strip of sand where a fire has been made, how much can he read when he looks into the face and the soul of a human being?

That fire had been put out so careful and the sign of it had been removed so well, that I think there wasn't another man in the world, outside of Clonnell and maybe one or two great Indian trackers, that could have noticed the thing. Yes, Clonnell was different from the rest of us, and my interest and my curiosity got bigger all of the time.

"I thought that I would look around in the sand, then," went on Clonnell, "because I hoped that there might be some sign worthwhile. After I had worked around in the stuff for a little time, I did get something that ought to be worthwhile."

Well, I was paralyzed, I was so interested. I could hardly breathe.

"Go on, kid," I urged.

"Well," he said, "you tell me first about how many men this fellow, The Doctor, may have killed?"

"Thirty-two, the count is, I think," I said.

"Thirty-two," he echoed, and his face fell.

"What's wrong?" I asked.

"Because I didn't think that it was more than half as many as that," he answered.

"Well, what has that got to do with what you found out?"

"It has everything to do with it," said Clonnell. "Because here's the thing." He took out a little piece of bone, and he handed it to me. I recognized it at once. It was about half of the inner curve of a bone handle for a revolver. The outer part had been burned away.

"Well," I said, "this looks like the unlucky devil that made the fire you're talking about dropped a gun into it. The Doctor would never have been fool enough to do that."

"No?" he said. "Well, I think differently about it. We all have our separate opinions about such things, you know."

That was fair, and that was right, as I couldn't help agreeing.

"But what has this to do with the number of men that The Doctor may have killed?" I asked him.

"Look again," he said.

I did look again, and this time I could solve the riddle. In the inside of that piece of bone there was filed a little row of notches. I counted them up. There were nineteen. Nineteen men had been killed by the man who had owned the gun of which this was a part. Nineteen! In that part of the world where everybody wore a gat and knew how to use it. Where even a fourteen-year-old kid could kill his man if he got half a chance. Nineteen scalps! Well, it fair made my hair lift and the cold sweat stand on me as I looked back to Clonnell.

"I thought," he was saying, "that nineteen was about what The Doctor might have killed. And so I thought that was his gun . . . and that I was really on the trail. But, of course, if he's killed thirty-two, then it means that I'm all wrong."

"Thirty-two? What do I know about that except the gossip?" I said. "But what I do know is that there ain't anybody else that's got even nineteen to his credit. Nobody but The Doctor. And it's a sure and certain fact that this here must have been his gun."

Of course, that was as clear as you could wish. It was The Doctor's gun, and a chill ran through me, so that I could hardly hold it. I could call up in my mind's eye the face with the short, gray beard and the big spectacles—all the devilishness of such a scholarly sort of a man being a real ruffian and killer.

Yes, it seemed to me that the fiend was watching me out of the shadows. All at once I had a powerful craving for the open air and the sunshine again . . . tons of boiling hot sun, and the perspiration of an honest horse in my nostrils.

But Clonnell seemed very pleased. "Do you really think that I've hit the right trail, then?" he said.

"You've hit it," I told him. "Except that I don't see how a fellow like The Doctor could have burned a gun by mistake."

"Perhaps it wasn't a mistake," said the kid.

I blinked, of course.

"Perhaps he wanted to get rid of the gun, nineteen

notches, and all. What difference does his gun make to him? Any gun would do for him. But the nineteen notches might give him away, you see?"

There was plain sense in that. More and more I felt that this kid had something to him.

"And if I'm right," he went on, "it seems to me that the proper thing for us to do is to get right on the trail and try to run it down."

I looked at him a little helpless, when he said that.

"All right," I said. "We'll hit the trail, if you think that we can find it."

He nodded, and in another minute, beginning at the point where the fire had been, he began to work in circles, widening out, and stepping along smooth and soft, like a fellow that knew exactly what he wanted to do. I cut for sign myself, but this brush sort of beat me. Because my work was usually out on the open range and the sign I followed rarely led into the brush, I didn't expect to find anything, and I didn't, but I had a mean feeling, all the time, that somewhere out of the shadows The Doctor might be watching us, grinning to himself, and getting ready to count off numbers twenty and twenty-one to add to his score. Not that I expected to be shot in the back, because, to give The Doctor credit, he always fought perfectly fair and gave the other fellow an even break. But what good would better than an even break be to me against The Doctor, even if I was shooting as straight and as fast as I had been that time in Chihuahua? No, I didn't want The Doctor's game or any part of it. Just when I'd about made up my mind to that, I hear the kid sing out: "Here's something again!"

"Don't talk so loud, you fool," I muttered under my breath, and I sneaked over to where he had sung out.

He was down on his knees between two trees, and,

when I came up, he pointed to a big, flat leaf, lifted it, and I seen a place where a knee had sunk deep into the soft ground.

"He was there, on his knees, about two or three hours ago," said the kid.

"Why two or three hours?" I asked him.

"Look at the blades of grass," he said. "They're still bent, but they're beginning to straighten themselves. It would take two or three hours for the sap to begin running in them again after they'd been squashed down like that."

I took a good look at the kid out of the corner of my eye. This was a kind of trailing that I'd heard about, but I'd never seen it before.

"And what would that mean," I asked, "outside of the fact that he's now three hours away?"

"Well, why would he kneel here?" asked the kid.

"To rest, I suppose," I said, "or to tie his shoe."

The kid shook his head and smiled. Not a mean smile, but pleasant and with his eyes twinkling. "No," he said, "nobody was ever heavy enough to make that deep a dent while he was tying his shoe. If you doubt it, put your knee to the ground there."

I did it, and I have to admit that I didn't sink very deep. I stood up again and swore a little. "What was he doing here, then?" I asked him.

"Well, something that made his knee sink deep," said the kid.

"What could that have been?" I further inquired.

"Lifting something, say?" the kid suggested.

"What the mischief would he want to be lifting?" I asked.

He pointed to a big rock, just in front of the impression.

13

"Lift?" I sneered. "Could anybody lift that?"

"The Doctor is pretty strong," said the kid. "But maybe you could lift the rock yourself."

I tried it. I have a pair of arms that no man need be ashamed of, but I couldn't budge that rock. Then I said: "Besides, what sense would there be in his wanting to lift that stone?"

"How should I know?" asked the kid. "I'm following a trail, not reading a mind." He got in position on one knee right in front of the rock. "I'll take a heave myself," he said. He laid hold. The muscles bunched over his shoulders, his coat seams creaked, and up came the rock. It told me what looked like plumpness on him was just all muscle. Every minute I was beginning to respect this kid more, even if he didn't pack a gun.

"Hello," I said, "here's something where the stone was resting."

I reached down and fished it up. With the dirt shook off, I seen that it was a strong canvas bag. There was a clinking inside as it moved, and, when I jerked the string away that tied the mouth of the sack, I found myself looking down into a face of glimmering little yellow lights.

There was a whole ocean of fives and tens and twenty-dollar gold pieces.

III
An Enigma

I took up a year's wages in the hollow of my hand and turned to the kid. There was a devil in me that said: "Why not tap him on the head and walk away with this stuff?" I weighed the sack. It seemed over fifty pounds, and that would mean close to six thousand dollars, if the stuff was all gold coins. Six thousand dollars! Those was not the days when every town had its millionaire. Dollars meant something, then. You could buy a house and a two-hundred-acre farm with that much money, and enough horses and stuff to work it, too. I had always hankered after a farm of my own.

I looked at the kid with the devil in my heart; but he didn't seem to guess that I might have any bad ideas. He simply said: "Well, we got something away from him. We've made a start, I suppose. Now maybe we'll be able to shoot for the whole wad!"

That brought me back to The Doctor. I'd pretty near forgot about him, so now I started, and I said: "We're on the trail of The Doctor. I'll tell you what we'll do! I'll call in the other boys in the party, and the whole of us will cut

15

for sign again and try to pick him up, although it looks to me like we got very small chances of finding him. The Doctor knows how to use a three-hour start, and he's left this heavy stuff behind him so that it wouldn't weigh down his wings."

There was sense in that, but the kid suggested that I go ahead with him.

"And why should I?" I asked him. "Do I want to run into The Doctor single-handed? And what good would you be, without a gun?"

He seemed to see the point of that, not that he got sore, but he agreed that I was right and that he was wrong. So I rode on out of the woods and seen old Phil Raeburn himself cutting across the top of a hill not far away. I caught his ear with a gunshot, and, at that signal, he fired a couple of times himself to call in the rest of the boys. Then we all streaked back into the woods, with me telling them at the top of my lungs just what had happened.

We got to the spot where I had left Clonnell, and there he was, stretched out in a spot half shadow and half sun and taking things easy with a cigarette hanging from his mouth. He got up and met Raeburn and the rest of the boys. Raeburn was in a rare stew. There had never been nothing that he loved so well as a fight, and the chance of rounding up The Doctor pleased him a lot, I can tell you.

As for the six thousand in hard cash that we had got, Raeburn hardly gave it a glance. He'd made so much in the last few years in El Paso del Tigre that money was just dirt to him. It was The Doctor that he wanted.

He said: "Clonnell, you've started a fine piece of work, this day. If you can help us to finish it, you'll have a place in history. Get your horse, and help us work out this trail."

Clonnell got his horse, but when the chief saw it, he let out a yell.

"Do you call that a horse? One of you boys take the gold back to the house and change horses with Clonnell. Joe, you take the gold and change horses."

Perhaps I'd ought to have felt happy because it was a sign that the old man trusted me even with that much money and partly, also, because I had the second best horse in the party. But I wasn't ready for that sort of a compliment. If there was to be a party that might round up The Doctor, I wanted to be in on it. He was too much for me alone. But with five of the Y Bar outfit along, we'd be too much for any gunfighter that ever breathed.

I started to complain, but I didn't really need to just yet because Clonnell said: "I'll tell you, Mister Raeburn. Argonaut and I have traveled around so much together that I'm used to him and he's used to me. I wouldn't feel at home on any other horse." He swung into the saddle on the back of that old cartoon of a horse that pricked up its ears and tried to look like the real thing in wild mustangs—only it couldn't.

Raeburn exploded again. "Clonnell," he said, "you're going to ruin everything. You've got the eye for a trail. You've uncovered his tracks. We got to depend on you. But how can we get near The Doctor and the sort of horse that he rides when you hold us back on that kind of a brute?"

"Does he look as bad as that?" Clonnell asked in his gentle way. "As a matter of fact, he's not so bad. He can keep up a jog for a good, long time. And as for Joe Riggs's horse . . . well, guns and mean horses were always out of my line."

Why, you could see the face of Raeburn wither up in contempt and anger. He turned blue with it, for he was a fellow that had built up his fortune by knowing how to pick fighting men and then using them to clear the rustlers

17

and the yeggs out of their old stamping grounds along El Paso del Tigre. He bought that range for ten cents an acre because the rustlers had always swept it clean, and he used his fighting men to turn the tables and make the rustlers hate our section of the country. You can imagine what he thought of Clonnell. But he didn't say anything. There's no use calling a coward by his right name when you have to use him.

He simply said: "Riggs, take the gold back to the house. Clonnell, we're wasting time. Come ahead and uncover the trail for us."

I would have argued with Raeburn to send somebody else back with the money and let me go on with the party, but I didn't dare. I could see that all the bad humor in the old boy was just gathering head. He only wanted some sort of an excuse to give a good scolding to somebody. So I watched Clonnell take the lead and saw the gang head away into the brush, and listened to the sound of their horses dying out. Then I started back for headquarters.

I cheered up, after I'd got started. Because it was pretty sure that no matter how clever in the head Clonnell might have been, he could never get enough pace out of that nag of his to come close to The Doctor. A hundred times posses had come close to that crook, and a hundred times he'd breezed away from them and slipped through their hands. This job would be just another case of it.

I felt better when I topped the hill and looked down into the hollow at the house. It was always a picture that done your eyes good. I've said that Raeburn had made a big fortune out of his range in the pass. When he decided to make a home that would be worthy of his money and good enough to please his daughter, he didn't spare the coin. He built a place big enough for a prince, all out of 'dobe bricks, Spanish style, with a red roof, and a cracking garden, and a patio that was something to dream about but never to expect to find on earth. It looked cheerful in February, and it looked cool in August. When the chief saw the place, he said—and I heard him—"Even Dolly will like to call this home!"

Well, I sashayed down toward the house, and, before I got to it, Dolly come out of a draw riding one of her Thoroughbreds and with the big wolf dog, Samson, running along to the side.

I got to stop here a moment. When I call her Dolly, maybe you get a picture out of that name of a pink and white pretty girl with a lot of golden curls, and dimples, and such like. Which is everything that she was not. She had only one dimple, and that was in only one cheek. She wasn't pretty—she was beautiful. But she had her father's black hair and black eyes, and, when I say that her horses scared even me, you get maybe a different idea from your first picture of her. This yarn has mostly to do with The Doctor and Clonnell and Dolly. So you should mark her down and underline her as important.

She come breezing by me, and then she pulled rein when she seen that it was me. She gave me a smile and a wave of her hand. At the wave of her hand, her chestnut tried to poke its head through the center of the sky, and, failing in that, he tried to stand on his head, and after that he just done a little first-rate bucking.

"That horse'll kill you some day, Dolly," I told her, when she'd mastered him.

She was white and her eyes was big and dark, not with fear, but with pain and shock, because that horse had been giving her a terrible beating. But now she smiled at me. She was always especially nice to me, because I was the ugliest and the meanest of all the hands on that rough ranch.

"He needs a little more exercise," she said. "I don't have enough time to keep my string working."

"How can you keep ten devils like him worked out?" I asked her.

"I wouldn't give a pinch of salt for a horse with no devil in him. I want the brand on the skin of my horse, Joe, and not in his heart," she said.

She had a neat way of putting things. She was smart, was Dolly. But more than that, she was honest, and, when I looked at those black eyes of hers, I knew that she meant what she said. She liked a fighting horse for the sake of the fight and not for the sake of the horse.

"You've given up The Doctor again, I see?" she went on.

"No," I said, "I've brought home a part of him."

She waited for me to explain, so I held out the canvas bag and shook up the gold coins. It startled even Dolly. "You've actually found some of his loot?" she cried.

"I didn't find it, but it was found by the queerest gent that even you, Dolly, would ever want to see in your whole life."

There was a flash of light across her eyes, like the passing of a lamp fast across a black window at night.

"Tell me!" commanded Dolly.

IV
A Threat Brought Home

I have to make a stop here to think back to things a little. What was it that made Clonnell so much in the eyes of Dolly? Was it maybe something that I said to her about him in the first place? It may have been that. Still, I only told the truth.

"Tell you about him?" I repeated. "No, I can't. You got to see him. Telling won't turn the trick."

"Try," said Dolly.

You had to do what Dolly told you to try. She was that way.

"He's a young man," I said, "maybe not more than twenty-five, stronger in the hands than any man I ever seen, and better at a trail than the slickest old Indian that you ever heard of, and dressed to look like a sort of second-hand dude, and hating guns and mean horses."

Dolly listened to this and frowned. "That doesn't seem to fit together," she said.

"No," I said, "it doesn't. His strength and his brains don't go with the lack of nerve in him. Matter of fact, Dolly, I suppose that he's a plain coward."

She shrugged her shoulders. "I don't believe it," said Dolly.

She didn't speak for a time, as we went on toward the house, but then she said: "There's a mystery about this Clonnell, and, if Dad brings him back to the house, I'll get at the bottom of it."

I smiled. I can't tell you why, but somehow the idea of anybody's being able to understand that young gent with his strange ways and his lazy smile seemed ridiculous to me. At the barn I got down and nearly had a leg taken off by Samson. I pulled a gun, and the devil of a brute backed away from me, snarling.

"Dolly," I told her, still covered with cold perspiration, "I'm going to have to kill that dog someday."

"Don't you do it," said Dolly. "Sampson is all right. He's only a one-man dog . . . and I like that kind best of all." She held up her hand, and Samson slunk up to her and squatted, watching her face, but with his lips snarled back and his eyes green.

"Do you know what he wants to do?" I asked.

"Tell me," said Dolly.

"He don't love you. He wants to cut your throat," I said.

She flashed a look at me, and then back to the dog—almost as though she was afraid that, if she didn't keep an eye on him, he would take a leap at her. One slash of those long fangs would about finish man or woman.

"Perhaps he does," said Dolly, "but the important thing is that he does what I tell him to do. Take my whip in, Samson." She held out her whip. Samson took it in his teeth and sneaked away toward the house, growling deeply in his throat. She passed a handkerchief across her face and took a deep breath.

"Dolly, you're afraid of him, yourself!" I couldn't help shouting it at her.

She looked at me, and, as she smiled, that one dimple played in and out in her cheek. Sometimes you would almost think that she was a man to hear her talk and see the fire in her eyes, but then there would come that dimpling smile and make you sort of dizzy and weak.

"I suppose that I am afraid of him," said Dolly. "Or better still . . . I respect him. I couldn't love a horse or a dog . . . or a man . . . without respecting him a little, Joe."

It would have beat you to hear her say it. But I could understand. I could understand better than most, because I knew what lay behind her. She was her father's daughter, and it wasn't so long ago, as years run, that Phil Raeburn had been known for one of the wildest gents that ever stepped into stirrups and pulled a gun. The things that he had done would have been the hanging of a dozen gents in any part of the world less wild than ours, and now the things that he had been doing was beginning to stand up and look him in the face out of the eyes of his daughter. Poor old Phil. I pitied him then, and I pity him now. But I never blamed him, and I never blamed her. They was just born with more power than they knew what to do with.

Take it all in all, I was pretty thoughtful after I left Dolly that day. She was like a storm in the offing all the time—you kept waiting for the thunder to start rolling and the lightning to begin to jump.

Along about the beginning of the dark, in comes the boys that had been riding the trail of The Doctor. They were dead beat, but they all agreed that the ride had been worthwhile and that of all the fine trailers in the world Clonnell was the best. He'd taken them right through that woods, and then away across the hills, following signs that they couldn't even see—and yet him not seeming to more than half try. He'd wound through the hills and all at once headed them straight south. They got to the edge of the river and there was the ferryman on the far side, with his boat sunk in the shallows. He told them that a big gent on a fast horse had been that way an hour before, and that, after getting himself ferried over, he'd paid the price of the ride and the boat, both, and sunk the boat.

There was nothing to do but for the boys to turn back. They were reasonable sure that it was The Doctor that had done that, and that Clonnell had been able to take them right along on the tracks of the crook.

"He's a bloodhound," said Shorty Meeghan to me. "The chief is going to keep him on and put him on the payroll, because he says that, if he can ever make Clonnell ride a fast horse, then the next time we take the trail of The Doctor, we'll sure have him as good as in our pockets. And I think so, too, and so would you, if you'd seen him canter his nag along, hardly looking at the ground, and yet sort of smelling out the way. It was a grand bit of work . . . and, Joe, ain't it a shame that he's a yellow hound?"

I agreed that it was. I couldn't help agreeing, too, that maybe we'd come across the fellow that would be able to put the finish on The Doctor. A trailer is born only once in ten years; and a perfect trailer comes along once in a century, I suppose.

About this time, along comes a message from the boss that he wanted me quick. I started in, and I went past the corral where Dolly was with one of her new buys in horse-flesh. It was a big gray devil, and, although Dolly had a rope and a snubbing post, that brute was giving her all that she could do. He was using his hoofs like a boxer's hands, and I wouldn't have been in the corral with him for a month's wages, if I could have dodged the job. But there was that girl tackling it for the fun of the thing.

No, she beat me. She beat me complete.

I went on into the house, and the chief called me right into his study. It was only a study by name, and not by use. The edges of the desk was all notched and blackened where cigarette and cigar butts had eaten in and taken a good, firm grip of the varnish and the wood. There was guns and horns and such things hanging on the walls, and not a sign of any books. But the chief had to have a room to himself, and the architect had called it a study, so what difference did it make if the bookshelves was used for gun racks?

The chief was in a stew again, but he usually was in a stew about something or other. When he seen me, he give me a glare and said: "Read this." Then he threw a letter at me.

I caught it on the wing, and, when I unfolded it out, I read:

Dear Raeburn:

Though I have done enough harm in various ways and to various people, I believe that I've never injured you. And you're the sort of a man who ought to have a little sympathy for men who don't ride by the straight and narrow way. I could ask you, for instance, how it happened that you ever got together enough money to start your cattle business, but I don't have to ask, Raeburn, because I know.

However, instead of showing me a little sympathetic understanding and, at least, turning your head the other way when I went by, you've done everything in your power to snag me.

You've sent out your best men on your fastest horses, time after time, to hunt me down, and you've financed and equipped your own posses for the sake of giving me a whirl.

25

I've endured it for a long time, but now I think that to stop your fire, I've got to get to the root of it.

I intend to pay you a visit, and, when I come, Raeburn, I'm going to hurt you in the worst possible way, if I can. Just how I haven't figured out as yet. Perhaps a bullet would be complete enough.

In the meantime, I present my compliments,

The Doctor

This was all written out fine and neat on a typewriter, without no mistakes, and it was signed the same way, but it never occurred to me or to the chief to doubt but that it must have come from The Doctor himself. There was something cold and reserved and thoughtful about it that seemed to show he had wrote it and sent it. When I finished reading it, I folded it up and looked at the chief very blank.

"Well, Joe?" said Phil Raeburn, biting at the wrong end of a cigar.

"I dunno," I said.

"Man, that's always the way with you. All right for little things, but you always fail in a pinch. And this is a pinch," he said.

I looked at him trying to light the wrong end of the cigar. "Well, Phil," I told him, "you can take a dozen extra hands and keep them watchful. But maybe that would do no good."

"No good?" shouted Raeburn. "What do you mean?"

I didn't answer, and pretty soon Raeburn answered for himself.

"Yes," he said, "The Doctor always finds a way to do what he wants. Joe, I wouldn't give a damaged nickel for my life."

V
Love at First Sight

Why, when you come down to it, neither would I. The Doctor's record was a lot too long and too perfect. He'd never been beaten, and I looked on Phil Raeburn as a dead man.

"Well," said Raeburn, "we won't sit still and wait for the lightning to hit us, anyway. We'll go out and meet it halfway, eh?"

I didn't see what he meant, but he began to stride up and down the room, still sweating, and still stopping now and then to try to light the wrong end of that cigar. It would only fume for a moment, and then go out.

He said: "Wait here, and I'll go mad. No, I'm going to strike back! I've got to strike back, Joe."

Still I waited to find out what he meant.

I only said: "Sure, it's fine to speak about striking out at him, but how are you going to know where he may be? It's hard to hit a single wasp when it's on the wing . . . but it ain't hard for the single wasp to hit you."

"Am I back in school in the first grade, maybe?" yelled Phil Raeburn, and he stopped and stamped, and damned his cigar that wouldn't work.

"All right," I said, because I liked Phil enough to take a lot of bad language from him, "all right, you have it your own way. Only . . . how are you going to locate him to hit him back? I'd like to know that."

"Ain't God put the weapon in my hands, Joe?" cried Phil, his voice squeaking a bit with his excitement. "Ain't God brought this here Clonnell to me just when I needed him? How else could you work it out, if God didn't mean for Clonnell to be useful to me?"

I didn't talk back. I ain't a church man. But I got a lot more faith in such like things than old Phil Raeburn ever did have. Only, Phil was superstitious, which I never was much. And Phil, when he got excited about things, was always pretty sure to drag in God by the heels and put the blame on Him and take the praise for himself. You hear Phil Raeburn talk, sometimes, and you would think that God was a sort of special agent for him.

"You're going to use Clonnell?" I echoed him.

"I tell you, old-timer," said Raeburn, "I got a big debt to you. Any ordinary cowpuncher would just have wrote this Clonnell down for a coward and let him go at that, but you had the sense to see that even a coward can be worth something."

"Is he really a coward?" I asked.

"Coward?" said Raeburn, his face wrinkling up with his disgust, "he's the worst that ever stepped in the skin of a man. I tell you, while we was on that trail, he would never ride first into a thicket or around a sharp corner of the trail. He stepped back and waved for some of the rest of us to go around first."

I could hardly believe that. Seemed as though shame would make any snake act better than that, but Raeburn swore that was the fact.

28

"All right, Raeburn. But you aim to use this sort of a gent against a person like The Doctor?" I asked.

"Take it easy, kid," said Phil Raeburn. "I didn't get you in here to think for me. I only wanted you to bounce ideas against and see how they felt coming back to me. Because, Joe, you was born to be wrong."

I didn't mind that. I just lay back in my chair and grinned at him. Me and Phil, we was pals.

"Go on and explain like I was five years old," I said.

"And how old did I take you for?" said the old man. He went on: "All that we got to do is to gentle down a couple of the best horses on the place, and, when we got a couple of them in fine shape for him, all as gentle as lambs, then we'll put this yaller hound on the back of them and teach him how to ride, and, after he's got accustomed to traveling on a decent horse, the first sign that we get of The Doctor, we'll head across the country for him, and we'll go on his trail with Clonnell to show us the way."

He said it like a man would say he had found a place where everything was sure to be gold.

"Is that the finish of everything?" I asked.

"It is," said Phil Raeburn. "The absolute finish, because why, I'll tell you . . . I've watched trailers most of my life. I've seen 'em good and bad and indifferent. I've seen the finest old Indian workers that ever hiked down the country following their noses. But I never seen nothing in the world like the way that this here gent, Clonnell, was able to cut across the country. He ain't no common man, and God made him weak in some ways because he's so strong in others."

He went on to expand and try to tell me how it was that Clonnell had led them the way across the country, and how he'd seemed to be able to read the sign a half mile away, and to know which way to take at every forking of the road—no matter how thick the trail might be, without so much as getting down from the back of his old nag.

I listened, and I could find it easy to believe because I knew that Clonnell was a queer one when it came to unraveling a puzzle.

Old Raeburn went ahead explaining his idea. "The Doctor is slick and he's smooth, but, whenever he moves across the country, he's so well known that he's sure to be marked down . . . and, wherever he's marked down, he's reasonably sure to leave some sort of a trail behind him, and that's all that I want. Give us the spot to start from, and this here Clonnell will run our bear up a tree for us. And leave us to finish the job, once Clonnell has brought us to grips with The Doctor."

Now, when you come to think about it, there was nothing so very far-fetched in the idea, and Raeburn barked at me: "Well, why do you look so glum?"

"Just because I don't think that it's The Doctor's year to be beaten. That's the way that I figure it. And then. . . ."

"I'm waiting and listening, but you talk terrible foolish, old boy," said Raeburn.

"Another thing is that I don't think that he aims to kill you," I said.

"Hey! Then why did he send . . . ?" Raeburn began.

"It just come to me while you was talking. If he'd meant that he intended to kill you, he would have said so right out, because he's that kind of a man. But he didn't mean that. He's figured out that killing is too easy for you. He wants to pay you off in heavier coin than that, and so he's working out his way. He simply says that he's coming to do you harm."

"What sort of harm could be as bad as killing, you sap?"

"I dunno. Do you suffer long after a bullet hits you?" I asked.

At that, Raeburn glared at me. Then he found out suddenly that all that time he'd been drawing away at a cigar that he was trying to light the wrong end of. He dashed the cigar down on the floor and stamped on it, and then he hurried on out of the room without saying no more. But I knew he was thinking that I must be right, and that he wanted to figure out what the devilish trick could be that was in the mind of The Doctor.

He was a grand man and a kind man, but he was harder than nails. Heaven knows how many dead men lay behind him in his climb to a fine fortune and the chances of an easy life. He was one of those fellows that his enemies hated worse than poison, and they could always add up a list of things a mile long—each item worth ten years in jail. But, on the other hand, his friends loved him just that much more.

I thought something about them things while I watched the old man going out of the room, and then I drifted on along behind him to see what might be happening next.

It was the thick of the dusk when I stepped out, just between the twilight and the dead dark. It was plumb restful to turn your eyes around and not have them aching with the distance of the horizon line. It's always a lot easier and nearer to look right into the heart of heaven than it is to see the skyline in the mountain desert. It was quiet, too, not that the range is ever noisy except with a storm, but somehow the daytime silence is a lot different from the silence of night.

Then I came upon Phil, leaning up against the corral fence and staring eastward, where the moon glow was just commencing.

"You're getting sort of poetical freezing to a fence to watch the moon rise, maybe?" I said.

"You idiot," said Phil Raeburn, "shut your mouth and use your eyes!"

He just hissed it, and I looked and seen something that would have excited me, too. For there was his daughter—which was more than two-thirds of himself—sitting at the top of the fence on the far side of the corral, and, as the moon poked up its rim, it put a gilding of yeller on her face and showed her laughing down into the face of a gent that was standing next to her at the fence.

Oh, that was nothing, just to tell it. But if you had heard the little, happy shiver in her voice, you would have known why the old man was shocked and why even I was scared, too. No, there was no need at all of asking questions, after that moment. Because all that gent had to do was just to sit down and figure it out and think things over for himself, and before very long he would see that only one thing in the world could possibly put that sound in the throat of a woman.

Dolly Raeburn was in love.

VI
A Surprise

"Who is it, for heaven's sake?" I asked as the soft, musical laugh comes drifting across the corral again and makes champagne bubbles spin up from my heart to my mind.

"Shut up," whispers the old man, very hoarse, "or I'll choke you to death here and now."

He was trembling, he was so terrible excited. No wonder, because that tall gent, whose back was turned to us, was mighty close to the girl on the fence. It was plain that he knew that she was pretty willing to let him say what he pleased.

It was a sort of horrible thing, in a way, to stand there and look on at that. I never felt so bad before. It seemed sort of terrible, you see, that a girl so strong-headed as Dolly Raeburn should suddenly be knocked right off her pins.

What the gent said we couldn't tell, because his voice was pitched so low, but, when Dolly spoke back to him, there was such tremors and breaks and trills in her speaking that you could see that she was like a nice, clean girl that had got drunk by mistake.

I pulled at the shoulder of old Raeburn to get him away. But he just shuddered himself out of my grip. He had to stay, of course, to see who that man could be, and so did I, too, because everything depended upon that. Give Dolly the right man for a husband, and she'd be the queen of all the women in the world. Give her the wrong man. . . . Well, I hated to think about that.

It was mysterious, too. I thought that she'd seen everybody on the ranch plenty of times, and certainly she'd never had any thrill out of them. As far as folks knew, men had never meant anything to Dolly. What one of the boys had she picked?

We didn't have long to wait to find out, because just now the moon rose up and brightened the corral, and just then the gent in front of the girl turned and we seen him in profile. You wouldn't guess who he was. I couldn't believe my eyes, and poor old Raeburn just drew in his breath like a dying man. It was Clonnell!

Somehow I got Raeburn to the corner of the saddle house, and he slumped down on a box. His head was hanging down, and he looked like a pretty sick man, which he was. So was I, too.

"It ain't typhoid fever or smallpox," I said sort of weak.

"No, it's worse," he said.

I had to agree, although I wouldn't say so.

"Women, they always got to . . . get interested . . . in the wrong sort of a gent first," I said. "It's the thing that grows them up."

"No!" said Phil.

I had to agree with him again.

He groaned: "Because there won't be no second affair for her. A first love and a last one. That's her style. Like me. Like me. God help her!"

34

Yes, that was the fact of the matter, right enough. You could see that she was his daughter.

All at once, he jumped to his feet. "Well," he said, "we can't leave her out there with that low, yaller hound. I'm going to get her and bring her in."

He started off with a rush like a bull. I grabbed onto him, and he dragged me along for about fifty yards.

"Phil, for heaven's sake, listen to me," I was saying to him. "If you cross her right at the beginning, she'll just balk, and then she'll run away with him. Let me go and persuade her into the house, sort of casual. Let me give her something to think about."

He seen the sense of that, all at once, and he stopped and grabbed me, and he said: "Will you do that, partner? Will you do that, God bless you?"

I said that I would, and poor Raeburn went on toward the house, walking, tottering and slow.

I tried to whistle. Pretty soon, I managed to hit up a sort of a tune, and I sashayed around the corral, large and liberal, and run into the two of them—by surprise, as you might say.

"Hello, Joe," said the girl. "Going to bed? So long, and sleep tight."

"Hello," I said. "The chief was wondering where you was. Hello, Clonnell."

"Oh," piped up Dolly, "are you Clonnell?"

It fair staggered me. She'd gone all of that distance with him without even finding out what his name was. It was about the worst case that I'd ever heard of, I can tell you. It was the worse kind of love at first sight, so far as the girl was concerned. She'd simply laid eyes on this big chap, and then nature had done the rest. She was crazy about him, I suppose, before she so much as heard his voice. His smooth, easy way of talking must have done the rest. But only to think of Dolly Raeburn falling in love with a coward, and a gent that wasn't afraid of letting the world know all about his cowardice—why, that was simply beyond imagining.

"Yes," he said, "Harry Clonnell is my name."

"Harry Clonnell," she repeated over to herself. She slipped down from the fence. "I have to go in," she added, very crisp. "Good night, Harry."

"Good night, Dolly," he answered.

All in a minute, here was Dolly walking along beside me. I thought that I was dreaming. I hadn't guessed that it could be half as easy as this.

She started right in. "When I met you today," she said, "I heard you say something about Harry Clonnell."

"I suppose that you did," I said. "Why?"

"Don't act so casual about it, because I think you know what I mean," she said. "What did you chiefly say about him?"

"I don't remember exactly. I . . . I don't know him well, y'understand, Dolly?" I hesitated. I was being about as clever as a gent could be in a case like that, because I wouldn't volunteer anything. I made her draw it all out of me. However, she didn't waste time beating about the bush, but came right straight to the point.

"You said he was a coward," said Dolly.

"Did I say that?" I asked.

"You did! You did! I hope that you'll say now that you were talking about a thing that you didn't know anything about. Because I wouldn't want to have any trouble between a man like you . . . and Harry Clonnell."

I wish that you had been there to hear the way that she said that name, making it rich and soft. Ah, she had a voice in her throat that would have tore a heart right straight in two.

After a time I said: "I don't want to do him any harm, Dolly. But . . . you won't make any trouble between us?"

"I won't!" she snapped. She stopped short. "Suppose that I went right back now and told him that you had called him a coward?" she asked.

"Well?" I said. "You might try it."

Because it seemed to me that I could do her and her father the best run in the world by breaking up this here love affair right where it started. Well, she hesitated for a minute, and I could hear her breathing hard. I hoped and prayed to God that she would go and do exactly what she had threatened, because I could see beforehand the sickening way that Clonnell would take water. She must have guessed that I was sure, because she had begun to hedge.

"He would fly at you," she said. "And his bare hands against your guns. . . ."

"Well, I'll give you both my guns to hold," I told her.

At that, she gave a little gasp. "You're a trained fighter, Joe!" she accused me.

"I never had a boxing lesson in my life," I told her truthfully.

"I don't believe a word that you've said!" she snapped.

But there was agony in her voice, and I knew that she was being tortured.

"Dolly," I said, "I don't want to knife any man behind his back, but I'll tell you what I'll do. I'll go and talk him over with your father and you. Let Phil tell you what he found him to be. That's all I ask. Otherwise, you can go back and tell Clonnell to his face what I've said."

That was fair enough. Dolly was as game as they come,

man or woman. She hesitated another moment, and then her nerve broke a little.

"We'll talk to Dad," she said, and went on into the house with me.

I was beginning to feel better every step of the way. Because after what I'd first seen, I thought that it was a lost cause, but now I had more hope, and I felt that the thing could be worked out with no harm done. Of course, it made me feel pretty good. It would fix me solider than ever with Phil Raeburn, for one thing, but, most of all, it would save Dolly from throwing her life away.

That was the way that it looked to me as we went into the house, because nobody could have guessed, at the time, how the miserable affair would finally turn out.

VII
Diplomacy

When we found Phil, I was afraid that he'd give away by his looks and his excitement that he knew something of what was up, but I hadn't given him enough credit for his gambling days, and he certainly played his hand fine, now.

Dolly cut right into the heart of the thing.

"Dad, I've just been talking to Joe about Harry Clonnell. I won't tell you what we've been saying, but I'd like to have you tell me what you know about him."

"What do I know?" echoed Phil, frowning a little. "That's sort of a queer question, Dolly. I never seen the man before today."

"Oh," she said, "you have eyes in your head, and you can read people fast enough. Just what sort of a person do you guess him to be?"

"I can tell you what I don't guess," said Raeburn. "He's the finest trailer that I ever saw at work. The state is six thousand dollars richer tonight because of the trailing of this same Harry Clonnell, and one of these days it may be Harry Clonnell that will be the means of running down

39

The Doctor. That's what I think of him as a man on a trail, honey."

It would have done you good to see her flush and her eyes shine. More than if a compliment had been paid direct to her.

"I knew that he was no ordinary man," said Dolly, with the new magic in her voice again. "What else do you know about him?"

It certainly surprised me a lot to see the way that Raeburn was working it. He couldn't have done it better. He started at exactly the right place to work up to what he wanted her to think.

"What else do I know? Why, dear, there's another thing. You know I've always been talking about Larry Chance, the strong man?" he asked her.

"Oh, ever since I was a youngster, I've heard you tell about the time he lifted the sack of cast-iron junk . . . but I'm not talking about Larry Chance now," Dolly said.

"Neither am I. The fact is, honey, that this Clonnell is a stronger man than Larry Chance ever was, though I almost hate to admit it."

Once more the eyes of the girl shone, and she threw a look of triumph at me. "And that's all that you know about him?" she asked.

"That's all, Dolly," Phil Raeburn replied.

She whirled around on me. "How have you dared to say what you did about Harry Clonnell?" she cried at me, and then to her father: "Dad, he dared to say that Harry was a coward."

She waited for some sort of an exclamation from Raeburn, but it didn't come. Instead, old Phil looked down to the floor and scratched his chin. It was very good work. I sure admired the way that he was handling this case. Like a real actor.

40

She broke out: "Dad, why don't you say something?"

"I don't know what to say, Dolly," he answered.

"You were with him all day in a manhunt . . . that ought to tell you something about his nerve. Didn't he lead the way for you all?" she asked.

"Except when it came to the blind corners, Dolly," said Raeburn gently. He made a pause.

Well, it was fine. He couldn't have improved his way of saying it, and it hit Dolly right in the heart. She winced and bit her lip, and the color went right out of her face. She looked at me with big eyes like I had poisoned a favorite brother.

"Look here, Dolly," I said, "don't take my word for it. Don't take your father's word for it. Go down to the bunkhouse and listen in to what the boys are talking about and laughing about. Why, this Clonnell ain't got the backbone of a yaller hound. And if you want a better proof than that, ask him to step out and get into the saddle of one of your horses tomorrow. Take any of your string. I don't care which."

That was a settler for Dolly. She leaned on the back of a chair for a minute. Then she started for the door, but stopped with her fingers on the knob. At last, she threw a look back at us and exclaimed: "Still, I know that you're wrong! Before the finish you'll find out that Clonnell is the bravest man in the entire range."

She went out and slammed the door so hard that it sprang open a little. So we could hear her running down the hall for her room and sobbing as she ran. We both listened to that, and it scared us worse than a pointed gun. I tiptoed over and shut the door very soft, and I hated to turn around from it and face old Phil again. When I did, he looked pretty sick, I can tell you.

But he was still game. He just said: "Well, it's sort of

41

funny, Joe. A while ago I thought that I was in the worst sort of trouble in the world. Now I see that it just wasn't any real trouble at all." He tried to laugh, but didn't make a very good job of it.

I said: "Raeburn, I see what you mean. It's worse than the danger of The Doctor to you."

"A million times, old fellow," he answered.

Then I said: "It means a good deal to me, too. I've seen Dolly pretty near grow up. I'd do a lot for that kid, and here's the chance for me to show it. Let Dolly have a day or two to find out for herself what sort of a man this here Clonnell is. The chances are that she will find out and that he'll be finished, so far as she's concerned. But, on the other hand, he may have her hypnotized complete. If that's the case, then I'll promise you that I'll take a hand in the thing."

"What do you mean by that?" said Raeburn, but he begun to lift his head again. "I don't try to buy the real services of a man like you, Joe. A partner can't be hired. But if you can help me out of this, you'll be more than a brother to me."

I nodded at him. I knew what he meant well enough. And I believed him.

"Just how I could manage it," I said, "I don't know. But if the job has to be done, I'll try my hand at it. I'll get this here Clonnell out in front of the girl and some of the others for witnesses, and then I'll pick a fight with him, and I'll make him crawl and take water worse than ever any man done before. If that don't cure Dolly, then nothing less'n the help of God will do the work."

Raeburn listened to me like a starving man that sees a chance for a square meal. He jumped for me and wrung my hand.

"Why, old-timer," he said, "there's nobody but you

42

that could work that deal. I know that you hate to play the bully, but now it's for the sake of the life of my girl . . . more than her life. I'd rather see her drowned tomorrow than married to a hound like Clonnell. Confound the day that ever brought him to our range."

We sat up for a time and talked over the details. It seemed pretty near a miracle to us that Dolly should have fallen in love so quick. What staggered both Raeburn and me was that Dolly should have made such a terrible mistake in the picking of her man. She'd had a chance to have her choice of the finest fellows that rode the range—rich and poor. The cleanest lot of straight-shooting, upstanding gents that ever packed guns. But not a man of them had ever got so much as two smiles out of Dolly. Here she was knocked right off her balance by this sort of a crawling imitation of a man.

Finally I sashayed out and started for the bunkhouse.

The moon was riding pretty high now, and showed me the black heads of the mountains where they were walking in double file down the Pass of the Tiger. Out of the north there was a driving wedge of clouds, like a high-flying flock of wild geese streaming down the valley. The whole place looked sort of mysterious and dangerous—the sort of a place where anything in the world might happen dead easy.

I got to looking back over the history of El Paso del Tigre and thinking of all the old stories that the Indians had to tell about the battles here, that had always ended with the massacre of one of the sides, and how it had gone on down, always filling up the pages that was crowded with black news, down to the days when the rustlers and the yeggs had kept things boiling here in the throat of the pass, and then Phil Raeburn had come along and put things to rights.

I pitied poor Dolly Raeburn, and I even pitied her father a little bit less. From one way of looking at it, you might say that he deserved a good deal of punishment for the bad things that he had done when he was a younger man—yes, and what he still done, from time to time. But I knew him too well to feel like that. He was worthy of being the father of Dolly, and she was worthy of being his daughter.

When I look ahead on what's to be told, I tell you that I only hope that I got the right words for the right places, to tell you just how things was when they happened and how to give you the feel of how queer and how different it all was. But words, they break down. Language don't count for much. So all I'll do will be just to tell out the story exactly the way it happened, one thing after another.

VIII
The Trial

I had news from the chief the next morning that was what we wanted to hear. Dolly had told him at breakfast that she was going to try out Clonnell with one of her horses that same day, and that, if he really didn't have the heart to ride a horse, she hoped that her father would send him away from the ranch.

"Good trailer or bad . . . a man ought to be a man," said Dolly.

That wise old Phil Raeburn had pretended not to like the bargain. Then him and me, we got into the best places that we could for watching the fun. We took balcony seats, posting ourselves up in the open door of the big hay barn that stood behind the stables. After a while we seen Dolly going into the stables with Clonnell lagging a little behind her. A minute later we seen her come out holding onto a sixteen-hand piece of thunder and lightning. It was a trick to see her swing herself into the saddle and catch the stirrups with her feet while she swung and banged the sides of that stallion. The next moment, the horse was

45

waltzing around the corral on its hind legs, with Dolly right in her glory.

Clonnell stood by, and we wasn't so far away that we couldn't see the smile on the face of Clonnell as he admired her, and I can tell you that she was worth admiring, every bit of her. She loved a horse, and she loved the fight that they could put up. It was a fine thing to see her sit that saddle like a little queen.

Pretty soon, she had the big horse eating out of her hand, and we could see her pointing into the stable and inviting Clonnell to go in and take his turn in bringing out a mount. But he just stood still, and Phil and me, we leaned against each other and laughed, it done us so much good.

After a time, there was no gestures. The girl just sat still in the saddle, and the man stood still by the fence with his head hanging. Even for a weak-hearted gent like that I had to feel more pity than contempt—him being so big and so strong and so smart in lots of ways.

What followed was something that Phil Raeburn and me hadn't expected. Phil was saying: "I'm kind of glad that I ain't down there where I can hear the words that she must be burning into that gent, old boy. She'll give him a roasting for a coward that'll almost make him brave."

I felt the same way about it, but just then she slipped down from the horse and waved to Clonnell, as though she was asking him to take her place in the saddle. That wasn't in the books.

"She said that she'd give him the run if he didn't play the man," said Phil. "She ain't living up to her contract, and I'm going to tell her so."

"Hold on," I said. "Hold on! You won't do anything of the kind, because the minute you start in opposing what she wants, you're through. She'll be eloped in five seconds.

No, the thing for you to do is to keep right on in the line that you started. Just be ignorant, and don't see nothing, and keep drumming up what a valuable man that Clonnell is on the trail, and that you're only sorry that he's such a coward . . . that's the stuff."

"Look!" said the old man.

If that girl wasn't helping Clonnell up into the saddle. Yes, sir, she stood there reining the stallion close against the fence, and managing his head, and offering him to Clonnell, but it wasn't any good. No, he would go a step or two forward, and then he would stop and shake his head. Even when the horse was standing still, it looking like a quivering flame, and that was what it was. Then Dolly pulled another trick that staggered us. She went into the stables with the stallion, and pretty soon she come back with the saddle and the bridle on a little bay mare called Anxious. She was a fast-footed little thing, and the gentlest of Dolly's whole string. She was so easy-going that Dolly was a little ashamed of owning her, and she never rode her much. But now she offered Anxious to Clonnell—and still he didn't want to take to the saddle.

Yes, sir, it made me blush even from that distance to watch the way that man held back, with the girl inviting him. The chief pulled out his field glass and turned it on them, and he lowered the glass and started in swearing. So I took it, and, when I'd centered the circle on them, I could see Clonnell gnawing his lip, although he didn't seem very pale. Just gnawing his lip and hanging his head and shaking it, and the girl rosy with shame and scorn of him, but still smiling and nodding to him. You could tell by the movement of her lips that she was reassuring him the way that a woman will reassure a little child. It made me wriggle and swear, just the way it had the chief.

Pretty soon she won out. Clonnell went up, and,

through the glass I watched her take a hard grip on the head of the horse. Then she stretched out her hand and put it under the elbow of Clonnell to help him up. You wouldn't have believed it.

"Gimme that glass!" ordered the chief.

"You go away," I said.

"It's my glass. I'm askin' you for my own property," Phil Raeburn said.

"Shut up and stop botherin' me!"

Because I wouldn't have missed for a million dollars the picture that pair made—Clonnell hunched up in the saddle like a scared monkey, and the girl leading the mare along and quieting her one minute, and looking back and smiling pure heavenly to Clonnell. . . . I didn't see the finish, because just then the chief grabbed the glass away from me, and, if he'd sworn before, the swearing that he did then laid over anything that I'd ever heard a man do previous.

They went around the corral a couple of times, and it seemed that Clonnell was beginning to lose some of his nervousness at the dancing of Anxious—because even Anxious was worthy of Dolly's string, and that meant that she was full of vinegar. Things was going along smooth in this way until a streak of evil busted in from the side and threw a change into everything.

It was Samson, the big wolf dog. He cleared the corral fence with a leap, and then he bounded across the corral and headed straight for Anxious and the man on her back. That was like Samson. You never could tell when he would bust loose like a mountain lion and try to cut throats right and left. There was a plain devil in him, and Raeburn was a fool for not killing the brute long before. But he dared not do it. Dolly would never have forgiven him if he took her pet wolf away from her.

Anyway, there was Samson aimed like an arrow for Anxious, and Anxious saw him coming. She didn't wait. With one rear and plunge, she was away from Dolly and halfway across the corral. Her first pitch brought a yell from Clonnell, and he rolled head over heels on the ground and raised a cloud of dust.

Into that cloud two things dived. There was Samson from one side, and there was the girl from the other.

With my heart in my throat, I had my gun out, ready for a long-range shot, and yet not daring to shoot, because I knew that nobody except maybe The Doctor could have been accurate at such a distance as that. It was a miserable thing to stand there and not be able to help. Then the wind cleared the dust cloud, and the first thing that we seen was that hound Clonnell scrambling on hands and feet for the corral fence. When he reached it, he got through it, and rolled away toward safety on the far side. We didn't give him more than a glance, though. What mattered was the girl, and I couldn't believe what I seen. She'd taken that rough monster of a Samson by the throat with one hand, and, while she backed him into a corner, she was whaling away at him with her riding whip and making him yelp every lick. She let him go with a final cut that made him pull his tail between his legs and scoot for the trees. Then she whirled around and bolted for Clonnell.

I really expected her to light into him the same way that she had lighted into the wolf dog. Heaven knows that he had deserved it for letting a young girl like that face a danger for him. But she didn't. No, sir, she reached him before he'd picked himself up, and she helped to gather him off the ground, and stood him up, and brushed off his coat, and you could see that she was asking him was any of his precious bones busted?

And the chief—why, I thought that he'd turn his guns loose on the pair of them. But all that he finally done was to lean his head against his arm and rest on the side wall of the barn, dead sick at heart.

I was sick, too. Not only because I seen that this girl was crazy in love with this sneak of a man, but because I seen that I would have to live up to my promise to old Raeburn and do a dirty job of house cleaning for him. I didn't like it a mite. I never have been accused of being a bully, thank goodness, and I didn't want to play the part for a minute, even for the sake of a fine woman like Dolly Raeburn. But my word was given, and, when the chief turned his sick eyes on me, I had to nod and say that I would do my trick.

IX
Chastening the Coward

I wanted a little time, to begin with, but Raeburn wouldn't listen to that. He pointed out that Dolly had gone mad about this man. He said that, if anything was to be done at all, it would have to be done before the disease got fatal. That was a fact. Any fool could have seen that, and it was plain that Dolly was on her last pegs, so far as common sense and this Clonnell was concerned.

When I met her later on that day, she said: "Joe, will you do something for me?"

"Sure, Dolly," I said.

"Try your hand at teaching Clonnell how to shoot, because it's a shame for a grown man not to know how to handle a gun . . . and dangerous, too, in this part of the country," she said.

You'd think that a girl would be ashamed of begging for favors for a man, but Dolly was a million miles past the point where shame ends. I tell you, I couldn't believe what I seen with my own eyes. I told her that I would do what I could, and that same day I started giving Clonnell lessons. I made sure that Dolly was there to see. I had a

51

terrible time making Clonnell even begin. Matter of fact, he wouldn't take a gun in his hand until Dolly had whipped out her slick little .32 and blazed away a couple of times at a post—and drilled it every time.

Then he took my gun that I was offering him.

"But," said Clonnell, "supposing that it should sort of explode. . . ."

It brought a groan from the ranch hands who was standing near, looking on, and Dolly simply turned white with disgust. But still she wasn't finished with him. No, sir, when it came to anything that she had to do with Clonnell, she was sure a glutton for punishment.

She stood by and persuaded him until he took the gun and aimed it. Then, if he didn't hold it in both hands and close his eyes when he fired it! Dolly looked down to the ground and bit her lip. But Clonnell had had enough. He wanted to quit right then.

He said: "Old fortune-teller once told me that I would take some sort of harm from a gun, one day, and I don't like the things. I have that reason for it, you see."

I couldn't speak, I was that disgusted. Even the girl had had a little more than she could swallow. We gave up the gun practice, and I was fairly sure that Clonnell was done for with Dolly. But I was wrong, as Raeburn told me a half hour later.

He'd had a talk with Dolly, and she had said that all Clonnell needed was a real chance to show his courage. She was sure that he had courage. She felt it in him, she said. But he was like a boy that won't learn to swim until he has been thrown into the water.

"I didn't argue with her, though it made my throat ache to hear her talk," said Raeburn. "I just said that maybe she was right, and that Clonnell was different from other folks. Which he is . . . he's the lowest skunk that I've ever laid my eyes on. However, the time is ripe to make the last try, old-timer. It's your turn to step out onto the center of the stage."

I saw that he was right, and that I would have to take my turn. Looking out the window, I seen that the stage was set for me, right now.

Dolly was riding her horse up from the corral, and Clonnell was following along slow behind her on his horse. I ducked out of the house and ran back to the corral. There I put the bars down and shooed my best cutting horse into the open. After that, I turned and ran back toward the place where Dolly and Clonnell was starting out on their ride together.

Half a dozen of the boys was in front of the bunkhouse, watching, because it was a sight worth seeing—to notice Dolly on one of her string.

I ran right up to Clonnell. "You thickhead!" I said to him. "You've left the bars down, and my best horse is loose!"

"Mind your tongue, Riggs!" Dolly said, turning crimson.

"Ah!" Clonnell said. "Your horse does seem to be loose. I'm sure that it isn't my fault, but I'll go catch him for you."

Yes, he would have turned and ridden down that way, but I wouldn't let him. I hated to do it, but, once started, I had to go through with my piece.

"Get out of your saddle!" I yelled at Clonnell.

Why, he got down as meek as a lamb.

"Joe Riggs, what do you mean? What do you mean?" called out Dolly, as white now as she had been red the moment before.

"I mean that he's a low-lifed, sneaking hound," I said, squaring up to Clonnell.

53

What a man he was to stand in front of. There was enough power in his arms and his hands to break me in two, but I knew that all of that strength was useless in a time like this.

"Let me explain, Riggs," pleaded Clonnell. "I really didn't. . . ."

"You lie!" I yelled at him.

Just then I remember that Sandy Slates come riding a big, strong, black gelding around the corner of the bunkhouse, and he pulled up to stare at us.

"I . . . really . . . Riggs, you're wrong," stuttered Clonnell.

"Am I? Here's where I prove that I'm right," I said. I hauled off and gave him a straight right, smashing square into the middle of his face!

What did he do? What I knew that he'd do. He just cringed back and held up his two arms before his face and begged me not to hit him again. I was so sick that I was paralyzed. There wasn't a sound from any of the boys that was watching—but, oh, what a set of faces—what a lot of sick men they was.

Then come a sob from Dolly, and she sank the spurs into her horse and went flying off down the edge of the draw. It was a regular precipice about fifty paces down, though some said that a Blackfoot Indian, being chased up El Paso de Tigre, had once slid a horse down the face of it and so got away. But Dolly was too blind with grief and shame to see where she was riding, and she sent her horse winging right along the edge of that cliff. She wanted to get away, and no horse could take her fast enough or in a straight enough line. She wanted to get away from the self that had loved this yellow-livered Clonnell. She wanted to get away from the shame of ever having set her eyes on such a man, and so she rode free and large and blind.

I looked back to Clonnell finally. He was standing up straight by this time, and he didn't seem to be paying any attention to me. He was wiping away a little trickle of blood that was running down from his mouth, and he was staring after the girl. You could see that he guessed what that ride of hers meant, and, all at once, I was terrible sorry for him, because, after all, what was wrong with him except that he didn't have nerve? What harm had he done to me? Or to any man else, so far as I knew? He was gentle and kind and good-natured. And I'd played the bully, and I hated myself for having done it.

Yet it was a great thing, if I'd won the game for Raeburn. I seen him standing off on the side of the group, looking very bright in the eye and happy. If The Doctor was to show up that minute and put a bullet in him, he wouldn't have cared much. He'd saved his Dolly from something that meant more than his life to him.

Dolly and her chestnut had turned the edge of the gully and was cutting across the fields beyond now, angling past us with the gulch between. We heard a wolf yell, and Samson darted out of some brush and dived over the edge of the cliff to cut across the hollow, and so take up with his mistress.

Clonnell gathered up the reins of his old horse, and he looked to be about to ride off when something happened that made us forget all that had gone before. It was the strangest thing that ever popped on the range. Even in El Paso del Tigre, where queer things had been stirring for the half of a century, there had never been an event like this.

Now that I come to the writing of it, I want to have everything exact, so's to miss none of the facts.

We was in the middle of a sort of a semicircle, Clonnell and me and Sandy, who had let his horse drift forward because it was a big, eager brute, always straining at the bit, after the fool way that some horses have. The rest—meaning the cowhands and Raeburn—was making the rim of the semicircle. And all was quiet except for the yelping of Samson as we seen him come out of the gulch and fly toward the course of Dolly.

The next minute we seen that it wasn't a question of going to meet his mistress for the sake of loving her. No, the devil that had always been boiling in that half-breed brute was now all turned loose. When he got to the Thoroughbred, he leaped for his head.

It brought a yell from all of us, and a groan from Raeburn. The horse reared, and, if Dolly hadn't been as fine a rider as any man, she would have been thrown out of the saddle.

We all had our guns out, ready, but what chance was there to use them? Old Raeburn himself came running forward, his eye straining and a rifle ready. But he didn't dare to shoot. It was a full quarter of a mile, and, at the rate that group was whirling, there was no chance to get in anything but a snap shot.

X
An Unexpected Turn

You could depend on Dolly, in a time like this. She didn't lose her head and grab the mane of the horse and start in screeching for help. No, as soon as she got her balance in the saddle, she snapped out her revolver and started to blaze away at the wolf dog, and whirl the stallion to keep him away from the knife-like teeth of Samson.

It was a fine piece of work, and it would have made most wolves head for the woods straight off. But Samson wasn't a wolf. There was just enough dog in him to make him know more than was good for his health. She was shooting from a whirling, jumping, bucking horse, for a platform, and that brute seemed to know that she couldn't land anything but a lucky shot on him.

He went straight for her throat, and leaped high enough to reach it, but Dolly—she'd fired her last shot, we learned afterward—turned the revolver in her hand and gave him the butt between the eyes. It made him miss his aim, for that time, but it didn't stun him. Only, he turned his attention to the horse.

It was all happening so fast that it blurs in my memory

and runs together. He darted at the head of the chestnut, and, when the horse reared, he switched around to the rear and gave him a slash that finished him as neatly as any butcher could have turned the trick with a knife.

The next instant, the big chestnut went down with a crash. It threw the girl heavily, and she lay on her back, clear of the struggling horse—flat on her back, with her arms thrown wide. A film of dust hung between her and our eyes.

The wolf dog had leaped clear as the horse went down. Now he whirled and went back to finish the life that lay inside the round, soft throat of Dolly Raeburn. And this last, mind you, in the split part of a second.

Then I seen a big arm shoot out in front of me. It tore the rifle out of the hands of Phil Raeburn, and I seen that it was Clonnell himself that had scooped the rifle away and pitched the butt in the hollow of his shoulder. All quicker than a flash, it happened. One move and the rifle was in place, and sighted, and the fire spurted from its muzzle—and Samson, across the gulch, leaped into the air and fell backward, and lay without a quiver.

I didn't have time to take heed of the full meanings of all of this. I didn't have a chance to wonder what had happened that the gent that didn't know anything about guns was able to shoot like this. Other things was following on enough to drive a man mad.

I was telling you that big Sandy was sitting on the saddle on the black gelding, but now Sandy disappeared out of the saddle and was pitched twenty feet away. In the saddle in the place of him was sitting Clonnell—the gent that couldn't ride even a tame horse, with a lovely girl encouraging him. Yes, there was Clonnell. Before he had found the stirrups, he was already driving his spurs home, so deep that the gelding was maddened with the pain and the suddenness of it and ran right where its new rider turned its head. And that was straight at the face of the gulch!

Yes, sir, over the edge of that cliff went the man that couldn't ride a lick, except on a rattle-bones ready to drop dead with age and weakness. Over the cliff and out of sight, and we run to the edge with a groan and seen him sitting back pretty, while he stiffened his legs in the stirrups and went smashing and crashing down toward the bottom and steadying the gelding something wonderful to see.

We got the course of that slide all marked out, but looking at it in cold blood is enough to send the cold shivers up the backs of most folks, though it ain't half enough to give them the picture of what really happened on that day.

I would like to show them Clonnell riding the black like a jockey, diving through thin air, with the rocks and dirt that he had loosened pouring down and rattling around him, and the big boulders beginning to bound down the face of the cliff. He reached the floor of the gulch. The gelding staggered, and a half-ton rock leaped past his head, missing it by an inch. Then those spurs tore the sides of the black open again, and it leaped across the gorge and scooted up the easy ascent on the farther side, and out where Dolly Raeburn lay beside her horse.

All of this happened while we stood there, paralyzed—though, after all, it took only a few seconds to happen. But yonder was Clonnell, the coward, the sneak, that wouldn't shoot a gun and couldn't ride a horse—there was Clonnell holding Dolly Raeburn in his arms, and her beginning to wake up. . . .

"Him . . . him!" gasped Raeburn, gurgling deep down in his throat. "Him the gent that I wouldn't have marry my girl. Him . . . a hero! A hero, Joe. We'll never see any man able to do a thing like this again."

Which we wouldn't, either. I remembered that I had hit

this man straight in the face. It made me pretty weak.

He stood up, and, holding her in one arm, he mounted the black gelding again, and come riding around the gulch toward us, cradling the girl, soft and easy, and somehow managing that dancing, half-crazy gelding with just his knees. I never seen a man before that could hypnotize a horse like that.

He come by us—us pouring out around him, and the first thing he said was: "Raeburn, she's sick and dizzy, but she'll be all right."

Then we heard a sobbing, childish sort of a voice saying: "I want Mamma! I want Mamma! Why don't she come? Oh, why don't she come?" All at once her wits must have cleared a little, and she cried: "Harry Clonnell! Let me go! I don't love you. I despise you. I hate you! You coward! You coward! I . . . I love Joe Riggs for having shown me the horrible truth about you. Will you let me go?" And she doubled her fist and beat at his face.

I stood by and seen and heard these things, but chiefly I seen the smile on the face of Clonnell as he carried her past, and it was as though she was holding him and kissing him—there was that much happiness in his smile, I can tell you.

He went on into the house. I got there with Phil Raeburn as fast as we could.

Dolly had fainted again. Clonnell carried her up the stairs to her room, and, on the way, he says, as calm as you please: "I know a good deal about these affairs. There's no danger. She'll come through very nicely. Only dazed by the bad fall. Here we are. Is that the door?" When he had laid her on the bed, he stood back.

She looked white and sort of strained about the mouth and the eyes as though she were suffering a good deal of pain.

"You'd better take care of her, now, Raeburn," said Harry Clonnell. "You can put a cold compress on her head. When she clears up a bit, she'll have a bad headache. But it will ease off in a little while. She's quite all right. Just be very gentle with her, and don't mind her if she says wild things now and then."

We left Raeburn and his daughter together, and we stood outside in the hall, facing each other. Clonnell would have turned away and gone down the stairs, but I wouldn't let him. I had to have this thing out, here and now.

I said: "Clonnell, God knows why you played the sneak. Being the man that you are, God knows. But you know what I've done, and maybe you know why I've done it. How do we stand?"

He looked into my eyes as quiet and steady as though I was nothing at all but a landscape, say, with a good many empty distances in it. Something in the Nevada mountains maybe.

He said: "I suppose that I ought to take you outside and finish the deal with guns, Joe?"

"You got the right to ask any sort of a fight with me," I said. "Knife or rifle . . . whatever you say."

"What about bare hands, Joe?" he said.

I couldn't help wincing when I thought of how those big hands of Harry Clonnell could tear me to pieces like shreds of boiled beef.

"It's all right, old fellow," he said. "I don't bear you any malice. I like you, Riggs. I like you a lot. You're honest, and I know that you hit me today because you thought that you had to."

"Will you shake hands on that, Clonnell?" I said, holding out mine.

He looked down at my hand, and then up to my face.

"That," he said, "is rather a different matter, you know," and he walked past me down the stairs.

I felt even worse than you can guess—worse scared, I mean. The Doctor, with a pair of drawn guns in his hands, wouldn't have scared me half as much as Harry Clonnell did that moment without touching a weapon.

I heard his long, soft stride go through the hall beneath, and then I heard a little cry from the room of Dolly. "Is it true? Is it true? Then I want him quickly! Call him! Call him, Dad!"

The door opened. Raeburn stood in the opening. "You go get Clonnell," he said. "Get Clonnell and get him quick, because he's needed up here."

XI
Unwarrranted Disappearance

Perhaps you have already guessed what I found when I went to search for Clonnell. Because, after all, everything that he had done from the beginning was just the opposite of what anybody would have expected a man to do. Now here he was having showed himself all that any man could want to be, and he'd won the heart of the richest heiress on the range, and he'd fixed the father of the heiress so that Phil Raeburn would have given away half of his ranch and the stock on it rather than lose this same Clonnell for a son-in-law. He'd fixed himself with all the gents on the place, including me, so that we figgered he was a little more than natural, he was such a fine feller.

Having arranged everything like that, you can guess what I found when I went down, grinning and glad of my message—because there was no Clonnell to find. No, sir, that gent had faded out complete. I thought that he would be in the bunkhouse, sort of sunning himself in the new respect that the boys had for him. No, he wasn't there. Then I thought that he must have gone out to the horses, but, though I hollered and screeched for him, he wasn't there. He wasn't no place, and in about half an hour it come smash into my head that fellow wasn't anywhere around—he'd gone!

I couldn't believe it. Who could think that a man would chuck away about a million dollars and the prettiest girl on the range? I went back to the house and got Phil Raeburn out of his daughter's room.

"What do you mean," he said, "by not bringing Clonnell back here with you? I've told her everything that happened, and she's in a fever to see him quick. Go get him!"

"He ain't to be got," I said.

"He ain't which?" asked the chief.

I explained how I had looked for him, and Phil Raeburn leaned himself against the side of the wall and stared at me. Then he grabbed me, and we went together into his study. We sat down beside a lighted lamp and smoked our pipes, and let them go out, and lighted them again, and didn't say much, except now and then to swear.

The chief said at last: "Will he never come back? That's the main thing."

I said after a while: "Well, Dolly's young. She'll get over this here affair."

"Lemme tell you something," said Raeburn. "When I met Dolly's mother, it was at a dance. I had one look at her. And that same night, an hour later, I was telling her that I had to marry her. She thought I was crazy. I got into trouble and had to hop. A week later I rode back in spite of the trouble and climbed up to her window and made love to her again, until she threatened to raise the house on me. For a year I was chased all over the map, but, at the end of the year, I woke up in the middle of one night and I knew that I had to have that girl or die. I gave myself a shave, saddled a horse, and started down from the mountains. I found her, stole her, married her . . . and that was how I got my start in the new life. Now you tell me that Dolly will forget this gent. But I tell you that Dolly is like me, only more so. I never seen but one woman that I could love. And she'll never see more than one man. She's sick now, and I shouldn't be surprised if she never gets out of that bed, if Clonnell don't come back. It'll break her heart."

I couldn't talk back to him, because I felt that he was right.

Right he turned out to be, though it didn't work out quite so bad as we had expected. Dolly was up and around inside of three days, but to see her you'd hardly know her. She'd always been a young tornado, smashing and crashing about the place, but she lost all of that. You would have thought that she hated to make a sound now. She walked about with her head hanging. Or else she would go off for a long ride across the valley, starting in the morning and coming back at night. Nobody with her all of that time, and all of us feeling that one day she wouldn't come back at all.

I had sort of an idea that when she rode out that way she had a dim sort of hope that maybe she would meet Harry Clonnell, racking across the hills on his rattle-bones of an old horse. But she never met him, of course. Because a gent that knew how to discover a trail as well as he did would sure be able to cover up his traces when he decided to disappear. So she got paler and paler. Then one day I found her in the corral, with her arms around the neck of one of her horses, sobbing like a baby.

I didn't have to ask what was making her cry, because it was in that same corral, and with that same horse, that she had given Clonnell the riding lesson.

I sneaked back to the house, feeling good and sick, and wishing that Clonnell had never been born. When I got in, Phil Raeburn met me, wild with excitement. He had a letter in his hand, addressed to Dolly Raeburn in a smashing, big, bold handwriting.

"It's from Clonnell!" I shouted.

"Shut up . . . do you think so, too?" he asked.

"I sure do."

"Does she get it?" he asked.

"Not before we've read it through," I answered.

We agreed that that was the right thing to do, because in Dolly's state of health it wouldn't have taken much to bowl her right over. We steamed the flap of that letter until the mucilage was softened, and then we opened it, very delicate, and we fished out the paper and unfolded it, and read like this:

Dolly, my dear:

Up to the other evening, I have been living at your place in a fool's paradise, but that day showed me that it was no use trying to pretend. I thought that I could be a new man. I found out that I couldn't. And here I am, knowing that I can never love any woman as I love you, knowing that you care a little for me, too, but knowing most of all that the worst thing I could do would be to ask you to marry me. So I got my courage together and rode away that night, and I know that I can never return again.

Forget me, my dear, and forgive me for not having quite the nerve and the strength to tell you the things that would not only make you stop caring for me, but would make you despise me forever.

Harry

When we read that letter through a couple of dozen times, the old man got the idea that something might have been wrote between the lines, and we baked it close to the fire, but nothing showed out.

"Anyway," he said, "she mustn't see it."

"Of course not," I agreed.

He put the letter into his wallet, and leaned back in his chair, looking his years as I'd never seen him look them before.

"It beats me," said Raeburn.

"And me," I echoed.

"Because he was a square-shooter," he said.

"The squarest that ever lived," I added.

"And gentle and smooth, Joe. So tell me, what was wrong with him? What was the thing that kept him from marrying our Dolly?"

Then it hit me in a heap. It hit me so hard and so quick that I had to jump up out of my chair and yell: "Raeburn, I got it!"

"You have?" he asked.

"Yes, I got it. It's the only thing that could make him back up. He's been married before . . . and he's got a wife living."

Raeburn—he turned pale.

"Man," I said, "can you imagine a young gent like him, with his looks and his ways and his foxy way of talking that wouldn't have to be married at his time of life? He was married . . . he found out that he had married the wrong woman . . . he left her . . . he sneaked away with a new name, most likely, and that's why nobody on the range ever heard of a gent by the name of Clonnell before. He come to this part of the country riding the rods most likely. All he wanted was to get shut of that other girl. He

67

met Dolly. He was crazy about her and she about him . . . and then all at once he seen that it wouldn't do. He couldn't go ahead making love to her while he had a wife living!"

Raeburn seemed to think that there was something in this. "But why would he play the coward?" he asked.

"That's simple, and it works right in with my theory," I explained. "Because the way of it was just that, when Harry Clonnell put on his new name, he decided that he would put on a new self, too. No doubt back in his home place he's known to be the bravest gent in the county, and all such. So he decided that he would disguise himself by changing his name and his ways, instead of wearing a new face. And dog-gone me if he didn't do a good job of it."

I couldn't help looking down at the right hand that had hit Clonnell in the face.

Raeburn admitted that perhaps I was right. He tried to poke a hole in my argument, but he didn't see any real weakness.

When he'd finally accepted what I had to offer, we agreed that the next thing to do was to try to find Clonnell. Because if we could only trace him to his home town, and find his wife, and who she was, old Raeburn had enough money to buy off a woman like that and persuade her to get a divorce, setting Harry free to take Dolly.

Well, it was a good idea. But somehow there seemed something wrong with it. We didn't know just where. Anyhow, we had reached the point of deciding that we'd put detectives on the job when we got the alarm from the sheriff that The Doctor was in our district again.

XII
The Doctor Again

I would sure not like to have myself wrote down as a heartless man, you understand, because I figure that I'm as kind as most, and nobody could say that Raeburn wasn't fond of his daughter. You would ask, though, how come that the pair of us could forget all about her in order to go pelting across the countryside in the chase of a crook that we really had no hope of catching?

I don't want to make more explanations, because I guess that they're no use. Anyway, in ten minutes there was five of us from the ranch, with Raeburn at our head, cutting across country on our best horses. Dolly was left behind in the big blackness of that ranch house.

What we knew was that by staying at home we couldn't do her much good, and, in the meantime, the hunt was all a fever in us. The sheriff had said over the phone that the word had just been brought in that The Doctor had been sighted by an old prospector east of Jedboro, and that he had been riding alone, as usual, just at the close of the day, and heading toward the Middle Pass in the Lawson range.

Even me, I got pretty excited when I heard that news, and as for Raeburn he was wild with it. Knowing the lay of the land, you would have been, too. The north and the south passes through the Lawson range was big, wide, easy ways, which most people always took. But the Middle Pass was a shortcut that even the devil would have had a shudder over. It looked as though the range had been broke in two across somebody's knee at that point. Most of the distance, there was granite cliffs on each side of you, and, now and then, a creek come down and turned itself to foam on the rocks in the bottom of the valley and filled the pass with roaring and shouting. There was a few turns to this side and that, but most of them was blind pockets. A fellow who took to the pass could be pretty sure that he would have to stay in it until he come out on the other side, or got turned back, unless he was swallowed by a rock fall or a landslide before he got through. Take it all in all, it was about the most unpopular pass that I ever heard of. But it was a shortcut, and the whole world knew that shortcuts was the special liking of The Doctor.

The sheriff's plan was good sense, too. He was riding with more than twenty men, and they would never stop spurring until they had reached the broad mouth of the pass on the Jedboro side. Then it was up to Raeburn, if he would, to get with his men to the farther side of the pass. After that, the sheriff would start feeling his way along the pass from one side and Raeburn from the other. There was at least two good chances out of three that one of the two gangs would run onto The Doctor in that pass. If we met him, there was at least nine good chances out of ten that he would die before the fight was over.

Of course, there had been a time when The Doctor had rode through fifty men without much trouble, he had the whole country so scared by the things that he was able to do, but it was all different now. The price on his head was a fortune, and the fame that would go to them that downed him was enough to make them known men the rest of their lives—no matter how many of them there might be. To be known as one of the party that was in at the death of The Doctor was the ambition of all the best riders and the best shots in the mountains. The sheriff knew just who to call out in a time like that, and he never made mistakes. As for Raeburn, he could pick any man on his place and not make no mistakes. The reason that he didn't take more than five was because he'd always felt, and we agreed, that numbers would never kill The Doctor. Only straight shooting would do that.

So the lot of us headed for the rear mouth of the Middle Pass and rode hard and fast until we had got into it, but, once we had the big, stiff-standing walls on either side of us, we knew that speed was no good any longer. The thing that we needed then was care and caution to sneak forward and try to surprise the great crook.

Three of us dismounted and slipped along on foot, to save all useless noise. Raeburn and one other came along behind with the five horses, at a little distance. It was three in the morning, and there was no moon when we reached the opening of the pass. We hardly covered five miles in the next two hours when the dawn began and brightened first on the upper crags, and then gradually lifted the gloom in the gorge a little.

But even midday sun couldn't make that place look anything but grand and dark. As we sneaked along, all of us told each other that, by something in our bones, we felt that The Doctor's last day had come. I suppose it was because the bigness and the wildness of everything around us seemed like a pretty good setting for that sort of a man to come to his end.

We had passed a waterfall, strung like a white rope on the side of the gorge, and we'd waded through an icy little brook—our feet slipping on the smooth faces of the rocks, and then Charley Hotchkiss, going on in the lead, whistled very softly. We didn't need anything more by the way of a signal.

We got our rifles ready and soft-footed up beside Charley, right quick. Raeburn left the horses behind with Tom Legrange and sprinted to catch up with us, and reached us, choking and gasping for breath, so that he was with us when we seen the great man coming down the pass. I say the "great man" because I felt that way about it. If you had seen him looming around the corner of a set of boulders on a great black horse, you would have felt the way that I did about it. Just his sheer bigness was enough to fill your eyes, but, even at that distance, there was something more than bigness, and the morning light glinted on his spectacles and glistened on his short gray beard as he rode in at point-blank range.

Just then, it didn't seem so wonderful that he had been able to do what he wanted for so long, and ride here and there, taking what pleased him. What was wonderful was that he hadn't smashed whole cities and ripped mountains apart. I mean that was how it seemed as we watched him with his horse striding down the valley, until it seemed to me that the booming of the waterfall was just the voice of The Doctor, laughing at us.

I got my rifle to my shoulder, but my hands was shaking with the worst case of buck fever that you ever heard of. When I tried for a bead, I wobbled from his head to the legs of his horse and up again to the morning sky. I was more like to shoot a hole in that blueness than to land a slug in The Doctor. I looked sidewise. Three rifles besides my own was leveled at The Doctor, and each of them was

72

just as bad as me—except for old Phil Raeburn, and he was steady as a rock. He'd been through such an agony with Dolly, lately, that this was a sort of lesser excitement to him, I suppose.

At any rate, I had just said to myself—*If The Doctor goes down, it will be Raeburn that does the trick.*—when Phil shouted in a great voice: "Fair play even to a murderin' crook! Doctor, run for it!"

That was bold and free and large. It made me shudder, I tell you, to hear it, because just then I felt no bigger than one of five crickets, with a great heel about to come down and scrunch us all flat.

The Doctor jerked in his black so fast and hard that the big fellow reared right up on his haunches, and that rearing saved The Doctor's life. Because just then three of us fired and sent our shots wild. But Raeburn, firing last and holding his shot very cool to see what the others had done, sent a slug straight at the head of The Doctor—and shot the rearing black steed.

The big horse fell in a heap, but not too fast for The Doctor to disentangle himself and leap clear of its body. That man looked bigger than human to us as he bounded to get around the nearest corner of the valley wall.

Raeburn and the rest of us had smashed another volley at him, but the chances was pretty large against us—he had been moving so fast as well as right across the field of our fire.

"The horses! Horses!" shouted the chief.

They were right at our hands. There was no lack of teamwork in a time like that, you can bet. Raeburn didn't have a man with him that wasn't able to think for himself, and the minute that the firing had begun, the gent with the horses had rushed them forward. They swung up to us, and we jumped for the saddles.

"Ride slow!" yelled Raeburn, his voice choked with excitement and hope now. "Ride slow! Ride slow! A slow hoss is faster than a fast man. And we want nothin' but straight shooting!"

So we took those horses down the valley at a jog, and, as we went around the corner, we got it. There was three shots so close together that you would have thought that four men had fired them. Down went Chick's gray, crushing the leg of Chick in the fall. Tucker's big brown gelding got a shot that ripped it across the haunch so that it whirled around and bolted down the valley like the wind, with poor Tuck tugging at the reins in vain. Charley Hotchkiss was writhing on the rocks with a bullet through his left shoulder.

We had been three, fine, brave men, a second before. Now there were two left—to face The Doctor!

XIII
A Climb to Fight

"But you faced 'em," you say. You sit back in your chairs by the fire and you cross your legs and you say: "You faced him, just the same. And there was two of you, which was odds enough against him, the poor devil." I can hear you say it.

Being brave indoors is pretty easy, usually. But being brave that morning in the Lawson Mountains was a different story. I was ready to quit, and a little bit more than ready. I would have turned my horse and bolted, right then and there, but I figured that it would be the same as making sure of dying if I stayed another half second inside of the range of that killer's guns.

I dived off that saddle and never was gladder than when I hit the ground. I'd lighted behind some rocks, and I started to crawl away when a hand grabbed my shoulder, and there was old Phil Raeburn barking at me: "Joe, where are you going?"

"Home," I said, "as fast as I can get there. Home!"

"You're gonna stay here," Raeburn commanded between his teeth. "You're gonna stay here and see this game through with me."

I sat and looked at him, feeling very blank, like a slate that has been sponged clean. Finally I got hold of a few words. I said to him: "Phil, old-timer, are you plumb batty? Are you aiming for the pair of us to tackle that wild man, and his guns that don't miss?" I pointed to the rocks around us. "Even a snake would get a sprained back," I said, "trying to get through those stones."

Raeburn didn't smile. He just narrowed his eyes and squinted at me and said: "Joe, you stay with me now, or we're through."

I seen that he meant it. I knew it was a fool job and that no good would come of it. Why, even Napoléon wouldn't have been wild enough to tackle an enemy in those rocks if he only had odds of two to one in his favor. He would have had more sense. He would just have tried to surround him and starve him out. But surrounding The Doctor would be like trying to surround a handful of quicksilver. He was sure to slip away.

"Raeburn," I told him finally, "I got as much courage as you have."

"Show it, then," he said, very ugly.

"I got more sense, too," I said, "but if you want to go ahead with this here game, I'll stick with you. Except that I know how it's gonna turn out."

He nodded and showed a good deal of satisfaction. "I nearly got him the first crack out of the box," he said. "With you to back me up, I'll be sure to get him the next try. He can't always win, the way that he has in the past, and something tells me that this is his day to die."

Listening to him, you would almost believe that he knew he was right. But I figured that he was a little bit crazy—what with all the trouble that had come to his house lately, and he felt that it was a case of him get The Doctor or The Doctor get him, since he'd had that note of warning. Now he was at grips with The Doctor, and he wanted to get it over with, some way or other. You could sympathize a little with that way of thinking, and, as much as I hated this party, I felt that I couldn't back down and leave the old boy to fight the thing out alone.

We gave one look to the boys that was down. They had pulled themselves around behind the corner of the valley wall, and there they were taking care of each other as well as they could, so that I didn't have even the desertion of them to use as an excuse to keep Raeburn back.

"He's lost his shooting eye," said old Phil, showing his teeth with a grin as he said this.

"Man, are you crazy?" I asked him.

"Crazy?" he asked.

"Didn't he turn five men into two with just three shots?" I reminded him.

"Them shots of his," pointed out Raeburn, "didn't kill anybody. I tell you, he's lost his shooting eye. He hit two horses and one man. I ask you is that a good score at point-blank . . . for him?"

Why, come to think of it, perhaps it wasn't. But then again, perhaps some folks attached more skill to The Doctor than he really possessed. The main thing was, from my way of looking at it, that five fighting men on good horses, with good guns, and knowing how to use them, had come around the corner of the valley, and there they had been hit by a tornado that scattered them and tore them to pieces.

"If only the sheriff would come up the valley from the other side," I said.

"Confound the sheriff," he said. "We're gonna get the credit of this all to ourselves."

"Why ain't there enough glory in this job to satisfy fifty men as well as two?" I asked, and pointed. "We got The Doctor sewed up in a bottle."

It looked safe enough, as a matter of fact. I would not have asked a better trap than that, to be made to order. It was just a deep crevice in the side of the cañon—made I can't guess how. There we lay in the mouth of the crevice, sheltered in our rocks, like breastworks. In the hollow of the crevice, where it narrowed to a point and cut into the face of the mountain, was The Doctor, wagging his gray beard and wondering how the devil would he get out of this scrape? He couldn't come out our way.

Raeburn had showed already that his hand was as steady as steel on his rifle. And since I'd fired once and been through the tightest part of the scrap, I would do as well as Raeburn, I thought, or a mite better.

"We've got him in a trap, but how do we know that there ain't a hole in the trap?" Raeburn asked.

"Look for yourself," I answered.

"Well . . . ," he began. He stared at the wall of rock, and then he shook his head, pretty satisfied. "Still," he continued, "though that trap has got a good bottom and we can take care of it on this side, the top of it is off."

I looked up to the dizzy head of the cliff. "You mean," I said, "that The Doctor is a fly, with glue on his feet, for working his way up to the top by that crevice?"

"I mean this," he said. "I've studied The Doctor and his ways. Do you know how he's always succeeded before?"

"Well, go on with your riddle, if it pleases you any!" I said, a little soured on him.

"Simply by always doing the thing that everybody agreed was impossible. He done the thing, always, that couldn't be done, and that's why he's grown old enough to have gray hair."

There was a sort of sense in this, any way that you looked at it. But I wasn't in the mood to applaud. I pointed out that nobody could ever get to the top of that crevice. Not for a million dollars.

"Life is worth more than a million," said the old boy.

Just then we heard the rattling of a stone that begun far up the inside of the crevice and came rattling and pounding its erratic way down to the bottom. I looked at Raeburn and turned a little pale, I suppose. I felt pale inside.

"What knocked that stone loose?" he asked in a snarl.

"Stones is always falling in a place like this."

"Well," he said, "I wish that one of them had landed on your head! Stones is always falling, is they?"

"The weather cracks 'em loose," I tried to explain.

"It's weather by name of The Doctor that has cracked that stone loose," he said, sat up, and glared at me. Then he jumped to his feet.

"Raeburn . . . you fool!" I yelled, and tried to pull him down. "He'll fill you full of lead!"

He wriggled and jerked himself away from me. "Sure," he said, "if The Doctor was there in that hollow, he'd have killed me twenty times before this . . . but he ain't there . . . and the proof of it is that I'm still standing here and living."

Why, it was a good enough proof at that. It was certain that if The Doctor had been back there, watching for us and our moves, he would have lifted off the top of Raeburn's head the minute that it showed above shelter, but there stood Raeburn, safe and sound.

I got to my own feet and followed him. He had scooped up his rifle, and he was running straight into the crevice. There we stood, the two of us, and moved back and forth, studying the way that narrow wedge of skyline appeared above us. Right at our feet lay the Winchester of The Doctor. He'd never have been known to leave a gun behind him before this, except for the burned one that Clonnell had found buried in the sand. It showed that he knew that he was making his last stand—or rather, his last climb.

Another stone busted loose and come thundering down. We jumped to get out of the way of it, and, as we jumped, I seen a man toward the top of the cliff—looking like a fly as a matter of fact at that distance, and seeming to be clawing his way up a surface as smooth as glass.

It was The Doctor, and Raeburn had been right. I yanked my rifle to my shoulder just as Raeburn done the same, and we give The Doctor our compliments with one voice, as you might say. But just then he had swung himself toward a jutting arm of rock, and, as he disappeared behind it, we couldn't tell whether or not we had hit him.

"After him!" said Raeburn. And he jumped at the rock!

XIV
The Sleuth's Surprise

Once I remember when the dogs run a mountain lion to earth in a dark cave—and me and Jim Christmas, we went on ahead into the dark and finally seen the eyes of the brute and put a bullet between them. But crawling through the dark of a cave was nothing compared with the climbing of that rock.

Shooting up ain't half as easy as shooting down, especially with a revolver, and, while we was climbing about trying to get in a slug on The Doctor, why wouldn't he be able to get in a few shots at us—him that never missed? We hadn't worked up fifty feet—me in the lead, but old Raeburn following along close at my heels—when there was a *clang* above us, and a bullet smashed into the rock ledge just over my head and knocked some stone splinters into my face.

I hung on, half blinded. "You see what this here is going to bring to us?" I said to Raeburn. But while I was talking, the old fellow worked right on past me.

I yelled to him that I was through, and that he would have to go on alone, if he wanted to commit suicide; but

Raeburn was like a bull terrier when it sees a fight. He wouldn't let up. He kept right on climbing and paid no attention to me at all, and so I had nothing to do but to follow him, little as I liked it.

That bullet that had knocked stone dust into my face had been meant to plow straight through my head, and would have, if I hadn't ducked just in time, and this sort of shooting was a little too straight to suit my ideas of a stand-up fight. However, old Raeburn was a madman. He kept plugging along until we got to a stretch where there was a sheer wall above us, and we had to work our way with our fingertips and toes, scratching at little, rough nothings, and inviting a fall every second. It was all that I could do to make headway, and I never yet have seen how the old man was able to keep up the work. But keep it up he did, muttering and mumbling to himself all of the time, and now and then stopping the work to hang on by one hand and, with the other free one, try a pot shot over his head. He hit nothing, I thought.

Then, as we was working up that sheer wall, we got it!

We couldn't see The Doctor, but it was plain that he could see us, and a shower of lead began to smash around us. I mean that it smashed around Raeburn, because he was in the lead, and no bullet could hit me that didn't first range down through him. I think that there were seven or eight bullets in that shower, and they all hummed past the head of old Raeburn, or else smashed against the rock wall close to him.

I expected to have his weight fall down on me every minute. I clung tight and I prayed for the end. I begged Phil to come down, but he kept struggling along all the time.

"He can't hit me! He can't hit me today!" shouted Phil. "I got a charmed life! And he knows that it's his day to die! Come on, Joe!"

Yes, Raeburn was a sensible man, and yet he wasn't ashamed to talk childish, like this.

He crawled on up, with me just beginning to follow, and then his gun banged, just as I was beginning to wonder if even The Doctor had a heart, and had been shooting only to miss and scare the old fellow. But the gun of Raeburn exploded, and I heard him yelp: "I sure got him that time, kid!"

I wouldn't believe it. It wasn't in the books for The Doctor ever to get wounded, but pretty soon we come along a stretch of crimson streaked down the face of the rock, and that was enough to convince a worse doubter than me. Certainly Raeburn hadn't been hit, and neither had I. There was only one possible explanation, which was that The Doctor had been winged by old Phil.

I got my heart up at that. We didn't have another glimpse of The Doctor while we was climbing up the rest of the way to the top of the cliff, but we made the best time that we could. When we got up there, we found that a made-to-order trail was laid for us. It was bright red lying across the surface of the bare granite, and it pointed, like an arrow, to a nest of rocks in the center of the little plateau. You wouldn't have needed any interpreter to tell you that was the place where The Doctor was lying up and bandaging his wound.

"We'll wait here," I said to Phil. "You wait on one side of the rocks, and I'll wait on the other side . . . and pretty soon he'll surrender. He'll be too weak to get far on foot."

Even Phil might have agreed that was sense, but I never seen a man go so crazy as he did, when he saw that he had a chance of finishing The Doctor. He was trembling with eagerness.

He said: "There's the skunk that said he would teach me a lesson. This'll teach him that Raeburn ain't to be fooled with. He'll send me letters of warning, will he?"

"Calm down, Phil," I said. "Look here. We're sitting pretty, blocking the whole neck of the peninsula here. He can't come by us. Sit down and take it easy, will you?"

"While he slides over the edge of the cliff on the far side and works his way down to the floor of the valley?" Raeburn said. "No, kid, I ain't that simple. I got my hands on him, and here's where I'm going to finish him."

All at once, he lunges forward and heads for the nest of rocks. I give one yell and a lurch after him. As I lurched, a gun whanged from the circle of rocks, and a bullet nipped a piece out of my ear. Very neat shooting, that was, and I pitched on my face and lay like dead.

You would think that was enough to warn back the old man, but Raeburn wasn't the stuff that takes a warning. He kept running ahead, and I heard the gun of The Doctor bang four times in a row—but still Raeburn didn't stop.

Why, there was something horrible about it, in a way. There was The Doctor, who simply didn't know how to miss his target, and he was firing point-blank at a man-size man, and yet Phil Raeburn wasn't killed.

When I seen that Phil was reaching the rocks, determined to die, I got up and tore after him, and I heard Raeburn swear long and loud and the noise of a scuffle— and I got to the rocks as fast as my sprinting legs would carry me. . . . There I seen Phil Raeburn tied hand and foot by the grip of a big man with spectacles and with a pointed gray beard—tied hand and foot so that he could do no harm.

But that was where I came in. The hands of The Doctor was full, and my hands was filled by nothing but a pair of big guns. I had them covering him in one tenth part of a second, and I was shouting at him: "Doctor, you're finished! Drop Raeburn and stick your hands up or I'll blow you to bits!"

He turned his head toward me, and his big shoulders twitched so that I thought for a moment that he was going to throw Raeburn at my head, like a log, and then come in to finish me.

But I had the drop on him with two guns, and though I was more excited than I had ever been before, still my hands was fairly calm.

"Steady!" I said to him. "I give you no time. Act now!"

The Doctor said in the deep, deep voice that he was famous for—how it sent the chills up my back to listen to it—"I think that you're right, and that I'm beaten." He dropped the old man and slowly pushed his hands up, shoulder high—fighting them upward, as you might say.

Raeburn, the minute he was free, yanked out one of his own guns, and jammed it into the stomach of The Doctor, then, with his free hand, he begun to fish out everything that The Doctor had in the way of a weapon. That was two pairs of guns and two big knives! He sure went loaded down with enough gats and cutting instruments. Even with his weapons gone, we didn't feel quite safe with him, till we'd got his hands tied behind his back. Then we paid a little attention to his wound. It was a double one. A bullet had snipped up along his right side, just grazing the ribs, and, whipping on up higher, it had flicked along his forehead.

"Gimme your canteen," I said to Raeburn. "I'm going to get this poor devil cleaned up."

"Let me alone!" The Doctor announced, very harsh and mean. "I don't need your care. These are only scratches."

"That's right," said Raeburn. Then he added: "Doctor, will you tell me one thing? Why couldn't you shoot straight enough to down me when I rushed you?"

The Doctor didn't answer, though that was a question that I was certainly a lot interested in. I'd soaked a handkerchief, and I went up and dabbed the side of The Doctor's face, and with the next swab, though he tried to draw back, I cleaned half of his beard. But as I did it, I let out a yell.

"Hey, kid, what's wrong?" gasped Raeburn, who was exhausted with work and with joy.

"His beard . . . it moved!" I said. Then, with a wild idea in me, I caught him by that beard and jerked. Well, maybe you have guessed it before—I dunno. That beard come away in my hand. I tore the big glasses off his face. . . .

And there was Harry Clonnell looking straight back at us with a frown.

XV
A Strange Situation

I stared at Raeburn, and Raeburn stared at me. I was upset, but Raeburn was just sick.

He said: "Confound it, Harry, that's why you shot crooked at me!"

Clonnell didn't answer him, but he looked at me with a queer light in his eye. "Do you bounce lead bullets off your head, Riggs?" he asked me.

"It glanced from the rock ledge just over me," I answered, knowing what he meant.

He nodded. It was as much as to say: "I had that bullet labeled for your finish, and I can't understand how you happen to be here talking to me." He went on: "You're through with me, I hope?" He raised his head and looked away across the heads of the mountains toward some trail that he was already traveling in his mind's eye.

Old Raeburn, without a word, picked up the guns that he had just took such a triumph in yanking away from Clonnell. He was about to hand them back without a word when I cut in.

"Phil," I said, "back up."

He glanced at me. "What fool idea is in your head now, Riggs?" he asked.

Raeburn stood back, scowling at me. I don't know how fast the brain of The Doctor could work under certain circumstances, but now he made a leap to scoop a gun out of the hand of Raeburn. If he got to that gun I knew it would be death for me. I fired point-blank—not for him, but just ahead of him, and the bullet must have fanned past his face not a palm's breadth away.

He stopped at that, and he whirled around on me and stood frowning and waiting.

"Riggs, you fool!" yelled Raeburn. "Have you got murder in your heart?"

"Steady up, Phil," I said. "The Doctor understands what I mean, even if you don't."

"I don't," Raeburn said, "but I intend to find out mighty quick."

"I mean," I said, "that I now got the upper hand of a gent that has sent twenty men to death. And I'm going to make him talk turkey to me."

"You want money, I suppose," said Clonnell.

"The kind of money that you could give me would poison me," I said.

"Wait a minute, Harry," Raeburn said. "Let him say his piece. I'm here to see that no harm comes out of him."

"You are?" I said to Raeburn, keeping both gats with their mouths turned on The Doctor and ready to speak six words apiece to him. "And how can you keep me from driving a slug through his head?"

"Joe," yelled Raeburn, "I swear that if you turn a gun loose on him, I'll tackle you myself!"

"You palsied old fossil," I said, "am I going to listen to

what you think that you can do? I say that I got Clonnell in my hands, and I'm going to keep him there until he talks sense to me."

Up from the valley below us there came a muffled beating of the hoofs of horses.

"It's the rest of the posse," The Doctor said quietly. "Whatever you have to say, say it quickly, or the others will take this matter out of your hands, Raeburn. . . ."

I chopped right in: "Raeburn ain't got nothing to do with it, because it's me that has the drop on you. Now, Doctor, Raeburn thinks that because you saved the life of his daughter, you're all right. But that don't go with me. I know how many banks you've raided, and what general evil you scattered around you. Raeburn, take a think. Would you want a murderer and robber like him married to your girl?"

"Murderer and robber!" snapped Raeburn, getting very hot and wild. "Why, you fool, every man has tools in his trade. And if some have the nerve to use guns for their tools, it shows that they have nerve . . . more than you and your kind, that hate work, but don't dare to play!"

Maybe there was enough truth in that to make me mad, but, anyway, it showed me one thing, that Raeburn liked this fellow, no matter what he was and what he had been. I liked him, too, though I was pretty scared of him as he stood there looking into my eyes, thundering calm and strong.

"Don't mind him. Talk to me," I said. "Tell me when it was that you took the place of the real Doctor?"

He watched me for a moment.

"About two years ago," he said finally.

I thought back fast as lightning. The worst things had come before that. Yes, all of the bad things had come before that—the things that could be called murder had all happened long ago. It was only the wild fights that had happened since.

"You mean . . . after the Phoenix affair?"

"Yes, after that," he said.

"Did The Doctor die?" I asked.

"Yes," said Clonnell.

"You killed him?" Raeburn asked.

"I trailed him, and I killed him."

When I thought of that, it gave me a little shudder, because I could think of the terrible war that it must have made—The Doctor making a trail to get away, and this clever devil unraveling the trail problems faster than they could be laid. Then the meeting between them.

I would have given anything to hear the story, word for word. I would have given ten years of life to have seen the fight.

"What happened?" I asked.

"I haven't time to tell you," he said, "except that The Doctor, when he was helpless, tried to talk down to me, and even tried to scrape a relationship, because he pointed out that we looked a good deal alike."

"Ah!" whistled Raeburn. "And that put the idea in your head."

"I had good reasons for not wanting to go back home. I was through there . . . I was through with all the people, and they were through with me," Clonnell went on.

I said: "I see through one part of it, I think. You sent a letter to Raeburn telling him that you were coming to make trouble for him. Then you planted yourself in the way of the posse when we was hunting. And you'd framed everything. You'd buried the gun butt, and you'd planted the sack of gold. It was worth that much money to you, if you could get at Raeburn's household without ever being suspected of what you were. You didn't dare to ride mean horses or shoot guns, for fear of doing it so well that you'd be suspected."

The Doctor shrugged his shoulders. "You have a way of looking into affairs, Riggs," he said. "I felt that you were a bit too dangerous. As for the rest, I could handle them. But when I felt your sharp eyes on me, I knew that I would have to play my part extra hard. I overdid it. And the result was that I had to show my hand."

"Ah," I said, "you showed your hand, then?"

He smiled at me in his gentle way. "I'd done enough to show the boys on the ranch that I had been playing a part. They would start asking questions . . . and once that began, they were sure to discover me, sooner or later. It simply had to be."

"Where was you born?" I asked.

"In Kentucky."

"It's pretty far east," I said. "Maybe so far east that you don't know that out here there is no questions asked of a man that does the sort of things that you done on the day when you saved Dolly Raeburn. There ain't a sheriff on the range but would be ashamed of even suspecting you of anything."

"Is that true, do you think?" murmured The Doctor, staring at me hard.

"Man, man!" broke in Raeburn, who begun to see for the first time what my drift was, "there was never a truer thing than that ever said. Was that the fear that drove you away?"

"No," said The Doctor. "The fact was . . . you may have guessed it . . . that Dolly had begun to care for me. And was I worthy of her? No, I saw that I wasn't. I couldn't dream of letting such a girl as that throw herself away on such a fellow as I. So I cleared out, Raeburn, for all of those reasons, though I'd come down to your ranch intending to have your scalp." He smiled again. "At least," he added, "I did no real harm."

"You done no harm," I said, "outside of leaving Dolly to die by inches. You didn't do no harm at all. We can watch her fading away from day to day, but we know that you don't mean no harm by it. A busted heart in a girl like that . . . why, what's that to you?"

"Hold on," said The Doctor. "I'm not quite a fool about girls. I know that broken hearts occur in books, but. . . ."

I held up my hand. The Doctor stopped.

"You mean it?" he said with suppressed eagerness.

"I swear to God," I said.

The Doctor sat down heavily on a stone, and old Raeburn come and dropped a hand on his shoulder.

"Harry," he said, "or Bill, or Joe, or Steve, or Pete . . . or whatever your name is . . . you've had a grand time of it for a couple of years, and you've raised your little bit of trouble, and I suppose that you sure hate to break away from it. But come down to us, lad. The mountaintops, they get cold in the winter. And you'll never find a truer heart than my Dolly's."

"What, man?" cried The Doctor. "Marry Dolly . . . and be discovered in a year or two. . . ."

"Out here, old son," said Raeburn, "a man's past don't never last more than three months on the shady side. If he can keep straight for that long, he's said to be a straight man. And every straight man is believed to have been always straight, unless it's proved against him. It's got to be proved to a jury that's got blindfolded eyes and cotton in their ears. Do you come?"

Well, I ask you, what could any man do?

XVI
Gathering the Ends

I have always been right glad to remember some days of my life—like the first time that I owned a gun of my own, and the first pair of long trousers, and the first girl that said she loved me. But I dunno that any day outshone the one when me and Raeburn stood by and watched pale Dolly Raeburn open a letter that came through the post, all wrote out in a big, slashing hand.

We had a main idea of what that letter said, but just the same it was good for us to watch the way that Dolly blossomed. She didn't say nothing to us. But she run up the stairs, the first step that she had moved out of a walk for days and days. Up there, we heard her voice come floating and bubbling through an open window as she sang out: "Hey, Steve! Hey, Steve!"

Steve Sloan hollered back: "Hello, Dolly. What's up?"

"Will you throw a saddle on the big chestnut with the white leg?" she asked.

"Hey, Dolly, that devil ain't had leather on him for ten days!" Steve said.

"Good!" she said. "I want something that'll explode!"

Explode was what the chestnut did, but Dolly sat through all the antics, and then took him tearing away, with an Indian yell trailing back to us.

Oh, she was a happy girl, I can tell you, and Raeburn was the next happiest person on earth.

After that, we waited, and along the morning of the next day, Dolly says casual-like: "Harry will be back tomorrow . . . maybe. . . ."

We just said: "Is that so?" Like we didn't know nothing.

"A queer feller," Raeburn said. "I dunno that I like the cut of that Clonnell, Joe."

"Nor me neither," I agreed. "He ain't got the look of the right sort of a gent about him."

Dolly jumped up from her chair. She could hardly speak. "If I were you, I'd be ashamed! I'd be ashamed!" And she flung out of the room.

"Tut! Tut!" said the chief. "Ain't she got it bad, though?"

Now the next day passed and along about evening time, when we was sitting around in front of the bunkhouse—all of us 'punchers talking over nothing in particular and getting ready for bed, a gent rides up and sits his horse far enough away to be blurred by the gloom of the night.

"Is Joe Riggs there?" said the voice of Clonnell.

"You're right he is!" I called back, and I made for him.

Well, sir, he was scared to death. He walked along with me to the house—his horse following him like a dog.

"Do you think it's all right, Joe?" he asked.

"Ask her father," I answered.

"Her father doesn't matter. But you have a clear pair of eyes. How do you see it?"

94

"Why, old fellow, you've had your fling, and you'll settle down fine," I said. "Come on in."

"Wait a minute," he said. "I want to talk to you some more. . . ."

But I dragged him through the door, and the next minute he seen Dolly, and she seen him—and the rest was easy to watch, I can tell you.

They was married the next week, Raeburn insisting that they should get together quick, and I suppose that he was right, because you never can tell about a fellow like that Clonnell. He, having more horse power than ten ordinary men, might get new ideas, so it was a good idea to tie him after daubing in the rope, before he got over the surprise of the new idea.

The very next week we had reason to thank our stars that we had him with us, because two dozen Mexicans from over the border had sneaked up through the mountains with their eye on El Paso del Tigre. Then they come whooping down to clean up the place.

The Doctor and five men happened to meet them at the head of the valley, and they split on Clonnell like water on a rock. They boiled and bubbled around him and the five for half a day. When the rest of us finally heard what was happening and come up, those Mexicans was ready to be swept away by any puff of wind.

The newspapers called it The Battle of the Pass of the Tiger. But we called it Harry's Scrap, which it was. After that it seemed, even to me, who was the most doubting of all the folks that knew, that Clonnell could feel that there was enough action here in the pass to keep him contented.

Sometimes when I seen him off riding by himself, with his eyes turned away to the distant mountains, I wondered if he didn't yearn to be follering the old, wild trails, with a thousand men hungering for his scalp, now and then.

One thing, at least, I was sure of. Dolly Raeburn Clonnell was the happiest woman in the mountains. And if there was a shadow on Harry from time to time—it disappeared in the face of Dolly's contentment.

A WOLF AMONG
DOGS

I
Rafferty—Lefty's Luck

A horseman swung his mount off the road and darted it between the hills at the ranch house that squatted in the hollow, with a blackened straw stack close at hand. He regarded neither of these disagreeable features of the landscape, nor the half blind, half desperate appearance of the front of the house itself. Instead, he made straight for the front door of the shack and raised a shrill, long whistle as he did so.

The whistle seemed to announce him, for, as he swept up to the house, the door was jerked open six inches and he had a glimpse of a half-dressed old man with a long rifle in his hands. The rider brought his horse to a halt with sliding hoofs.

"They're after him!" he gasped out at the old man.

"Who's on the trail?" came the inquiry.

"Chic Harley."

"That houn' dog?"

"He's comin' hell-bent. He's got about eight gents with him, all on good hosses and all ridin' the life out of 'em."

"Hey, stay here and gimme a hand saddlin' up the. . . ."

99

The messenger, however, waited for nothing more. Somewhere in the distance a horse neighed. Perhaps it was the only one in the fields that felt the first chill of the dawn and rejoiced in the coming of the day. But perhaps it came from some horse hard ridden down the road. The neigh broke off short, as it usually does with a running horse. That was sufficient for the bearer of the ill news. He wheeled, spurring deep. There was a violent scratching of gravel, and the sweating horse careened off around the corner of the house and was gone with an echo of hoof beats behind him, sometimes seeming far off, sometimes, for a moment, flung back in a loud echo from the hills.

The old fellow at the door remained for a moment, undecided. Then he jerked the door shut, tossed the rifle into a corner, and hurried up the stairs, calling.

A door was yanked open before him. There was seen a boy's frightened face as he stood shivering in the morning cold.

"What's up, Dad?"

"Shut up your yappin'. Get in there." He paused, with an afterthought as he went by the door and, shooting out a grimy hand, he fastened it upon the shoulder of the shrinking youngster. "You ain't heard nothin' . . . you ain't seen nothin'!"

The boy swallowed and winked, then he slammed the door and the father rushed on down the narrow upper hallway to the front room—his own room, although it had been turned over to a most important guest for the night. He did not knock, but, tossing the door open, he stormed across to the bed and began to shake the figure of the sleeping man by the shoulder.

"Lefty! Lefty! Wake up!"

Lefty groaned. In the fire of his anxiety, the old fellow half lifted the body from the bed, but Lefty was as limp as though his brain were stunned, and his head fell back slack from the shoulders.

"Lefty! D'you hear me?"

"Lemme be," breathed Lefty. "Won't you lemme be for a minute?" And he was sound asleep again, even while the hand of the master of the house tore at him in a vain endeavor to rouse him.

At this, seeing the light of the day freshening every moment, the old fellow desisted from his work and stared down at the haggard face of the sleeper—perspiration beginning to stream out on his forehead.

"He's plumb spent," said the rancher bitterly. "Lefty!" he screamed.

"Comin'," moaned the sleeper, and dropped away into his stunned slumber again.

The other ran to the window and looked out. The road from this second-story window was visible. It stretched past the front of the ranch twisting over the hilltop into the valley, then visible again, as it streaked behind the trees on the farther side of the hollow. Still there was no sign of a band of horsemen rushing along it. But the warning could not be wrong, and, once the riders came into view, they would be swarming about the house in a trice.

He hastened back to the bed. "Lefty! Lefty! They're comin'!"

Not a stir of the sleeper. Indeed, he merely smiled and made a slight gesture with his hand, as though he recognized the call of a friendly voice.

Then, in despair, striking a hand against his own face, the rancher cried: "Harley! Chic Harley!"

The effect was magic. The sleeper opened his eyes. The agony of the waking was only a moment so great as to keep him motionless. Then he kicked his feet over the edge of the bed and swayed to a sitting posture.

"What about Harley?" he mumbled. "Wha's masser?" He was like a drunkard, so thick did exhaustion make his speech.

"He's comin'!" yelled the old man, cupping his hands at his mouth to give his voice volume. "Chic Harley is comin'!"

At this, there was a gasp from the other. He got to his feet, reeling. Reaching for the shoulder of his friend, he steadied himself. "'Tain't possible!" he muttered. "Not Harley."

"They just brung me word."

"But Harley was clean across the state the other day."

"He might have come by train. He'd come a million miles for the sake of a trail, I guess."

"Gimme my hat," said the hunted man, and, when it had been jammed upon his head, he was escorted through the doorway and swaying, bumping, down the stairs.

"How long I slept?"

"Three hours. Can you sit in a saddle, Lefty?"

"Don't ask questions . . . gimme hoss."

When they reached the open air, the chill of it straightened out the exhausted man a little, but he was still walking with sagged knees when he reached the barn. The morning light revealed him clearly. He was a man of middle height, rather thin, with a high-arched nose, eyes sunken with weariness, and a mouth worn by much suffering to an expression of sadness.

In the barn stood a brown horse and a gray. To the brown ran the rancher, dragging a saddle off the peg.

"Hold up," said the fugitive, leaning weakly against the wall. "Gimme Rafferty ag'in."

"Not him . . . not the gray," said his friend eagerly. "They're trailin' you by that hoss, old son. They dunno your face. It's the hoss that's fetchin' 'em after you, Lefty."

"Gimme Rafferty," muttered the other. "He's my luck. Gimme Rafferty, or I won't try to ride."

"Rafferty's spent!"

"Is he plumb fagged?" said the fugitive sadly, and, walking with uncertain steps to the gray, he laid a hand on the hip of the animal. Rafferty stood with braced legs, his head hanging, until, at that touch and that voice, his flagging ears pricked up and he lifted his head.

"He'll pack me a ways," said Lefty. "Besides, I dunno that I care much if they get me. Let Rafferty see the last of me."

The rancher, with his free hand, made a gesture of despair. But the time was drawing very short. There was no leisure for argument, so he threw the saddle on the back of the gray.

"Are you gonna make a fight of it if they . . . I mean, if *they* have the luck?"

"Am I gonna let 'em string me up, d'you think?" snarled out Lefty. "Not me!"

The saddled gray was brought to the front of the barn, and Lefty mounted. They made a dreary figure—the exhausted horse and the exhausted man. The dust of yesterday's ride was still thick on Lefty. The dust of yesterday was turning the gray dingy, also. But still, with his master in the saddle, he lifted his head a little and came heavily up on the bit.

"Good boy," said Lefty, touched, and ran his hand down the neck of Rafferty.

"Good luck!" cried the rancher, looking anxiously down the road. "Good luck, Lefty, and remember to . . . hey," he broke off with a yell. "I hear 'em! I hear 'em,

Lefty!" He raised a hand for silence. Out of the distance was the muttering drum of hoofs of horses upon a road muffled with dust.

"If they get you here . . . !" he yelled frantically. "Ride like the devil! Get out of here! Get out fast, Lefty!"

In spite of that approaching sound of doom, Lefty spared the time to smile down upon the other with infinite scorn and with infinite knowledge, as of one to whom all the wrinkles on the face of danger have long been known, one who has often flirted with death.

"You get back into bed," he said. "That'll be best for you. Good-bye, old-timer. I ain't gonna forget. . . ." He sent the gray into a trot, and not a fast trot at that, while the rancher stood aghast at so slow a pace with that rush of pursuit drawing momentarily nearer.

But only at a trot Rafferty was sent straight back among the sheds, and not out toward the roads—back among the sheds and so was aimed at the broken hill country beyond. By wits and not by speed must Lefty be saved upon this day, if saved he might be.

Realizing this, the old man gave another look toward the road, a sidelong glance of dread, and then bolted for the house.

II
A Promising Trail

That "hound dog," Chic Harley, leading a posse, came down the road; the cool of the morning had not been able to temper the fury of their hard riding. They stormed straight up to the rancher's shack and summoned him with a brief clamor.

"Mort Carey!"

He had no time to pretend to be wakened from a sound sleep. The front door crashed open and the thunder of their heels was on the stairs before he could reach the entrance to his room. They met him there, a flood of rough men who tossed him back before them to the farther side of the room. He retreated instinctively in the direction of his rifle, but he was commanded away from it with a gesture. Chic Harley himself was in the forefront, and, where Chic Harley stood, other men were prone to forget that they went armed. To make a motion toward a weapon was as good as a death warrant, so terrible was he with his guns.

This was the sort of a moment for which he lived, as every man in the mountain desert knew, and, if he had an opportunity to do mischief, he would not have to be invited twice before he seized upon it. He was like a savage dog, always ready to tear. There was, with all of his courage, a sort of detestable caution in Chic Harley and a lack of impulse that made all men hate him as much as they admired his fighting qualities. Another man, with his love of destruction, would have run amuck and been ruled out of society long ago, but Chic Harley never permitted his passions to carry him away with them unless he were strictly behind the fence of the law. He had been known to swallow insults from a man of not half his prowess, simply because he was not quite sure that the law would back him up if he destroyed the man. Indeed, he would not fight unless his legal retreat were perfectly secured. Then he proceeded with a terrible surety that made him all the more loathed.

Under such circumstances he could rarely fight. There was only one field in which he could give a free rein to his talents, and that was as an agent of the law in the pursuit of criminals. This was the delight of Chic Harley. As for business affairs on his ranch, they were never allowed to stand in his way. He was ready to mount at the first alarm, and he would ride horses to death, outstrip his companions, rush on with the fury of a mink on the trail until he closed with his foe. When he overtook the fugitive, he had no desire to make a capture, for death was what he wanted. Death was the thing which he loved, and which he had so often dealt out to fugitives. But in him, his battle hunger never became a blindness—if he rushed along the trail like a furious weasel, when it came to the moment of combat, he held back and fought like a fox, wickedly and safely. He was young—not yet thirty—and of a fine presence of which he was very proud and scrupulously careful in his dress.

At sight of him the heart of Mortimer Carey failed in his breast, and he looked desperately around him, but he was hopelessly cornered.

"Now, Carey," said Chic Harley, "we want the gent and we want him quick. We'll listen to what you got to say."

Carey swallowed hard. "I dunno," he said, "who you're drivin' at."

"Search the place," snapped out Harley over his shoulder. "The fool ain't planned to talk to us. Go through it from top to bottom, and make it quick." He continued to Carey: "You're lyin', Carey. We know that you're lyin'. A gent on a gray hoss put up here last night."

"A gray hoss?" said Carey blankly. "I dunno nothin' about that."

"Look here," said the deputy sheriff grimly, "you ain't in too good standin', Carey. They's some folks in these parts that figger you know more'n you talk about concernin' a pile of crooked work that goes on in the mountains. I'm givin' you a hint that might turn out to save your own hide. Talk up, Mort. It's worthwhile for you to talk, and that's a fact!"

But Carey shook his head. The dread of the unknown was chilling his blood, but still he shook his head and made his firm denials. He could not betray one who had so recently been his guest, for although your city dweller may forget that there is something sacred in hospitality, he who lives on the edge of the wilderness cannot forget. Every man's house must of necessity be a tavern open to the public, and open to those in need, free of charge. It is a matter of turn and turn about.

"We've found Carey's kid," the returning searchers announced, "and they's a bed in the attic that's been slept in."

"Who slept there?" snapped out the sheriff.

Carey rolled his eyes for a thought. "Sam Dufferin," he said at last, blinking. "My cousin, Sam Dufferin. He come in last night, and he left early."

"What trail did he take?"

"He rode east, I guess. I didn't see him off, but that was his aim, last night."

"You're a mighty slick liar, partner. What color of a hoss was he ridin'?"

"Come to think of it, he was riding some sort of a gray . . . but it was dappled pretty black."

Chic Harley shook his head, as one who cannot be persuaded. "Where's the kid?" he asked suddenly. "Somebody bring me up that kid, will you?"

The kid was brought, and stood blinking and scowling around him, frightened, but savagely at bay and ready to fight like some wild young animal.

"What's your name?" asked Harley.

"Nick is my name," said the boy, whose eyes had stopped roving and who was staring at his father as though striving to read the mind of the latter and find out what it was that he was expected to say.

"Nick," said the manhunter, "d'you know who I am?"

"I know you," said the boy, still staring like a somnambulist at Mort Carey. "You're Harley. You're the killer."

Harley flushed, as much in pride as in anger. "Well," he said, "you know what I do to folks that don't tell me the truth."

At this the boy turned sharply upon him, his face working. "Are you tryin' to scare me?" he said furiously. "Mister Harley, I'm a Carey, and the Careys don't scare!"

There was a little approving murmur from the others in the room, and the eyes of Mort Carey went black and bright with pride. As for the other members of the posse, they detested the methods and the manners of Harley as much as they admired his skill and the results that he obtained. He was what they considered a necessary evil. He had brought peace into a district of the mountain desert where there had been confusion and a thousand crimes before. Indeed, Harley had selected that district with care because it was the scene of so much wrongdoing that he was guaranteed many a ride along fugitive trails. That promise had been fulfilled, and, for his part, he had worked so industriously that what had once been a favorite resort of criminals was now shunned by them like a plague.

The feast had been cleared from the table, and it was generally expected that Chic Harley would now move on to more promising scenes. If people appreciated him, they detested him, also. No one in the world was such a friend to Harley that the latter would not have rejoiced at an opportunity to take his trail the moment he fell under the legitimate ban of the law. And the world knew it. So the men in the room could not help muttering their approval of little Nick until the glance of Harley flashed at them and checked them, like the side look of a suspicious animal.

"Did somebody spend last night here?" snapped out Harley at the boy, eyeing him up and down as though he regretted that the youth of the child prevented sterner measures at once.

Nick hesitated a fraction of a second, looking at his father again. "Yes," he said at last.

"Who was it?" asked the deputy sheriff.

Again the eager, questioning eyes of Nick flashed at his father. He was met by a warning frown. But speak he must. He cast swiftly around him. "Tom Parks was here," he ventured sullenly.

Chic Harley turned to the father with a broad grin of triumph. "Looks like Sam Dufferin has changed his name," he said. He added with a roar, as though to overwhelm the boy in his confusion: "What color hoss was he ridin'?"

"A sort of a . . . bay," said Nick in despair.

There was another grin from the deputy sheriff. "I guess that'll do," he said. "That's enough to show that the pair of you are lyin'. Harborin' gents that are wanted by the law . . . that's what you been doin'. Refusin' to help the agents of the law when duly summoned . . . maybe that'll be a jail sentence for you, Carey. I dunno." He turned on his followers. "Scatter, gents. We gotta find the trail of him that was ridin' the gray. And we've lost about three miles of time already."

He himself was not an expert trail master. For that reason he looked to the horses while the rest of his men cut for sign. They began around the house itself, and then rode in increasing circles. Perhaps the hearts of some of them were not in this work of trailing, but their professional pride as cowpunchers and hunters was now called into question, and they did their best. Out of the tangle of horse trails old and new that surrounded the shack they had to find the newest leading away from the house, and five minutes later an excited yell announced that the trail, or something which seemed very like the right trail, had been located.

Then Harley called a swift consultation. There was a brief exchange of views among the oldest heads among the trailers. Finally they agreed that the trail was really promising. In an instant they were sweeping through the sheds behind the house at a canter. Carey and Nick, from the shack, watched them going with sullen eyes.

III
Turned to Face Danger

The first mile convinced them that they were right. The trail was freshly made, and it drove straightway from the home of old Carey—there could hardly have been a mistake about its identity. At the end of the first mile, it dipped over the first crest of the hills and stopped on the bank of a stream. The hunters spread at once. Some rode up the stream and some down. Some forded it and cut for sign along the farther bank.

In ten minutes they picked it up. The fugitive—for after the making of this trail problem he could hardly be anything else—had ridden simply down the stream for a hundred yards, then put his horse to the bank up a series of hard rocks from which, when the water dried, there would be no traces left. But where he had passed from the rocks to the ground beyond, the signs were found cut deep by the plodding hoofs of the horse. It was easy to follow these plain markings.

They journeyed on without haste. It was plain by the number of times the fugitive's horse had stumbled that the animal was tired out, and they needed merely a trifle of

111

patience rather than risk the exhaustion of their own mounts by an overuse of the spur. For the early morning rush through which they had put their cow ponies had worn them badly. Your true cow horse is not meant for sustained efforts at speed; it will jog all the day at a dogtrot, and it will rock along at a tireless canter that does not cover the ground much more quickly, but it does not stand up under a fast pace. It has not the legs for such work. The long, rolling stride with which the Thoroughbred wings effortlessly through the fields behind the flying pack would break the heart of the mustang in no time. Accordingly, the posse spared its horseflesh carefully and campaigned them through the hills with a vigilant care.

For another half hour they plodded along a trail that freshened constantly, then they struck a plateau of flinty rock where the trail had gone out. There was a full twenty-minute delay until separate riders had cut around the edge of the plateau and found a spot where the fugitive had doubled back very near the point at which he entered the rocks and headed away over the sandy hills once more.

Now, with set jaws, feeling that their prey was in danger of slipping from them in spite of the nearness with which they had come to it at the shack of Carey, they hurried on with slackened reins, and in three weary miles found themselves at the edge of a raw-faced cliff, while on the floor of the valley, a hundred feet below them, they could see easily the trail of the fugitive's horse. A scant hundred feet—but how wide a gap to them. They could circle some four miles to the side and come back into the trail once more, but four miles doubled for the going and the coming meant eight, and an eight mile handicap added to what their horses had already gone through would be fatal to their chances of success. Three men besides Chic Harley volunteered for the desperate effort. They were cool riders themselves, and their horses were goat-footed mountain climbers. They worked their way, sliding and stopping by fits and starts, to the bottom of the cliff. From above, the rest of the posse gave them a cheer of admiration mingled with envy. Then they went on again.

It was a more serious matter now. Their numbers before had been enough to make all resistance ridiculous, but four men composed a different story. Any good shot, with an efficient rifle, might sit at his ease behind a rock and pick them off. They were forced to strike on more carefully, studying the trail before them, regarding every nest of rocks with suspicion. Then one of the horses went suddenly lame; three riders went on together.

But the strength of three is not the strength of three-quarters of four. It is less than half in power. For while three men fall, the fourth man kills the assailant. The problem that three men cannot solve is apparent to the fourth. Chic Harley, doing his best with horse and with trail, discovered that his companions had fallen silent and refused to answer him as he urged them forward. It was a bad sign. Except in the actual face of danger, silence is apt to indicate a failing heart. There was more than this to be considered. The slowness with which they rode and the manifest weariness that they showed might be held as an index to point out the serious lack of confidence that they had. Nothing he said could cheer them on. He tried the power of sarcasm.

"A fightin' gent like you, Shorty," he said to one of them, "sure has got an appetite for trouble. That's why you're singin' so much. That's why you're dog-gone near ridin' your hoss to death to get at this gent of the gray hoss?"

Shorty answered heavily: "I dunno what you're drivin' at, chief. If you mean, am I feelin' fine about mixin' with this gazabo we're after, I'll tell you that I ain't."

Chic Harley was staggered. After all, it required an infinite courage to admit fear, and Chic never for an instant doubted the integrity of the bravery of Shorty.

"For why?" asked Chic. "Why ain't you feelin' like mixin' with this gent we're follerin'?"

"Speakin' personal," said Shorty, "I ain't never for mixin' with no desperado."

"You follered Champ Hanson with me," said Harley. "You follered Lew Cutting. I aim to think that they was both desperados, as folks say."

"They wasn't," answered Shorty with the calm of immense conviction.

"Well?" queried Harley, raising his voice like most men when they are face to face with something that they don't understand.

"Champ and Lew were just common folk gone wrong. Common folk, Chic, like you and like me."

"How come you to make out the meanin' of desperado, old-timer?" asked Chic, frowning.

Shorty considered, and the horses of the entire party fell to a walk, with that of Harley leading as usual. "I'll tell you," said Shorty finally, making a mental discovery, "a desperado is a gent that has been like you and me and the rest of us, maybe, until along comes a time when he gets up against a pretty stiff deal with his back to the wall. Three men corner him, say. He's scared stiff, while they're chasin' him. But after they've cornered him, he gets all cold and cool. Maybe he ain't ever been much of a shot, but when he gets in a pinch, he can't miss. His arm is like a rock. He's fast as chain lightnin'. His guns help him to do his thinking. Understand?"

Chic and the third member were both silent, considering. Shorty went on: "They all talk about desperados. Well, they dunno what they're talkin' about. They ain't been more'n one or two, all put together."

"One or two?" shouted the other two in one voice.

"Well, maybe a half a dozen," qualified Shorty.

"Why," began Chic, "I could name a. . . ."

"A hundred that have been called desperados. What was they? Gents that could shoot straight and knowed it. Bullies that took advantage of their strength. Swearin', ravin' fools that was hungry for a killin'. But that don't make no desperado. Them fellers don't raise their voice. They stand and wait when the time comes for trouble. And when the fightin' starts, they just start killin'. They're rattlers without no rattle. Killin' a man don't mean no more to them than choppin' down a tree. They got no conscience . . . not while they're fightin'. They're quiet. Mighty near gentle, you might call 'em. Look at this here gent on the gray hoss. He's that way. No loud talkin'. He just walks into the bank with a mask over his face and puts a gun on the rail. He says mighty soft and easy to the president . . . 'I'm in need of some cash. Have you got any to spare in here?' That's the way he puts it. And the president, he looks up and takes it all in. You know that there president, Calkins. They've tried to rob his bank before. He's killed seven men in his day, and his day ain't over. He's a fightin' fool. But when he heard that feller behind the mask, it turned his blood cold. He seen that he had to give up. And he surrendered. He opened the safe and told the boys not to make no foolish moves. This here gent on the gray hoss gets thirty thousand, and then drifts out of town. He was desperate . . . cold desperate, that was all. You got to hand it to him. He froze up the town . . . it was half an hour before they come to and started climbin' onto their hosses to foller him. Y'understand?"

115

"Why did you ever start on this here trail?" asked Chic Harley furiously, but still controlling half of his wrath.

"Because I hadn't figgered it out," answered Shorty frankly. "It looked like a game to me . . . till I seen the way he mixed up his trail for us, and till I seen that he was ridin' the same old gray hoss. That made me know that he was queer."

"How come?"

"He could've got another hoss from old man Carey. He could've got a fresh cayuse, not a plumb fagged one like the one that's been stumblin' along this trail. But he stuck by his old hoss. Why? Because he's queer! Because he's different from the rest of us, I'd say." He added with an enthusiasm of conviction: "And I say that we ain't gonna catch him. If we do, he'll slaughter the whole three of us . . . easy."

Harley glanced at the third man and saw a confirmation of Shorty's mood in the other's face. Then his rage broke in a flood. "To the devil with the pair of you for a couple of yallerlivered cowards and skunks!" he stormed at them. "I never took a trail and turned back on it. I ain't gonna begin with this one. I'll go and get him by myself!"

Touching his horse with the spurs, he leaped ahead down the trail. At the next turn he could look back without moving in the saddle, and he saw the two sitting motionless in their saddles, watching him. They had not been shamed into following. He hardly cared. In his present mood, nothing could have served to deter him for a moment upon his path. He wanted fight, and the quicker the better. He wanted fight, and heaven save the man who stood in his way! Besides, the glory would all be his. Plus the reward.

So, blindly, he rushed his mount over the next hilltop, and there in the hollow beneath he saw a masked man

116

upon a gray horse sitting in the saddle, waiting for him. As Shorty had prophesied—waiting for the danger to roll down upon him. Why he waited might be read, perhaps, in the braced legs of his weary horse. But if he did not choose to ride on, rather than stand and do battle, the man might have taken to his heels and disappeared among the rough rocks. He could have made almost as good time on foot and left a less legible trail, by far. But flight was not in his mind. As Shorty had said, he had turned to face his danger.

Chic Harley drew rein and jerked the rifle from its scabbard.

IV
Two Guns Are Proffered

But, in the very act of raising his rifle for the shot, he paused with a shock of surprise. Making no effort either to retreat or charge, the stranger sat quietly with his own rifle balanced at the pommel of his saddle. It was very strange.

Chic Harley pitched the butt of the rifle into the hardened hollow of his shoulder and fired. It was an easy shot. Not exactly point-blank range, but very near it. He was already lowering the rifle and about to urge his horse forward, when he saw that the stranger was not falling. No, there he sat, still, with the rifle balanced across the pommel of his saddle and with the wind furling the brim of his sombrero. Chic Harley exclaimed, with a catch of something like fright in his voice. Then he jerked up the rifle again. Just as his finger was curling around the trigger the winged terror struck him. He fired, indeed, but he fired blindly. Then he lurched out of the saddle and fell in an odd heap on the ground.

*   *   *

When he opened his eyes again, he lay on his back under a small tree, and beside him sat the masked stranger.

"What's up?" asked Chic in a strange, far voice.

"I hit a bit higher'n I aimed," said the masked man gravely.

"I'll come through, then," said Chic eagerly.

The other shook his head. "You're a dead man, Harley," he announced.

"It's a lie!" screamed Harley. "It's a. . . ." His voice stopped without his will. "How long've I got?" he whispered.

"I dunno. I bandaged you up and stopped the bleedin' mostly."

"You're white," said Harley, speaking thick. He closed his eyes. Then he opened them again suddenly and gasped out: "You ain't gonna leave me, old-timer?"

"Not I, old son. I'll see you through . . . unless them pups that was ridin' with you come along and scare me out."

"To the devil with them," moaned the dying man. "Oh, they'll burn a million years in hell for this. But you don't mean it . . . not about me, stranger. I ain't checkin' out. . . ."

"You're dead, Harley."

Harley moistened his lips. "Who might you be?"

"Why, they call me Lefty."

"I remember . . . the shoulder you put your gun ag'in'. . . . Lefty, might I see your face?"

"I guess not."

"It'd make it easier to die, somehow."

"Well. . . ." The hat and the mask were removed, and Harley stared up into the worn features and then at a close-cropped head above them.

"You're fresh out of the pen, I guess," he said.

The slayer nodded.

"And you're headin' straight back for it," said Chic Harley faintly.

"I'll never go back to it," answered the other. "Maybe they'll land me, but they'll never get me back. I'll have my fling," he added with a fierce composure. "I'll have my good time. Maybe it'll be a week . . . or a month . . . or a year, but before I'm through I'll give 'em reason to remember me by. Leave off talkin' about me. What kin I do for you, old-timer? You're in a bad way. Look here . . . if the pain. . . ."

"It's terrible," groaned the dying man.

"Take a swig of this."

Lefty poured a stiff swig of whiskey down the throat of Chic. The latter choked, and then the muscles of his face composed.

"That's better," he declared. "I can stand it better now. It sort of takes the horror off of things, Lefty. What might make you so keen to gimme a hand like this . . . when I was ridin' you down before?"

"You done your duty."

"I was huntin' you for the fun of the huntin'," said Chic with the resolution of one who is already facing all that may be feared in life.

At this confession, a scowl formed on the brow of Lefty, but it disappeared almost at once. "I dunno what was goin' on inside your head," he informed Harley. "But I seen you come on and take your chance all by yourself. I aim to figger that you're nine-tenths man, partner."

Chic Harley sighed and looked away past the head of the other to the pale blue of the sky. Could he hold his destroyer until the companions from the posse moved up within range? For surely they had heard the rifle firing and were coming up with all speed to the place from which they had heard the noise. Or, perhaps, if Lefty rode on, he, Chic Harley, would survive the bullet long enough to describe the slayer to the rest of the posse. These were the hopes that were forming in the mind of Chic Harley while he watched the sky. But all of these hopes might fail him, and there was another way in which he might, perhaps, entangle the enemy.

"There is one last thing that you might do for me, Lefty," he said.

"Lemme hear it," Lefty said gently. "I'm sure willin' to do what I can, partner."

"These here gats of mine," said Chic feebly.

"All right."

Seeing that Chic moved his hands toward his Colts, Lefty drew them forth and raised them before the eyes of the dying man.

"I've done my work with them guns," declared Chic mournfully.

"I reckon you have," Lefty agreed.

"The last thing I want you to do . . . would you swear that you'd do it, partner?"

"I would."

The death agony thrilled through the body of Chic Harley, but he fought it back. He must take the thought of his revenge with him to the grave. "Are you one of them that believe in God?" he gasped out.

"I believe in God," Lefty stated solemnly.

"Put up your right hand." It was done. "Now lemme hear you swear, partner, that you'll take these here guns to the gent that I name."

The hand was raised. The eyes of Lefty glanced with awe into the pale heart of the sky with a feeling that the thin clouds that blew there drew the outline of a shadowy face, immense and beautiful and terrible, staring down at him. His breath grew shorter. It was with a quiver of dread that he repeated: "I'll swear that, partner."

"Take these here guns to my brother and. . . ."

"But if he knows them guns, he'll want to hear how I come by 'em!" cried Lefty, beginning to guess the trick that had been used to trap his conscience to the destruction of his body.

"You'll take them guns and put 'em in his hands," said Harley, speaking with difficulty. "You'll take 'em to . . . Gus Harley!" he cried in a horrible voice, and died as he spoke.

Lefty, looking up from the body, saw a horseman streaking to the right of him, driving hard to cut him off, and another to the left, riding with equal vigor. Lefty watched them as a wolf watches a pair of dogs that have come out from the town to harass it. His fingers automatically closed hard upon his rifle. That was a tooth that could bite them both to death, but still the time had not come to use it again. He threw himself on the back of the weary gray and sent that gallant animal at a slow gallop full of labor, not up the road between those two racing enemies, but straight back in the direction from which they had come that day. He heard yells of rage. The pair wheeled their mounts about and stormed straight after him again. How wild and rash they were, and how neatly he could subdue all of that passion by two light touches of his forefinger. But, for the time being, he withheld his finger.

He turned in the saddle and looked back at them and grinned at them as the wolf grins when it sees the bull moose floundering and helpless in the snow. Still he would not shoot. Something held him back by the force of a mere thread. How narrowly it held him, and yet it had power enough to keep him from the fight. He wondered then what it was. He was to wonder many times thereafter.

But they came fast, fast, as though their horses had not been in the least fatigued by their labors of the day, or as if they saw the prey and were eager as their riders to come up with it. So Lefty, twice turning in the saddle and gripping his rifle, finally, with a groan, headed the staggering gray for a steep pitch of rocks that tumbled down a hillside, and there he swung himself out of the saddle and began to run forward on foot up the slope.

Rafferty, the good gray, followed like a dog at his heels. How much was he heartened and strengthened by the release from that crushing weight in the saddle. He could breathe deeper and more freely once more, gallant horse, and he went up the slope fast enough, even speeding up to the side of Lefty as the latter ran.

A shower of lead began to spatter around them as the two pursuers opened fire. Lefty dropped to his knees and called the gray, and Rafferty, like a circus horse, lay down behind a big rock while his master fired in reply from the corner of the boulder. He did not kill, but he had never fired with so sure a hand in all his life. He slashed open the very crown of the sombrero of one rider; he nipped the rump of the other's horse with a wasp sting of a bullet and sent the beast away plunging and bucking. This was more than enough. The two bolted, and Rafferty was left alone with his master to rest and grow strong for the next day's march, the next day's journey from pursuit.

V
Drifter Subs for Rafferty

There was no immediate pressing of the pursuit. When such a captain as Chic Harley falls on the field, his followers pause in some dismay unless, out of the excess of their love for him, they rush forward at once to gain revenge. But there was no excess of love for him among the followers of Mr. Chic Harley. They were merely downhearted at the fall of so formidable a companion, and, when they had all drawn together at the end of a day's savage riding, they decided that there was only one thing for them to do, and that was to bury the dead champion at once and make forward to the nearest town to tell the story of his fall.

So the trail was cleared for Lefty. He doubled straight back through the mountains and came, at dusk, three days later, to the sight of the shack of Mort Carey and the smell of the smoke, which trailed from his chimney, oddly mixed with the fragrance of frying bacon. The mouth of the fugitive watered and his eyes grew dim, but, drawing his belt tighter, he shook his head with resolution.

At the door of the shack he knocked heavily. It was answered by young Nick, who yelled with surprise and with excitement at the sight of the new arrival. "Hey, Dad, here's Lefty come back! Here's Lefty! Jiminy, Lefty, but it's fine to see you ag'in!"

Mort Carey came running, and stood panting before Lefty. "What's brung you back, Lefty?" he gasped out.

Lefty regarded him with a sigh. Plainly his last stay at this house had worn out his welcome forever. "I got a hoss here," he said, "that I ain't needin'. Not right now. I'll leave him here with you, Mort."

Carey shook his head in the greatest perturbation. "Lefty," he complained, "they know the looks of that hoss even if they don't know you. They'd be out here lookin' around mighty quick. They wouldn't give me no rest, Lefty. I . . . I can't keep Rafferty for you. But . . . come on in . . . have . . . have a bite to eat, won't you?" He bit his lip in his anxiety, pulled one way by fear and another way by desire to appear hospitable.

"Take Rafferty out to the corral, Nick," said Lefty. "I want to talk to your dad."

Nick, very anxious, went out the door and took Rafferty, turning back now and again to fix a wistful eye upon his father as though to plead that the traveler might have the best usage that was possible.

When the boy was out of earshot: "Mort," said the outlaw, "I reckon you know what Rafferty means to me?"

"You figger that he's a good hoss," said the rancher.

"Well, he is. But they's other hosses better. If I was you, I'd shoot the gray that they're trailin' you by and leave it in the mountains while I went off and got me another hoss. Understand?"

"I understand," said Lefty bitterly. "I know what you mean, right enough. But lemme tell you, old-timer, Rafferty and me has been through hell . . . together! We've pulled each other out. I've kept myself from goin' nutty by havin' Rafferty to talk to. You'd have me ditch him after that?"

"It don't sound pretty. But better the hoss than yourself, I say."

"Listen," said Lefty slowly, denting the air with his forefinger with the greatest possible emphasis, "that hoss has as much right to live as I got. Or more. What wrong has he ever done me? For why should I knife him because he's worked his best for me? Can you tell me that?"

Carey, staring at the excited face of his companion, merely shrugged his shoulders and said nothing, as though he realized that here was a brain entirely out of touch with his own. "All right," he muttered at last. "But how about me? What'll they say when they find out that I got the gray ag'in? They're watchin' me like a hawk all the time."

"You'll say that the hoss was turned loose into your fields. That's all. And they can't prove no other ways. Ain't I right?"

"I don't like it."

The flame of Lefty's temper ate through the thin wall of his self-control. "To the devil with what you like! You'll keep that hoss, Mort. It's overdue, after some of the things that I've done for you!"

So he turned on his heel while Mort, behind him, stammered apologies. But Lefty had heard enough and seen enough to put the thought of Mort Carey behind him among the small-hearted and the faithless. Then he started on his next trail across the mountains on foot, a seven-day journey. He crossed the range and descended through the lodgepole pine forest, through the belts of upper and lower evergreens, and down to a lower region of rolling foothills where he found Bantonville lying at its ease beside a slowly winding stream, itself as quiet as the little river.

In two thousand miles of cattle country, he could not remember such another spot as Bantonville, so favored by the gracious hand of God. In the hollow valleys nearby, where the soil was deep and rich, there were farms, and over the hills roamed cattle by the thousand, sleek-sided, mild-eyed. To the practiced eye of Lefty, they looked like dollars—many a hundred of them. It was a very paradise of peace, this landscape; even the forests had not been cleared away too much. The evergreens still straggled across the hills, here and there, like vanguards thrown out from the solid black masses of the trees that clothed the sides of the higher mountains.

Here he was, then, in sight of his goal, but he could not go into Bantonville on foot. It might be too necessary to leave it with all possible speed. He passed two ranches, looking over their horses that strayed in the fields as he went. One does not need to see all the horseflesh on a ranch in order to judge whether or not there is a good mount on the place. By one horse or by two the lot may be judged. Either a rancher goes in for simple "hossflesh" which is capable of "toting" the 'punchers to their work, or else he is ambitious to produce animals of speed and pride. The first two places that Lefty passed were of the former variety. At the third he needed only one glimpse across a field where half a dozen horses were grazing to know that here he could get what he wanted, a horse that he could rely on in times of peril.

He found the owner and found him not at all amenable to reason. He bred horses for his pleasure as well as for his work, and the thought of parting with any one of them was not to his taste. He cast a dour eye upon Lefty, therefore, as the latter explained carefully that a roan he had been riding through the mountains had put its hoof into a hole and broken its leg—at such a distance from civilization that he had been forced to leave the saddle cached away near the spot.

"My hosses, speakin' personal," said the rancher, "ain't for sale."

"Nobody," said Lefty diplomatically, "that has anything worth keepin' wants to get rid of it."

A 'puncher, hurrying from the bunkhouse toward the barn, paused to hear what the stranger had to say.

"Those gents up the line," said Lefty, "had ought to pay agent for takin' their hossflesh off their hands. But these here hosses are real."

The rancher squinted at him, as though in doubt as to what was intended and what was true. "You knowin' hosses?" he suggested with a covert sneer.

"A little," said Lefty.

"Suppose we was to let him go down to the corral and pick out the best hoss there . . . by the look of 'em?" suggested the 'puncher.

The rancher grinned and nodded.

"If you'll let me buy the one I pick out," said Lefty.

The rancher frowned. "At a price," he said.

"What's that?"

"Three hundred iron men, young feller, is cheap for any hoss on my ranch, but, if you *do* pick out the best of the gang, why . . . you get him for a gift." He bit his lip, seeing that the use he had made of the pronoun had limited the sex of the "best horse" at least.

"But if you make a miss," added the rancher angrily, "it's five hundred dollars you'll need to take a hoss off'n my place!"

"Good!" said Lefty. "I'll make a pick, and, if it ain't the right hoss, it'll be worth five hundred to me."

"What might be your line?" asked the suspicious rancher as they went toward the corrals.

"I've done everything," said Lefty slowly, "from prospectin' to ridin' herd. And they ain't nothin' I've tried that wouldn't have come easier with a good hoss between my knees."

"You've saved a good many months' pay," said the other dubiously.

"I had a streak of luck at faro," answered Lefty at once. "That's how come I collected the dough."

They stood at the fence of the corral; it was a fifty-acre field, rich in pasture, and the horses were scattered across it in knots, feeding or clustered under the trees for shade, for it was the bright middle of the day.

Lefty put a hand on a fence post and vaulted lightly into the enclosure.

"He's a hoss *rider*," said the rancher, looking at the slightly bowed legs and the rather waddling gait of the tall stranger.

"He's a *man!*" said the 'puncher, remembering the ease with which Lefty had lofted himself across the fence supported upon one hand.

Lefty, in the center of the enclosure, waved his hat with a yell that started from the bottom of his lungs and re-echoed from his palate like the scream of a wounded Indian. The horses broke into wild flight and milled in a huddling race around the edges of the field.

"Hey!" shouted the rancher, seeing the purpose of this stratagem. "I didn't agree to that!"

"Take it easy," muttered the cowhand at his side. "Old Drifter, he won't put on no special speed for this sort of a game."

The rancher, after a moment of keen suspense, took a long breath and leaned against the fence again, grinning. A young bay filly, delicate and beautiful as a naiad, flaunted her tail in the face of the others, running lightly at the head of the sweeping procession that tore along the fences of the corral. Behind her two magnificent geldings, both of them brown, worked in fine harmony, shoulder-to-shoulder.

Lefty surveyed the sweeping train for a moment, and then returned to the fence.

"Might be you've picked your hoss? Might be that they ain't none there good enough for you?" queried the rancher with a double mockery.

"Gimme a rope," said Lefty. "I'll take the horse I want."

The 'puncher brought a rope, and, with it, Lefty sauntered forth to the center of the corral once more. A wave of that rope shot the gang ahead at full speed.

"Rope a hoss in a fifty-acre lot . . . with a standin' start!" sneered the waddie.

"Wait a minute, young feller," said the rancher. "That gent has used a rope before . . . dog-gone my hide . . . he'll get me a few busted hosses, that way."

For Lefty, breaking into a run suddenly, headed the leading animals into the narrow end of the corral. The rush of those from behind swept all into a confused jumble until, in wild panic, each broke away and sprinted individually for liberty, after the fashion of panicky horses. Then the rope that Lefty had been trailing carelessly behind him as he ran was brought whipping forward. It darted as a snake darts. The noose, as though with wits of its own, opened, and a tall chestnut stallion ran his head and long neck through the opening.

There was a yell of despair from the rancher. "He *did* get Drifter!" he shouted.

VI
Lefty Meets
Jo Morrison

There was dignity about Lefty as he rode into Bantonville on the back of mighty Drifter, with a mouth of iron tugging at the bit and a body of flexing steel springs quivering and crouching at every step. There is always dignity in a man when he takes his life in his hands, and so was Lefty doing on this day of days. For he was going to take the weapons of Chic Harley, according to his promise to a dying man, to the brother of Chic, to none other than Gus Harley himself, the sheriff of the county, the hero of the range, the most famous and dreaded fighter up and down the sweep of the mountains. His fame began where that of his brother ended.

It might have been said that there was something lacking to prove that Chic Harley was truly formidable, since he had achieved his reputation in the pursuit of fugitives, whose nerves, it might be supposed, would be destroyed by the mere impending shadow of the hand of the law. But Gus Harley, forty-five years old, hardened, tempered by dangers of a thousand kinds, and always master of men and events, was a problem of another nature. There could be no doubting of Gus. Lefty, cool and crafty warrior that he was, fearless, with not a nerve in his body, knew instinctively that against such a man as Gus Harley he could not stand. To confront him would be suicide. Yet his problem was to place the guns of his dead brother in the hands of the terrible sheriff and then—escape!

He had with him one prime requisite—he had beneath him a horse that could truly be called one in ten thousand. Rafferty had been fast enough, but the greatness of Rafferty was the greatness of a wise head and a loyal heart. Rafferty was as clever and as true as a dog; Drifter was terrible and strong as a lion. There was no kindness in his little fiery eyes. There was no beauty in his long, bony head. His heart did not swell with love for any creature. God had given him a matchless barrel and adorned it with four matchless legs. He was a running machine *par excellence,* and that running machine might whirl Lefty away from the danger of the sheriff's guns. If only he could manage to bridge the gap between the presentation of Chic's weapons to Gus and the saddle safe on the back of the big chestnut!

That was his final problem, and he turned it back and forth in his mind. He could find no expedient. He decided, like the true tactician that he was, to wait until the moment came and he found himself upon the battleground. Having made up his mind to that, he could be almost gay. He stopped to talk to a pair of urchins who were arguing heatedly over the possession of a rubber slingshot. The elder and larger, having possession in fact, was using his size to make up for the doubtful quality of his rights.

"I *had* a slingshot, didn't I? I lost it right here in this grass, didn't I? An' ain't it as like to be mine . . . this here one . . . as it is to be yours?"

"I can show you the notch where. . . ."

132

"*Anybody* can put a notching in something," sneered the older of the two.

"Look here," broke in Lefty, leaning an elbow on the pommel of his saddle, "why don't you fight it out?"

"He don't dast to fight," scoffed the elder.

"He's bigger'n me," said the youngster.

"Nothin' is big enough to go around callin' you yaller," said Lefty. "Soak him, kid. I'll show you how to lick him."

The younger of the pair cast at his slingshot a despairing glance of desire, at Lefty a wild look of hopefulness and bewilderment, and then, hoping for a miracle, closed his eyes and rushed in—against the well-driven fist of his antagonist. It met him squarely on the end of the nose and sat him down in a puff of dust, rubbing his face with the back of his hand.

"I'll show you!" taunted the big boy joyously. "I could lick about a dozen like you, I guess!"

"Get up," said Lefty. "Get up and tackle him. He's scared of you. Get up and hit him in the belly. That'll make him quit."

To a boy of ten the voice of a mature man is an oracle. The youngster leaped from his place in the street. His first fall had been a mere chance, he told himself. Such a man as this stranger could not be wrong. This time he kept his eyes open, and he struck his enemy fairly in the stomach.

Even a grown man can hardly stand such a blow, but to a child whose body is uncushioned with stout muscles, such a stroke is sure to be the end. The freckled fist sank up to its wrist in the anatomy of the robber who rolled over and over in the road, and the victor ran home triumphant, incredulous, the slingshot grasped in both of his hands.

Lefty jogged on down the street until he became aware

of watching eyes. She stood at the gate in a dress as white as the sunshine and mottled with black shadows from the tree above her, so that it was no wonder that he had not seen her at the first glance. He knew, by something in her face, that she had been there for some time—long enough to see the entire affair of the fight, at least. She did not wait for him to address her, and her very first words told him very distinctly what her attitude was.

"I guess you're aimin' to see a lot of fights," she said coldly.

Had she been anyone else, he would have answered nothing, but hurried down the street to avoid her tongue, for even in his youth he had established the wise maxim that a woman is not to be argued with. But, being what she was—he paused and found himself compelled to listen, dragging the hat slowly from his head.

She was not beautiful. Her nose was too short, and her mouth too wide for that. But her blue eyes were as bright as a mountain lake, and as pure and as deep, and they looked Lefty through and through with scorn. He felt that it would be well to go on—very well, indeed. But, in spite of himself, he could not stir. The longer he remained there, the more clearly he saw how the sun shone through the thin lawn collar and cast a rosy shadow on her throat, and how round that throat was, as though it were filled, even now, with song, and how her head was poised lightly at—his comparisons failed him. The heart of Lefty began to stir, and then to thunder.

"I dunno that I'm interested in fights," he said mildly to her.

Anger flushed her face and flared in her eyes. She could not speak, for the moment, but mutely pointed to the spot on the street where the dust still carried the deep prints of the boys—the spots where they had fallen, the spots where they had planted their feet to strike or parry. Then she was able to cry, recovering her breath: "D'you mean to say that to me . . . right after I saw you?"

Perspiration rolled out upon the brown forehead of Lefty. He stared at her with wonder that so delicately made a creature could be so terrible.

"D'you believe in stealin'?" he asked her sadly.

"What's *that* got to do with it?" she demanded hotly. For she could see that he had weakened before her, and there is no tyrant so merciless, no bully so overbearing, as a woman over a cringing man.

"That big boy . . . he'd swiped that slingshot, you see," explained Lefty in agony.

"And then you let the poor little boy fight for it?"

"You see," began Lefty, "it's always appeared to me that it's better for a boy to sort of learn to fight his own way than to get under. . . ."

"There! There! There!" cried the girl, stamping with every word to emphasize her anger. "I knew it'd pop out pretty soon. You *like* fights. If you were in Mexico, you'd go to those terrible bullfights . . . where they kill horses . . . that's where you'd go!"

She swept him from head to heel, and there her glance lingered upon the spurs, as though seeking to find something dreadful in their proportions. But they were equipped with most indifferent rowels, and the silken flanks of Drifter had not been ruffled by the spurs of his rider. She turned her attention to the horse itself. There was a wicked look in the eye of Drifter that must reflect the character of his master as well, she told herself, so she frowned more darkly upon Lefty.

"What might your name be?" he was asking.

"Josephine Morrison," she said.

"Mostly folks call me Lefty," he said. "I'm glad to know you."

"D'you aim to stay on in Bantonville?" she asked him without enthusiasm.

"I was figgerin' on passin' through," he replied. "But I guess that I'll be comin' back," he added slowly, looking at her more earnestly than ever. For he was telling himself, reluctantly, that he had encountered fate in the person of this slender girl, and that he must see her again, even if her home was the town of terrible Gus Harley himself.

"Anyway," said the girl with a sudden softening, "Tommy is a little bully . . . I'm glad he was thrashed."

"Sure," said Lefty heartily. "Might I drop around someday and have a talk with you?"

"About what?" she asked in the most unfriendly manner.

"Why . . . about boys . . . and fights," said Lefty. "Seems like you don't understand me, Miss Morrison."

"H-m-m!" she said. "Maybe not."

"Good-bye," said Lefty.

She merely waved a curt hand to him and turned away down the path, while Lefty let Drifter prance on down the street. When he had gone a little distance, he glanced back and saw that after leaving the shade of the tree she had passed in the full glare of the sun and was looking after him. How brilliant a figure she made in that white dress, shimmering like fire in the sun! With a great feeling of triumph, he raised his hat and smiled, but she turned sharply away and hurried on toward the house.

VII
Delivering the Colts

He found Gus Harley in his office—a little ten-by-ten room occupied by two straight chairs and a desk whose surface was gouged by many deep scars. The sheriff himself was now canted back in his chair, and upon the top of the desk rested his spurred heels, accounting for new scars on the varnished wood. He was not like Chic, his dead brother. He was as swarthy as Chic had been blond, and his worn, seamed face was garnished by a long pair of mustaches that moved up and down when he pursed his mouth—an habitual expression.

His greeting to Lefty was a mere tilt of his sombrero that allowed it to slide far back on his head. Then he hooked his thumbs through the armholes of his vest and waited for his visitor to introduce himself.

"You're Gus Harley, I guess."

"I'm him."

"The boys call me Lefty."

"You're Lefty Richards, maybe?"

At this, Lefty started a little and looked more fixedly at

the other. "What might make you think that?" he asked with a scowl.

"Maybe I could guess. Maybe I've seen your picture. It was you that Calkins got sent up to the pen."

Lefty snarled like an enraged dog. "It was Calkins that sent me," he admitted. "There wasn't no proof ag'in' me . . . but Calkins sent me up!"

"That was hard."

"It cost me five years! Calkins . . . maybe it'll cost him something yet!"

The sheriff nodded noncommittally. "What you want out of me?" he asked.

"I want to give you a message. But first I want to know what sort of a chance have I got around this here town?"

"How d'you mean?"

"If I go to work near by here, are you gonna watch me like a crook every minute and lay everything that happens inside of ten miles to me . . . because I've been in jail?"

The sheriff smiled. "I never take nothin' for granted," he said. "You'll get a square break with me, Lefty."

The ex-convict sighed. Looking into the face of the man of the law, he was confronted by an iron honesty that stirred something in his own heart to respond. "I wish to heaven," he broke out, "that there was six more like you in the mountains, Harley. Then a gent like me would have a chance."

"You aim to get work around here?"

"Yes."

"And you ain't gonna let folks know . . . what you been doing with yourself for five years?"

"What would *you* do, Sheriff?"

"I'd tell 'em the truth, partner. I'd let 'em know the truth and to the devil with them that wouldn't give you a chance to make good."

Lefty blinked. This was a manner of reasoning which he had never encountered before.

"Tell 'em that I'm just out of the coop?"

"That's it. Then fight your way up."

"Fight? Oh, I see what you mean. Take twenty-five years to prove that I'm square. That it?"

"You know folks around these parts. This ain't the East. You play fair and square for six months, and see what happens. They'll take you for what you seem to be."

"You mean that?"

"Sure. What made you fix on this here town?"

The impulse to confess stormed big in the heart of Lefty. No man can see a pretty girl without wishing to talk of her if he cannot talk to her.

"I come along here to bring some news to you. Then, ridin' down the street, I come up with a girl that looked like home to me."

The sheriff grinned. "I see," he said. "Go on."

"There ain't more to say. I seen her, and I didn't look good to her, I guess. But I'm gonna stay and stick."

"And get her, Lefty?"

"And get her!"

"Who might she be?"

"Josephine Morrison."

"Jo Morrison!" exclaimed Harley. Then he leaned suddenly, became very busy with the contents of an open drawer, and looked up at last rather grimly at the other.

"What's wrong with her?" asked Lefty Richards sharply.

"Nothin'. By my way of thinkin', she's the finest girl in town."

Lefty sighed. "And not about to get married to nobody?"

"Why, no girl is married till the preacher has finished his talkin'," said the sheriff wisely and a little sadly.

"She's engaged to somebody," said Lefty in desperation. "Who might it be?"

The sheriff changed the subject suddenly. "What might you want with me, Lefty?" he asked.

Having been brought to the climax thus abruptly, Lefty recalled to himself the story as he had planned it, a simple story. With the grace of God, he might manage to have it believed. Let it not be thought that he was a timid man when it is confessed that for the moment all thoughts of the girl disappeared from his brain. He concentrated upon Gus Harley, the destroyer of men. Even from the short time he had been talking with the sheriff, Lefty had judged him. The strength of honest resolution was in Gus—a strength like adamant. It was no wonder that he had crushed formidable men. Lefty himself felt like an incapable boy in front of the older man.

"I was comin' through the mountains ridin' my roan," began Lefty smoothly, "and, comin' through a break in the hills, I seen a gent in the hollow beneath me, sittin' on a gray hoss with a rifle balancin' across the pommel of the saddle. Just then over the next hills beyond the. . . ." He paused to clear his throat and gather his resolution. At the mention of the rider of the gray horse and the balanced rifle, the sheriff had rocked forward in his chair, dropped his armed heels to the floor, and sat up, full of nervous attention.

"You're gonna tell me that you seen my brother killed," he said quietly.

"That's it," said Lefty.

The sheriff pointed a forefinger at Lefty. "That gent on the gray hoss . . . how close was you to him?"

"About a hundred and fifty yards . . . maybe two hundred."

The sheriff sighed. "Then you couldn't make out his face?"

"Nope. Not exactly."

"What sort of a look did he have?"

"He sat sort of loose and easy in the saddle. You know what I mean. He had a sort of lazy look on a hoss."

"Yep," said the sheriff, very thoughtful. "That's the way that some of the boys have told me about him. How big would you say?"

"I dunno. Maybe about my size. No," he added carefully, "I guess he was a good deal taller."

"By what they tell me," said the sheriff, "I aim to guess that he is." He measured Lefty at a glance, slowly, coldly. Lefty endured the scrutiny. So successful was the lie up to this point, and so beautifully circumstantial, that he felt a redoubled courage and trust in his wits.

"The other gent that come was your brother. I didn't know it then, or I might've drilled the crook on the gray hoss. But I didn't have no way of tellin'. I couldn't see that his face was masked, because he had his back to me, you see? All I seen was that the fight was. . . ."

"He got in the first shot?" asked the sheriff.

"Nope. Chic Harley fired first. The other gent was takin' his time. You'd've thought that he knowed that Chic's gun was loaded with paper. Then he fired and dropped Chic out of the saddle."

"What did he do then?"

"Rode up to him and started talkin' to Chic."

"What did you do?"

"I stayed where I was put. There wasn't nothin' I could've done."

"Except take a hand to get the gent that done the killin'!"

"How could I tell that it was a killin'? I seen the gent on

141

the gray hoss takin' care of the other one. It looked all right to me. I figgered he was only wounded . . . stunned, maybe. Then I seen a couple of men come tearin'. Him on the gray hoss jumped into the saddle. When I seen the others come, I guessed that the gent on the gray hoss was runnin' from a posse. But I still wasn't quite sure. Then I seen him start straight back down the way he had been ridin' in the first place. . . ."

"You got the lay of the land that way?"

"Sure. When I seen the pair of 'em tearin' along after the gray hoss, I rode down, too. But when I come by the gent that was lyin' on the ground, he hollered to me. I went up to him, and he told me that he was about done for. I seen by his face that he was. Well, I asked him what I could do. He said there wasn't nothin' except to take his guns and bring 'em to you, because you'd never leave the trail till you'd got the gent that. . . ."

"God help me if I ever quit that trail," said the sheriff quietly.

Lefty, staring blankly at the other, realized that a simple truth had been spoken that put his life into a double jeopardy. "And here's the Colts," he added in conclusion. He drew out the long weapons and passed them onto the top of the desk. Then he waited. It was the time to which he had looked forward as the crisis. For it had seemed to him that some message must be carried by the guns to the brother of his victim.

There was no crisis whatever. The sheriff accepted the pair of Colts without a word, glanced them over, and put them into a drawer of the desk. "That was all?" he said finally.

"He didn't have no time for talk," said Lefty honestly. "He was about done for when I got to him."

The sheriff rose and walked to the window. Then he

came back. If there had been any great wave of emotion, it was conquered before he faced the killer again. "Lefty," he said, "it looks like I owe you something. You settle down right here in Bantonville. If it comes to gettin' you a job . . . why, I'll try my own hand at it, partner."

"You're a white man, Harley," said Lefty huskily.

The sheriff accompanied him to the door. "What's become of the roan?" he asked, eyeing the big stallion with some surprise.

"He busted a leg in the mountains. I had to cache the saddle and come along on foot. I got this out the way I. . . ."

"From Jim Thomas. I've seen that Drifter hoss before."

And so the peril was ended—for the moment, at least.

VIII
Made for Taking Chances

But fear, which had been put into the background for the moment while Lefty was leaving the sheriff, returned again before he reached the hotel. He reviewed his story. It was simple enough in the telling, but there might prove to be great flaws in it before the end if any strict inquiry were made. Suppose, for instance, that they asked him where he bought that roan horse and from whom? Or suppose that the sheriff inquired from those two men of the posse what tracks of a stranger's horse they had seen near the body of dead Chic Harley? These two possibilities were the first that came into his mind. It might be, of course, that the first question would never be asked. It might be that the men of the posse had not thought to examine the ground around the dead man and inquire into the nature of the tracks that were there.

If the truth were ever known, he was no better than a dead man. He had faced a hundred fighting men before, but something told him that before the sheriff he would be helpless as a child. He had lied brutally to an honest, kindly man. That lie, he felt, would be like another gun

144

turned against him if the battle ever came. In the meantime, all common sense demanded that he should leave Bantonville at once and strike away through the mountains. A thousand miles would be no more than a comfortable gap between him and terrible Gus Harley. But if he left Bantonville, he left the blue eyes of Jo Morrison. Go he could not! There was no power in him to leave.

So he went on straight to the little hotel and signed his name on the register—Tom Richards. The proprietor knew at once.

"You ain't Lefty Richards?" he asked.

"Yes."

The eyes of the proprietor narrowed to a squint. There was no doubt about what was going on in his mind. However, it was not from this man that he might get a job.

He came down from his room after he had washed the dust from his face and the grime from his hands. He went into the dining room, and a burly youth with a great jaw and little wicked eyes followed him and leaned over his place.

"You're Lefty Richards?" he asked.

"I'm Richards," said Lefty defiantly.

"Look here"—the other grinned—"I don't mean it that way. I'm in on the know. Maybe you've heard about me? I'm Sam Tucker."

"I dunno that I've ever heard about you," Lefty answered cautiously.

A shade passed over the face of the other. "Why," he said with astonishing frankness, "I'm the gent that done the Lewiston job three years back. I handled the soup there."

Lefty Richards stared at him.

"That ain't your line," said Sam flatteringly. "You ain't

got the time to run a mold and stick in the soup and crack
the safe. You like to make it sweet and easy. Well, old-
timer, that's a pretty good way, except that they's only one
chance in ten of gettin' away with it. What's your lay right
now?"

"You mean. . . ."

"Sure. I'm ready to hire out or go partners. I need a job,
old man!"

"I've got no lay," Lefty responded shortly.

"Sure you ain't," chuckled the other, standing erect
again. "But you take your time and look me over. You'll
find out about me. I'm a square bloke, Lefty. If you want
to get a trick turned, I'm the man for you, and don't you
make no mistake about that. I'll do your trick and do it
right. Take your time, though. Make up your own mind
about me. And when you're ready, I'm ready." He
winked broadly and sauntered away, trailing behind him
the stifling sweetness of Turkish tobacco—most foul in
the nostrils of Lefty Richards, trained as they were to the
sharp sting of native tobacco.

It was a sample of how other men were to receive him.
The crooks would open their arms to him. He was one of
them. But the honest men?

The proprietor had given him an ample hint of what
was to come. That afternoon, he jogged his horse out into
the country and stopped at three ranch houses. All three
needed men, and all three frankly told him so and looked
over him and his horse with approving eyes, but, when
they learned his name, there was a change. It always ran
in one tune.

"What's your name, partner?"

"I'm Richards," he would say bluntly, taking the sheriff's honest advice. "I'm Lefty Richards."

"Lefty . . . not him that . . . ?"

"I've just done time for five years," he would answer harshly.

The invariable reply would be: "When I'm needin' a 'puncher, I'll take a look around for you, Lefty."

All three of the ranchers made the same return. Then Lefty rode back to the town. He was in a black humor. It was not that he needed money to live on. The loot from Calkin's bank was still his—a constant peril to him if he should be arrested and searched. But, in the meantime, he had nothing to fear in the way of a lack of funds. It was not for the monthly pay that he wanted to work. It was to rehabilitate himself in the eyes of little Jo Morrison, and perhaps to win back some of the genial respect of his fellow men that had disappeared on that day when he was taken to the penitentiary.

There was no chance for this. He was blocked on all sides, and in the evening Sam Tucker sat down beside him on the verandah, waiting, smoking, saying nothing. But now and again his little bright eyes rolled at Lefty, full of a mute questioning. A black spirit rolled up in Lefty. If the world would not have him as an honest man, why might it not receive its own reward and see him turned permanently into a plunderer and a destroyer of the rights of others?

This seemed to him a fair exchange enough. He went forth on the second day, however, to make still another attempt. His reception was the same, or a little worse. The news of his coming had spread before him. They recognized him, now, when he approached, and he saw the recognition and the hostility in their faces before they uttered a word. If it was this way with them, how would it be with the keen sensibilities of Jo Morrison when she learned of the past career of Lefty?

"Well," said Sam Tucker, when they sat together on the

hotel verandah that night, shunned by the others. "I've found a plant that only needs a little work to turn into a crop, old-timer. Might you be interested?"

"What's in your head?" growled out Lefty sullenly, hating himself for giving way to temptation, hating the whole world for having forced him to this point.

"About fifteen thousand berries," said Sam Tucker gleefully. "That's all. Only fifteen thousand iron men floatin' around and waitin' for a couple of gents with a little talent to come along and pick 'em off. You hear me, bo?"

His language and his manner were highly offensive to Lefty, but when one has thrown in his lot with rascals, one cannot afford to be overly nice. So he swallowed his rising anger as well as he could and nodded.

"The sound of that," he admitted, "is fair enough."

"I've found it and staked it out. But we'd split it fifty-fifty," suggested Sam Tucker generously.

"What sort of a job?"

"A cinch, old-timer. One of them tin safes that old ladies used to keep their imitation jewels in. I could open it with my pocket knife. They ain't nothin' to it. A can opener . . . that's the size of that job, Lefty. But I need somebody to gimme a hand with a couple of. . . ."

The heavy step of the proprietor advanced toward them. "Lefty Richards here?"

"That's me."

"Somebody wants you," said the other.

"Who's that?"

"Somebody wants you . . . up at the corner," said the hotel man significantly, and went away.

Lefty hitched at his belt and rose.

"Don't be a sap," whispered his companion. "They got some gag to work on you."

"What sort of a gag?"

"I wouldn't trust 'em. No town that has gents like Gus Harley floatin' around in it is any happy huntin' grounds for you and me, old-timer."

This genial inclusion in the same class with the yegg made Lefty Richards set his teeth. "I was made," he answered abruptly, "for the takin' of chances. I aim to take this one."

"Why wouldn't they come right up to the hotel if they didn't mean some kind of a low trick?" asked the other sharply.

Lefty, who had not thought of this angle of the affair, nodded gloomily. But, no matter what reason said to him, there had been a touch of mystery to the voice of the proprietor that appealed to him irresistibly. He could not avoid that appeal. So he took a step away.

"All right, kid," said Sam Tucker, shrugging his thick shoulders. "If you want to take the chance, I'll go along and help take care of your fool self."

Lefty paused again. What instinct was this that sprang up loud and strong in him? "You stay where you are, Sam. I'll handle this little job, whatever it is, that's coming along."

Sam Tucker with a grunt sank back in his chair, while Lefty drew his belt a notch closer to his ever-gaunt belly and strode off the verandah of the hotel.

The eyes of the other loungers followed him with side glances of keen malice. He was the ex-convict. He was the wolf among dogs. They hated him as dogs hate wolves. But he, knowing their hatred and scorning it even though it made his heart ache, drew himself up a little more erectly and went on as though his pride were only increased by this burden. So he came around the corner of the hotel away from the street, and there he found Josephine Morrison waiting for him and waiting alone!

149

IX
Mighty Fair and Square

In such a great event all the small details are remembered eagerly afterward, although they are hardly noticed at the time. What Lefty Richards saw at the moment was only the girl, but afterward he remembered all the picture and never tired of putting it together bit by bit. It was just after the red time of the dusk. There was still a flushed streak in the west, and all around the horizon a pale strip divided the night sky from the earth, and the tallest mountains lifted above that strip and joined their heads to the large, deep sea of the central sky. There was just enough light to show the coming of the dark. It was the pause between life and sleep when the day has passed into its old age. The business of that day had ended; the children had come out to play in the street; from far-off kitchens could be heard the clatter of pans that were being washed; back doors slammed as the scraps were carried out to the chicken yards; a coyote yelled in the distance, and the dogs raised a sullen chorus in response. All of these noises came, but they were lost and muffled in the overhanging thickness of the night. Even the wind was tired and walked like a ghost from tree to tree, whispering to each as it passed.

In such a moment he stood before Jo Morrison and felt his body tremble with the vigor of his heartbeat. She was wearing that same white dress. It shimmered like a sheaf of moonbeams in the shadow of the trees.

"Lefty . . . Mister Richards?" she asked timidly as he came nearer.

He tugged the hat from his head. The pulse in his temples stopped thudding so steadily. "I'm Lefty," he admitted.

"I'm Jo Morrison," she said.

When she did not speak, he began to grope wildly for something to say, and he found nothing. He began to stammer something. Was it about the coolness of the evening? His own confusion reassured her. She cut quietly into the muttering of his talk. "When I saw you today, Lefty, I didn't know. I guess you thought. . . ." She paused, and then stamped as though angered by her own lack of coherence. "I didn't know!" she breathed suddenly.

"About what?" he asked.

"Gus Harley told me."

"About me?"

"Yes."

"He told you I was a crook . . . a gent just out of the penitentiary?" he asked her.

Perhaps the sheriff had told her, likewise, that it was the sight of her that had persuaded him to stay in the town. If Gus Harley had given her that news which brought her now to scoff and mock at him, he would have the life of the sheriff even if it took his own to buy it. He set his teeth and looked sternly at the girl.

"If I'd known about you," she said, "I'd never have

talked to you like that. I didn't know, Lefty. I wouldn't've treated a dog like that. Honest!"

He made out with vague wonder that she was apologizing. For what? He was too used to verbal kicks and cuffs even to resent what she had said to him.

"I didn't know," she reiterated. "If I'd guessed what you'd been through to make you bitter . . . and make you like fighting . . . I wouldn't have let myself say such things."

"You mean me bein' in prison?"

"I mean . . . all the hard life you've had."

"I got what was comin' to me, I guess."

"Gus Harley says that there was never a good case proved against you."

It was a thunderbolt to Lefty. He could hardly believe his ears. "Did the sheriff say that?"

"He said a lot more. He says that you'll have a hard time getting work, Lefty."

"I'm having that hard time right now."

"They don't trust you, I guess?"

"They don't. I'm a yaller dog to the ranchers around these parts."

"Poor fellow," she murmured.

Ah, balm on a wounded heart, that gentle voice.

"Gus thinks that I could help you. So I talked to Dad. He says that he'll be glad to give you a place on the ranch, punching cows. Will that be good enough for you?"

"Me? Anything is good enough for me," said Lefty.

His heart grew great with emotion. After all, he told himself, the world was sure to be like this. It might seem hard and cruel to the underdog, but if one were patient, the inner goodness was sure to appear. Or was it only because there was this administering angel, this figure of light, this frank-hearted girl? No, for the sheriff was at the root of it all—that sheriff whose brother he had killed. It made him shiver to think of it.

"Look here," he added hastily, "does the sheriff talk everything over with you?"

"Gus and I talk most things over," she said. "I guess we'd ought to, you know."

A sudden fear struck at Lefty. "For why?" he asked, hardly able to hear his own voice.

"Well, we're going to be married in about six weeks, you know."

What else she said at that moment he heard in a great distance, as one hears a single voice through the curtaining thunder of the chorus of a cataract. This was the clue to it all. The sheriff, out of the greatness of his surety that the girl was his, could be generous to a despised rival—had even made it possible for Lefty to remain near the town and near the girl. No, more than that, must he not have a profound reason for wishing to keep a stranger in the town—one, above all, who had professed an affection for the sweetheart of Gus himself?

It was more than a probability. It was a certainty. The sheriff had a deeply lodged suspicion of Lefty. Until that suspicion was verified, he wished to bait a trap and catch the man and hold him safely. He had baited the trap with his own fiancée. Dark rage and cold grief swept over Lefty. Yes, and, if this were true, the girl herself had been apprised, and she was here, now, playing a part. In his honest indignation, Lefty took a long stride nearer to her; she shrank back with a gasp.

"What's wrong?" Lefty said, feeling that start was the signal of conscious guilt.

"Nothing. Only . . . it seemed to me for a minute that you were . . . angry . . . I don't know why."

"Me? Angry?" asked Lefty. "Why should I be?" He

laughed heavily, mirthlessly. At this, she came to him and laid a hand on his arm and looked up at him, standing so close that a fragrance entangled in her hair came to him mingled with the pure sweetness of the pines. It was a sad, sweet thrill to the outlaw.

"You're mighty queer," she said. "I don't know what's in your mind. But . . . I've got no right to ask questions. You've been hurt. I had a fine horse once. But somebody had treated it badly when it was broken. I had to watch it all the time . . . for years . . . and finally it loved me, Lefty, but there was always something wild in its eyes. I guess maybe that you'd be like that. There's something wild in you. You been hurt so badly. Why . . . I'm mighty sorry for you, Lefty. I'm mighty sorry."

When he thought of it afterward, these were just such words as any of a hundred persons might have spoken. Yet, uttered in that soft and musical voice, they were robed with magic that unarmed and unnerved him. He grew weak before her. A base thrill of self-pity shot through him. Then he was seized upon with a mighty wave of a new emotion—utter scorn for himself, utter belief in her and her goodness. He was a wolf, and she a white swan.

"You talk mighty fine and square," he said at last.

"I mean every word ten times over, Lefty."

"I guess you do."

"And you'll go to Dad?"

"I'll go to him."

"Tomorrow?"

"Or next day."

"No, no. Promise me tomorrow . . . before you do something wild."

"Did the sheriff tell you that I was apt to?"

"Gus? He doesn't know. Poor old dear, he's blind, almost. But I can tell. Oh, Lefty, you're busting with hate for the whole world, aren't you?"

Now, when a coward is cornered, as everyone knows, he is apt to fight back desperately. And when a mute man is touched deeply enough, he may say a surprising thing. Lefty, cornered so that he could not escape and then deluged with this womanly gentleness, felt something rise in him at last. It mastered his shyness. Then he caught her hands and pressed them between his. He stood over her with his body rigid and trembling. His voice, when it came, was like a groan, so that the sound of it shook him to his feet, and shook the soul of the girl hearing him as it shook Lefty to utter that speech.

"God bless you, Jo," he muttered. "God bless your heart. You're gold."

To such a thing as this, there is no answer. An answer or a comment destroys it. But Lefty did not leave suddenly for that reason. He only knew that something was breaking down and crumbling to pieces in him and that he must get away by himself. So he fled—stalking stiffly across the opening toward the hotel verandah.

X
A Change in Jo

If he had sneaked back, he might have seen various things of the greatest interest to him. He might have seen Jo Morrison dabbing her eyes, after she remained for some time transfixed on the spot. Then he might have seen her go home slowly, pausing often. He might have seen her enter the Morrison house at the end of the village with a smile on her lips so strange that, when her mother saw her, she cried out: "My goodness, Jo, what is it?"

"It's nothing!" said Jo, and went straight to her room.

What there was changed in her, her mother could not tell. But the very atmosphere of the room was altered after Jo passed through, and Mrs. Morrison sat for some time fumbling at the sewing in her lap and staring at the black, glistening square of the windowpane that obscured the night, and the white, crinkled square of the newspaper that obscured her husband.

Then she got up, gave her husband a guilty glance as though afraid that he might guess what was going on inside her mind, and went in to her daughter. She found Jo lying on the bed in a darkened room, silent. From the window the faint pallor of the starlight illumined obscurely the white dress of the girl. Her hands, folded upon her breast, were like dull brown shadows. Mrs. Morrison felt that her own entrance had passed unnoticed to her daughter. She waited at the door. There was not a word of greeting. Yet she knew, by an electric something in the air, that Jo was not sleeping. Mrs. Morrison became a little awed, a little frightened. She went softly to the bed and sat down on the side of it. The springs protested with a great, noisy creaking.

Then she said: "Jo, what's happened?"

There was no answer.

"Jo!"

"Yes . . . Mother?"

"Jo, what's happened?"

There was no answer still. Mrs. Morrison grew cold with fear. Then she knew, with sudden wonder, that her voice was simply unheard—a disturbing noise to her daughter, no more. She was just far enough from her own girlhood to have it like a dream in her mind. But she was not far enough away from it to remember that there are some things in girlhood to which all that happens to a mature woman is as nothing. She remembered; no woman can quite forget.

"Jo," she repeated for the third time, leaning closer, "what's happened?"

At last there was a stir. "Mother?"

"Yes, darlin'. Yes, Jo."

"Sit close here."

"I will."

"And don't leave me?"

"No, no! Jo, what's happened?"

"Mother. . . ."

"Yes?"

"Gus Harley . . . he's a good man . . . he's a. . . ."

"Oh," murmured Mrs. Harrison, tears of relief running from her eyes, "is that it?"

"You think he is?"

"A mighty fine good man."

"But. . . ." The voice of Jo trailed away.

"But what, Jo?"

"Nothing. There's the moon coming up," she added with a sort of dreamy content.

Mrs. Morrison was not irritated by this sudden change of the subject. She looked away through the window. Beyond and behind all the confused words of the girl, there was a steady current of feeling and of meaning. Just what it was, the mother could not yet make out, but it was surely there. Now through the eastern forest, the red moon climbed and rose like a fire through a huge pine, and, standing for a moment resting on the spear tip of the tree, it turned to rich orange-gold before it started its ascent of the steep hill of the heavens. It rose higher. It turned half the world to black; it turned the world to richest frost silver. It cast a shaft of light through the window that flooded across the girl's dress and made her slender warm hands turn white. Tears of another kind came in the eyes of Mrs. Morrison and an ache in her throat.

The voice of the girl began again, full of pauses, with a new note in it, rich and stirring. "Gus Harley . . . he's a good man. But there's something he. . . ."

"Yes, Jo?"

"Does he want to please me . . . or it is just because . . . he and Dad are old friends . . . do you think?"

"Silly girl, dear girl! Everyone loves you."

"I don't want to be loved that way."

Mrs. Morrison caught her breath.

Jo went on: "Gus is kind."

"The kindest man in the world, next to your father," said Mrs. Morrison.

"D'you think that a kind man can love a . . . can love a . . . girl?"

"A kind man? What are you talking about, Jo? Gus is good to everything . . . even to horses and dogs!"

"That's it," said the half drowsy voice. "That's the difference. . . ." The voice trailed away, but not in sleep, the mother knew. There was a hidden emotion, the deeper for being voiced so quietly.

Mrs. Morrison hung over her daughter like a discoverer over a strange coast, half afraid of what she might learn. She said gently: "I remember when Gus first. . . ."

"I don't want to talk about Gus!"

"Oh!" said Mrs. Morrison.

"I'd better just . . . lie here . . . I want . . . to think."

"What's happened, Jo?"

There was a long pause. "Do you smell the pine trees?" whispered Jo at last.

Mrs. Morrison felt that a great river flowed between her and the girl; the nearer she sat, the more impassable it was. She stood up softly, and stole to the door, all her heart crying out in silent entreaty for her daughter to call her back. But there was no such call. She was allowed to open the door slowly, and shut it behind her, feeling that she was shut out from the life of Jo and some vital secret. She hardly knew what—she hardly dared to let herself know. She went back into the living room, and, gathering up her sewing, she sat down.

"Them explorers," said the deep voice of Mr. Morrison behind his paper, "is found."

"Yes?" said the wife dutifully, hearing nothing.

"They was all dead, except one."

"Yes?"

"I dunno what gets into folks to want to travel down there to reach the pole. What *is* the dog-gone pole, anyway? Just a plain chunk of snow and ice. What's it good for? Some folks is plain queer."

"Yes," said Mrs. Morrison.

The paper rustled down. Mr. Morrison was revealed from behind it. "Well?" he asked.

"Well what?" snapped out his wife with unnecessary irritation.

"What's wrong with Jo?"

She started. "Jo?"

"Yes."

"Why, nothing, of course. What *should* be wrong with Jo?"

"I thought there was something. . . ."

"*Humph!*" said Mrs. Morrison.

"She was sort of different."

This confirmation of Mrs. Morrison's own opinion angered her more than it pleased her. Besides, how could her husband have noticed anything—through that newspaper? But it was often like this. Just when she had definitely written down the rancher as a man blind to all saving his business, there came a flash of uncanny insight—such as women are supposed to have the sole right to and possession of. It was hardly fair, she thought. Just at that moment, with her little world spinning about her ears, she did not wish to be bothered.

"I don't know what you mean," she said stiffly.

"Nothin'." He raised the paper, and presently spoke from behind it again. "It was just something in her way of walkin' across the room and sayin' nothin'."

"Do you want her to talk . . . to a newspaper?" snapped out Mrs. Morrison.

"*H-m-m,*" said her spouse. "Has that rheumatism been botherin' you lately?"

"Of course not! At this time of year? I'm not *quite* as old as that, I'd have you know, Mister Morrison."

Mr. Morrison growled. "Gettin' so a man can't open his mouth in his own house. Dog-gone that girl, I'll have to go speak to her."

"No!"

Her husband jumped. "Why not?"

"She ain't feelin' too well."

"Darn it, I knowed she was sick! What's wrong?"

"She's got a headache," said Mrs. Morrison. "And . . . open the window wider, won't you? The air is full of the pines tonight."

Mr. Morrison stared at her, then hastily erected the barrier of his newspaper between himself and his better half. He said aloud: "They's enough air in this here room right now. It's comin' on chilly." He said to himself: *Who in the devil can understand a woman? Not even themselves.*

XI
The Game of the Fox

Lefty, when he reached the verandah of the hotel, dropped into a chair heavily at the side of Sam Tucker.

The latter waited for some time, listening to the hurried breathing of his friend. Then he suggested kindly: "All trouble don't make noise. I guess you had your bad time, Lefty?"

"Leave it be," said Lefty.

"Look at that moon comin' up," said Sam Tucker. "That'll bring out all the young folks in town billin' and cooin', I guess."

Lefty started up. "The devil, Sam," he said, "sometimes you talk plumb disgustin'!" Then he strode from the verandah and went up to his room. But there he found no content. The air was close. No wind blew though the door. The slant light from the moon filled the chamber with a lonely emptiness.

He sat on the edge of the bed trying to arrange his thoughts but finding that, in spite of himself, they moved like a treadmill, back and forth, gaining no ground. He had started out from prison to get revenge upon an unjust

162

world. He had struck two blows in that course. He had taken a large sum of money from the very bank that had caused his imprisonment for no sufficient cause, and he had slain the chief of those who had pursued him. He had reached this town, deeper in the course of revenge. But now he was checked. There was another purpose in his life—he only wished, now, that the money he had stolen was safely back in the vault of the little bank. An odd feeling of good fellowship had been growing in him. Even Calkins, the arch villain Calkins, did not seem a devil of so black a dye, just now. Who could tell? Perhaps Calkins had been moved only by a desire for justice from the first. Perhaps he had really believed that Lefty was guilty of the first robbery.

Meanwhile, the fruit of the second robbery was still in his hands. It rose before him like a mountain. On the other side of the mountain was Jo Morrison. To be sure, there were other obstacles. Gus Harley was the chief of these. But Gus Harley might presumably be disposed of. No girl was married to a man until the wedding ceremony was actually completed. Up to that time, she might change her mind. So reasoned Lefty. But this stolen money—it was a stain upon his honor, and with such a stain he could not even come to her as a friend. There would be no explaining of it, even to her lenient ears.

He took out the wallet. It was odd that so much money could be compressed to so thin a bulk. Here in his hand, between thumb and forefinger, he held lightly a whole ranch stocked with cattle—happiness—comfort for life—all that money could buy, to his simple seeming. Until he could restore it to the rightful owners, he must get rid of that fatal money. He cast about him. He might cut open the mattress of the bed and sew the wallet inside it. But suppose the mattress were changed the next day and taken away and the wallet found? The hair prickled on his head at the thought. He might hide the wallet in the closet by removing a board and nailing it into the wall, but then he recalled some wonderful stories he had heard of how such things were discovered. No, he dared not hide it near his person. There must be some other place found.

Lefty hurried out of the hotel, went down the back stairs, and out the back door. Then he waited in the yard, trying to find an idea, listening with half his attention to the babbling of the two Chinese servants, the cook and waiter. Then he went on idly.

He jumped the fence. He walked across the field. He entered the trees. Still he found nothing that would do. Yonder was a rotten stump with a hollow in its side. But that very stump might be cut up for kindling wood very soon. Its dryness would be an object.

He strolled on for half an hour. Then he crossed a little hollow below a hillside, and in the center of the hollow there was a large rock, three feet high—a blunt triangle. It must do for him. He rocked the heavy stone upon one side. In the moist, black cavity beneath, he cast the wallet. Then he hurried away.

At the top of the hill he turned to look down at the hiding place again, and there, revealed in the clear moonlight, was the shadowy form of a man leaning over the very rock that he had so recently left—yes, leaning over it and twisting it strongly to one side. Lefty reached impatiently for his revolver. Then, realizing that the distance was too great, that he must not risk a bullet, after all, he dropped the gun into the holster and raced back down the slope.

Near the edge of the hollow he reduced his pace again and stole cautiously ahead to catch the spy at his work of examining the contents of the wallet, but, when he peered around the thick trunk of a pine tree, he found that the clearing was empty. The stranger was gone! He listened for a moment. There, in the near distance, he heard the faint crackle of underbrush. The man was retreating, then, at a round pace, but not so fast that Lefty could not overtake him. First, however, he must make sure that nothing had been left behind, so he leaped to the rock and pushed it aside. There lay the wallet in its place—but empty, of course. No, it was as fat as ever, to the pinch of his fingers. Lefty snarled like a cornered wolf. How clever was yonder spy to have gone even to this detail to deceive him, in case he returned again that same night to put his spoils into a new hiding place. He drew out the wad of contents—and it was money. Fake money, then? No, here were the very bills that he remembered so well, every bill so often scanned that it was like a page out of a book to him. Here was his money, but was all of it here? One greenback, extracted, might mysteriously prove substance enough to destroy him in a court of law and bring down on his head enough guilt to put him in prison for the remainder of his life. He began to count hastily. Twice over he flicked the sheaf through his fingers. No, there was not an item missing. He who had seen the wallet had allowed it to remain there, with all its wealth still fattening it.

Lefty turned cold with the fear of the unknown. For what could be in the mind of the spy? To mark the stolen goods and then bring a witness before he took them forth? That might be the idea. All thought of pursuit departed from Lefty. He concealed himself hastily on the edge of the clearing and waited. But no one came. The chill of the mountain night entered him. A hunting wolf, coming up the rising wind, almost blundered upon him in the covert and leaped away with a terrified snarl. An hour passed and another. But still the clearing was empty.

Then Lefty gave up the question. It was far too mysterious to be penetrated by his brain. He went back toward the hotel. If a rock had served him once, it must serve him again. Under another boulder among the trees, he concealed the treasure. Now let the spy come forth the next morning to take the wallet by the light of the day. He would have thin air for his pains.

But who and what could he be? What was his idea? Was it Sam Tucker, perhaps? That suggestion stuck in his brain like a burr. When he reached the hotel, he asked on the verandah: "Where's Sam Tucker?"

"Over yonder," someone answered. "He's been here all evening. Asleep, I guess."

It was not Sam Tucker, then. Let him sleep in peace. It was not Sam Tucker, but who else was there who could have done the trick?

He could not close his eyes that night in sleep. If the thought of the mysterious stranger was not tormenting him, there was the memory of the girl to make his heart ache. He had made a fool of himself before her, he decided. She had been stunned by his egregious bluntness— his stupidly emotional talk. Lefty grew hot with the shame of it.

In the morning, when the first light of the early summer dawn touched the window, he was out of his room and downstairs. Then away from the hotel to the hollow, skulking like a hunted thing—or a hunter. He went to the second rock. His wallet was still there under it. He looked away from it, taking care to cover his trail. He went to that other rock in the hollow where he had first hidden the money, and nearby he picked up the trail of the spy and followed it. Whoever it was, he had skulked around the back of the village. No honest man, surely, would have walked on such a trail. Lefty followed until he came behind a long, low house from the chimney of which a thin wisp of smoke was rising, showing that breakfast was cooked early in that house.

He passed to the front of it to make sure. But his first surmise had been right even from the rear. It was the house of none other than the sheriff himself. It was terrible Gus Harley who had stalked him on the preceding night, and who had located the treasure and left it there. Why? What reason under the blue heavens could have induced the man of the law to do this thing?

So Lefty, dazed by all of this, went back to the hotel. There he flung himself on his bed and tried to think it out. But there was no solution. Here was a man known as the most honest sheriff in the whole range, and yet he allowed a man who he knew to be a bank robber to go for hours unarrested.

"He wants something else out of me," said Lefty to himself. "He wants to get something else out of me, then he'll pick his time and grab me, when I figger that I'm safe. But I've seen the game of the fox, and I'll match it. I'll find some way of matchin' it."

All of this was logical enough. There was only one flaw. It left the reason of the sheriff hidden in as deep a mystery as ever.

XII
The Shadow of a Man

Surely in all the world there was never another man so tantalized, so utterly maddened, as young Lefty Richards was now. Reason told him to mount Drifter and flee across the mountains as fast as the horse could take him, and instinct told him not to leave the girl. Not that any hope of winning her came into his conscious mind, knowing that she was so close to marriage with the famous sheriff, but still in his unconscious mind there *was* a hope, and he clung to it. He might win Jo Morrison if he stayed in Bantonville.

Thus, he remained. He went the next morning to the ranch of Mr. Morrison. Everyone could show him the way, for it was a large and well-known property. He found that Morrison himself, who stayed in the town house now that he was past his youth, had not driven out that morning. But the foreman was there, and the foreman talked to Lefty in a terse and most unpleasant way.

"You're Lefty Richards," he said, when he saw the robber.

"I'm him," said Lefty.

"You've come here lookin' for work?"

"That's me."

"Old-timer, you ain't wanted."

"That's makin' it fine and quick," Lefty responded, flushed with anger and with disappointment.

"I don't want you," said the foreman, "and the boys don't want you, but old man Morrison, God knows why, has sent out word that we're to give you a job if you come around this way. What in the devil are you good for on a ranch?"

"I can ride a horse," said Lefty slowly, "herd a bunch of cows, or lick the devil out of any fool that talks too much about me or anything else."

The foreman took the hint, but he did not give ground. He was a little terrier of a man, and he thrust out his jaw and glowered at Lefty. "I got to take you in," he said, "but if it wasn't for the orders that I got, I'd see you damned before ever I took you onto this here ranch. This is an honest crowd, Lefty!"

Lefty had no doubt of that. He did not want it to be anything else. But, from the first moment, he found himself ostracized. The other cow waddies did not want his companionship, and they showed it unmistakably. At the noon meal, those who sat next to Lefty had not a word to say to him, and silence to a stranger is the worst of insults in the West. That was not all. He had only to approach a laughing, chattering group in order to have them fall quiet until he had gone by.

These things angered him, but he stuck with his work and said nothing, did nothing to irritate directly those who were around him. Two-thirds of his attention was turned away from the ranch toward the town of Bantonville. He was waiting for the coming of the sheriff. He waited for five days, doing his work regularly on the ranch and, when he was out of earshot from the others, trying his hand at a little target practice to keep his shooting eye in proper trim.

At the end of the fifth day he slipped on Drifter and rode off to examine his buried treasure. It was dry sand under the rock, and the wallet was unhindered, unchanged. Lefty went methodically through its contents. His feeling was beginning to change. Since the world frowned so blackly upon him, would he not be justified in marrying Jo Morrison, if God gave him that opportunity, and living upon the money he had wrested from hostile society itself? He assured himself that he *was* justified in such a course. He went back to the ranch that night with his mind made up. The first thing was to find the heart of Josephine Morrison. And for that he waited and planned.

There was the ranch work to be done, and he maintained his share of those labors with a most scrupulous care. Moreover, by keeping to himself and paying no attention to the fashion in which he was slighted by the others, he began to win some measure of their esteem. But all of this was very slow work until it chanced, on the ninth day of his work at the ranch, young Terry Swain arrived at the ranch full of moonshine whiskey and primed for concentrated trouble. He had enough liquor in his system to make his brain as wild as a March hare's, and yet his tongue was not thick and his hands and his feet were not fumbling. It was only his wild red eyes that betrayed his condition—that and his breath.

He announced, when he entered the bunkhouse, that he was a tornado, and that he had come to twist things. A moment later he declared that he was the Colorado River on a spree, and still again he invited all the men on the ranch to attack him at the same moment. Numbers meant nothing to him, he said gleefully. His ordinary custom was to destroy half a dozen waddies for exercise before he ate in the morning. Such was the manner of Terry Swain when the door of the bunkhouse opened and Lefty Richards walked in.

A deadly hush passed over the crowd of cow waddies. A moment later Terry had become dangerous. What he wanted was bloodshed, at once, and here was a man pledged by reputation not to avoid his challenge. Here was a famous gunfighter—Lefty Richards. So he began to plague Lefty with violent words, while the cowpunchers stood by holding their breaths and expecting the sudden destruction of Mr. Swain.

To their amazement, Lefty Richards sat for fifteen minutes on the edge of his bunk smoking cigarettes and listening calmly to the wild torrent of abuse that streamed from the lips of Terry Swain. Then, as calmly as ever, while Terry called him all manner of coward and a "yeller-livered skunk," Lefty went to bed and was snoring before Terry ceased raging.

The next morning Terry was half sick and half frightened. He knew what he had done, and he expected death for it, but he was too much of a man to run away, and he was too foolishly proud to apologize for his remarks of the evening before.

"He wouldn't pull a gun on me while I was drunk," said Terry, "but he'll come out rampin' for me this mornin'."

So he waited near the door of the bunkhouse for Lefty to come back from the corral where he had been tending to the wants of Drifter. Back came Lefty Richards, but, when he saw Terry, he merely paused with a grin.

"You done your tongue a lot of good last night, kid," said Lefty, and passed on into the bunkhouse.

Terry Swain groaned with relief, and from that moment

he became a firm ally of Lefty. Half the enmity of the others, also, disappeared. In another day or so they were accepting Lefty as an equal comrade. It does not take much for a cowpuncher to install himself in the hearts of his companions. Very soon reports came in which made Morrison nod and grin.

"A lot of these crooks only need a chance to show that they're white," he declared with a large generosity. The sheriff agreed with him, emphatically.

Such was the news that came to Josephine Morrison just as she was starting for the dance with the good sheriff.

"Do you think Lefty will turn out square?" she asked Gus Harley.

"He's doin' pretty fair," said the sheriff, and changed the subject.

That same night Lefty Richards had dressed in his best and ridden in for the dance, but his heart had failed him when he came within the verge of the glow of the lighted windows of the schoolhouse where the dance was held. He climbed up to one of those side windows and watched the crowd swirling, watched the elders and the young folk seated along the walls, and saw the beaux and the belles of the district whirling in the center of the room. Or he watched the orchestra frantically at work, the fiddler with his eyes closed, swaying his head with the rhythm of the piece. These things he observed, not because they were interesting in themselves, but because they were part of the background of Jo Morrison. She herself was the center of all observation. She was the very queen of the ball, and the eye of Lefty gloated over her. The more he stared at her, the more impossible it seemed to him that Gus Harley should ever be her husband. He was so much more fitted to be her father, thought Lefty.

He waited until the crowd broke up and went home, and he followed Gus and the girl to the Morrison house. Sneaking close behind a tree, without shame, Lefty listened.

"Good night, Gus," said the girl.

The sheriff leaned above her.

"No!" she said.

"Jo, Jo," murmured the poor sheriff, "you ain't never gonna have no fondness for me."

One could hear the grit of the gravel on the path under her stamped foot.

"I'm going to marry you, Gus. Isn't that fondness enough?" And she flaunted away into the house.

The sheriff remained for some time where he was, with his head debased and his figure motionless. Then he went off up the street without a sound. At another time Lefty might have pitied him, but now Lefty was merciless for this was the affair that is as cruel as war.

At Jo's window he waited until the door brushed open, making a sighing through the room, and he saw the dim form of Josephine entering. With a whisper he alarmed her and brought her to him. She did not come very close but paused nearby, leaning toward him.

"Lefty!" she said. "I've felt you at my elbow all evening. Where have you been?"

"I was outside the school. Did you guess I was there?"

"Why didn't you come in?"

"Would you have danced with me?"

"Lefty! Of course!"

"I didn't know," lied Lefty. "If I'd been sure, rawhide lariats couldn't have stopped me."

"Hush!" she urged. "Is that someone on the street?"

"I don't know."

"Lefty. . . ."

"Yes?"

"You've got to go away from Bantonville."

"Why?"

"It'd be a lot better."

"D'you know something?" Lefty asked with a furious eagerness.

"Yes," came the alarming answer.

"What about?" asked Lefty. "If they're talking about me, I got a right to know what they're sayin'."

"It's only that it's safer to have you gone."

"Oh, Jo, what do I care about bein' safe? I've been in danger before, and now. . . ."

"Hush!" said the girl again in a trembling voice.

He could feel, somehow, that she was very weak, very unsure of herself, oddly within his power. It filled him with joy.

"It's not about you, only," she began to explain.

"Who is it? If I'm to leave town, who is it for outside of myself?" gasped out Lefty.

"For me," breathed Jo.

"For you."

But she had fled away into the darkness of the house and left Richards alone, with only his half-guessed discovery to keep him company. He turned away from the house, almost glad that he had not the time to press on his inquiry after her meaning. There was enough delight in what he was guessing that lay just before him. Then—as he turned from the window—he saw a shadow slip behind a nearby tree, the shadow of a man.

XIII
Lefty Is Called
a Poacher

A moment before, the night had been most neighborly, filled with pleasant sounds from among the trees. But it was all quite changed by the mere flitting of that shadow. Lefty Richards, when he glimpsed, dropped flat upon his belly, without regard for dignity, and wallowed through the darkness and through the garden mold, until he came to the shelter of the big trees himself. There he paused and crouched, waiting for some sound to apprise him of the movements of the other, but no warning sound came. He was surrounded by the absolute quiet of the night, broken only by the distant laughter of the people streaming home from the dance.

After a decent interval, to allow his nerves to grow quieter, Lefty Richards advanced toward the rear of that spot where he had seen the shadow of the stranger, and, after five minutes of careful stalking, he found to his utter amazement that the fellow was gone. There was no sign of him among the trees. Truly like a very shadow he had come, and like a shadow he had gone. All the nervous straining of Lefty's ears did not suffice to detect any sign of his departure, although the ground was strewn with dead leaves ready to make noise enough under even the lightest foot. Lefty began to shudder like a child who fears a ghost.

What he did next was very odd, but not altogether unexplainable. He did not even pause to hunt through the surroundings of the garden, but, as though taking it for granted that it was useless to hunt on the trail of this mysterious stranger, he set off on a trail of his own that led him through the woods and down the village, behind the hotel, past a hollow, and into another in which he found a familiar rock. He kicked it upon its back. In the white hollow of the sand beneath it he saw—no sign of anything! He thought, at first, that the wallet might easily have been covered from view by working down among the sand, but, when he scooped his fingers through the sand, they brought him no treasure as a reward.

Lefty got to his feet again, stunned. He did not even care to replace the rock in order that the second-hand thief might not know that his theft had been discovered. There in the sand he left the big stone lying on its side, while he took stock of his situation. He who held that wallet held the life of Lefty in his hand. The wallet itself was a sufficient guarantee. It established the identity of Lefty beyond a doubt, and damned him as the long-wanted bank robber. At that stroke, Lefty would be turned back into prison and Jo Morrison would be taught to look upon his memory with horror.

There were several things that he could do, but none of them was satisfactory. He might leave the town and take to flight—thereby giving up Jo and all his hopes for a new life. Or he might wait until the morning came, and then attempt to track the thief—which offered a small chance of success. Or he might beard the danger where he most suspected that it lay, that is to say, he might go straight to the home of the sheriff for an explanation. But this alternative was not very greatly more promising than either of the others. To face the sheriff was to face a wall of fire. In a word, Lefty Richards was thoroughly frightened, unhappy, desperate. Being desperate, he rather naturally turned to the most dangerous expedient of all. He went to face the sheriff in the sheriff's own home.

Gus Harley was at home. He sat oiling and cleaning a Winchester near to the window. There were no newspapers in his life. As he was fond of saying, what he heard from other men was as good and as reliable as what editors of newspapers heard from other men. Besides, he did not have to know what went on all over the world. His own world had to do, actually, with the happenings in one county, and, although that county spread over more territory than some European principalities, yet it was not too large for him to glean the principal items of interest by word of mouth. Sometimes the news came in rather late, but when it arrived, it had an aroma, it had a freshness, it had a suggestion that could never have been found in a newspaper. Therefore, for all of these reasons, newspapers were not in the house of the worthy sheriff. Instead, he preferred to occupy himself as Lefty now found him— with his guns. If his guns gave out, he had his thoughts to turn over and over while his fingers performed their more than half mechanical duties.

He looked up and gave Lefty a smile as the latter entered. "I hear that you been doin' fine," said the sheriff at once. "All the boys from out on Morrison's ranch has been sendin' in fine reports. It sure tickled 'em because you didn't carve up young Terry Swain. They said you had call enough for choppin' him up pretty small."

"Just a mite irritated, he was," replied Lefty, sitting down. "What he said didn't do me no harm. Matter of fact, I figgered on cleanin' him up on the next day when he was himself ag'in, but when I seen him standin' up there waitin' for me, like a soldier about to get shot in the line of duty . . . why, it was too much for me, Sheriff. I told the young fool that we was friends, and he allowed that we was."

The sheriff nodded, and wrapped a rag tighter around the end of his ramrod.

"Might be," suggested Lefty, "that you're one of these here gents that takes a fancy to the night, Sheriff."

"Like what?" asked the sheriff, still without looking up.

"Why, one of them that likes to stroll around by themselves."

"Me?" the sheriff mused thoughtfully. "Why, I been to the dance, Lefty. Dog-gone me if this here dancin' game ain't gettin' a bit too much. I never used to mind it. Now it gets pretty foolish."

"Sure," said Lefty. "You ain't a kid no more. I feel sort of froze over myself when I step out on a dancin' floor. Who was you dancin' with . . . Jo Morrison, I guess?"

At this, and certainly it was not a trick of his imagination, he saw the glance of the sheriff turn sharply up at him, but he pretended to be very busy with the rolling of a cigarette.

"I took Jo to the dance, of course," said the sheriff softly. "Who else would I take?"

"Why," Lefty responded, "I dunno who." He leaned back in his chair, in which he shifted a little to the side, so that the right-hand holster swung clear of his hip and the butt was near his hand. "But it seemed sort of queer," said Lefty.

"What seemed queer?" asked the sheriff without emotion.

"Nothin'."

"You're talkin' a mite funny, Lefty."

"Maybe so. I was thinkin' of something."

"What was that?"

"That you and Jo must've gone spoonin' behind the trees around the house."

The sheriff sat bolt erect, glaring at the lounging form of the robber. "How d'you mean that?" he asked furiously.

"Take it plumb easy," Lefty cautioned. "But look at that." He pointed, but the sheriff, glancing down, appeared to notice nothing that was at all out of the way. "Look at that smear of black mud," suggested Lefty.

"What of that?"

"Maybe you ain't noticed that most of the ground around here is *gray* or sort of reddish gray. But they's one patch that's plumb black."

"I dunno that I foller you," said the sheriff, beginning to frown and lose some of his dignity and aloofness at the same time.

"Try again," Lefty said. "It ain't likely that you're very far off from the truth about this here. That there black mud got onto your boots under the trees beside the Morrison house."

The sheriff said not a word, but hitched his body a little to one side, so that the holster for his revolver fell clear of the chair. There could not have been, as a matter of fact, a more emphatic answer or one that Lefty could have understood more clearly. It was to be a battle, then, and only postponed for a few moments. He might use that delay to get at some of the important facts.

179

"You been onto me for a long time, Sheriff," he suggested.

"For a spell," Harley said.

"It was you that sneaked out yonder and got the dope on where I'd put that money the first time?"

"That was me," admitted the sheriff with the most perfect frankness.

"Lemme find out where you learned that I shifted that wallet and where I put it?"

"I waited right there in the brush for a time."

"When I come back to the hollow?"

"That's right."

"You seen where I took it to, then?"

"I did."

"What put you onto me in the first place, Sheriff?"

"I dunno. The looks of Chic's two guns, I guess."

Lefty blushed. "It was a fair fight," he said huskily.

The sheriff, upon this rejoinder, waved his hand—his left hand, for the right was kept steadily near his holster— and waved the protest away. "Sure it was a fair fight," he said. "Chic had it comin' to him for a good many years. Nobody that takes to manhuntin' for a sport deserves anything better'n Chic got. It was comin' to him. He run you down, and you plugged him. I guessed all of that while you was tellin' me that yarn."

"Still you went and got me a job in the town?"

"I did. When I made out for sure that you was the crook that held up the bank. . . ."

"Well, what the devil was inside your head?"

"I figgered that you was comin' on pretty well right here where you were, and that there wasn't nothin' better you could do than to stay on here and take a chance at doin' something for yourself. I aimed to return that money to the bank . . . sort of anonymous. Then you could turn loose and prove yourself an honest man. I didn't wish you no bad luck. Not until. . . ."

"What, Gus?"

"You begun to hunt on my ground," said the sheriff, "and, when I seen that you was a poacher, I made up my mind that you was to die, Lefty."

XIV
No Doubt Remains

After that, of course, each of them stiffened a little. They cast swift side glances about the room to make sure where every chair and every table was posted so that, in case of a hurly-burly, each would feel himself to have only a small chance of tripping over anything. But these surveying glances were as brief as possible. On the whole, they viewed the room from the corners of their eyes, and then stared steadily at one another. Neither was accustomed to making the first move in a fight; neither was prepared to make the first move now. They were ready to kill, but they were not ready each to be the assailant.

"A poacher," Lefty stated grimly, "is a gent that takes what another gent has the only right to."

"Like me," said the sheriff, "being engaged to the girl."

"You," said Lefty, "bein' old enough to be her father and comin' pretty close to breakin' her heart."

"You lie!" Harley cried.

"You've sneaked around enough to find out the truth," said Lefty. "I'll tell you what, Harley, it's because you're scared to admit that what I say is the truth that you want to get rid of me."

The sheriff grinned and showed his teeth, as a bull terrier grins. "You're talkin' fast, Lefty."

"But not foolish, I guess."

"That's by your way of thinkin'." With this, he reached his left hand inside his coat, keeping his glance earnestly on the other all the while, and drew out a wallet that he cast on the floor. It was a worn and battered bit of leather, newly gouged with many deep scratches.

Lefty recognized it with the slightest glance. It was his own.

"Afterward," said Gus Harley, "I'll tell 'em that you resisted arrest and that we had to fight it out, and then that I took this here wallet offen you."

"Afterward," said Lefty. "I'll tell 'em that, while we was talkin', you got foolish with your gun you was workin' over, and it went off and drilled you clean!" He added: "They'll believe me."

"Not in a million years."

"Jo'll believe me," said Lefty.

The sheriff groaned. "Get your gun!" he commanded.

"Grab your own," said Lefty. "I don't take no advantages."

"It's nigh onto one o'clock, Lefty. When the damned old clock begins to buzz, you get ready to pull your Colt. When it strikes for the hour, we'll shoot. Is that right?"

"That's square," Lefty agreed.

They sat silently, staring at one another, never moving, never speaking. Each felt that if his steady stare relaxed for a single instant the other would gain a crushing moral advantage. Each dared not let his glance so much as flicker.

The time passed slowly—more slowly than it passes for

the runner in the race who feels his strength flowing from him and the goal still far, far in front. Once an owl hooted outside, and the sheriff blinked. Once a mouse squeaked behind the wall, and Lefty started. But aside from this, both were rigidly motionless until the clock in the hallway, the big old-fashioned grandfather's clock in the hallway, began to *whirr*. Then they rose, of one accord, to their feet.

The clock struck. The guns leaped from the holsters. Before the echo died, two gunshots roared through the little chamber. The sheriff crooked his finger to fire again, but there was no need. Lefty had whirled around and around and collapsed along the floor. He was only momentarily stunned. When the sheriff leaned over him, he said with perfect calm: "You got me, Sheriff." His head was a mass of red. Even the sheriff shuddered.

"Are you done for, Lefty?"

"Not a bit. It just grazed my skull. That's all, I guess. It only knocked me out."

"Thank heaven for that!"

Voices and feet approached the front of the house, knocked, shouted, and entered. Half a dozen men poured into the room. They found the sheriff on his knees beside Lefty.

"What's up?" they demanded of Gus Harley.

He was too busy to answer.

"What's up?" they asked of Lefty. "Can you speak, Richards?"

"Who fired that shot . . . the sheriff?" asked another.

For so perfectly had the guns been pulled that the explosion had come at the same exact instant.

"I was foolin' with my gun," Lefty stated clearly. "The damned thing went off in my hand and slammed me."

"Hey, Gus, is that right?"

The sheriff turned upon them with a scowl. "The devil," he said, "what other way could it have happened?"

In ten minutes the excitement was over. The people were gone. The sheriff and Lefty were alone in the room, Lefty with a thickly bandaged head.

"What made you say that?" he asked.

"I dunno," said the sheriff. "I dunno. It was Jo, I guess. Now get out of my house and don't never let me see you ag'in! Here's your stolen money. You mail this back to the bank."

Who could say what went on inside the head of the sheriff that night after Lefty Richards, badly hurt, white-faced, and his mind full of wonder, went back to the hotel? Whatever the reflections of the sheriff might have been, Lefty Richards, it was certain, sat up all the night and among other things wrapped a little stack of money in thick paper and addressed it to a certain bank of which a Mr. Calkins was the president.

In the morning, the sheriff was not in town. He was gone. The first Lefty knew of it was a note that was brought to him early in the day.

I've changed my mind, said the note. *I'm too old to win. You go on, Lefty. I dunno what else you are. But you fight clean. Go on and win, Lefty.* It was signed: *Gus Harley.*

Lefty went straight to the Morrison house and found Jo in the orchard. She tried to flee to the house when she saw him, but he headed her off.

"Gus Harley told me I could see you," Lefty declared quietly. "So I've come to tell you that I love you, Jo."

She grew very red, looking him in the eyes, then she grew very white, noticing the bandage around his head.

185

"Oh, Lefty!" she cried. "Suppose he'd shot a little straighter!"

By that, Lefty knew that Gus Harley had written to the girl as well. There could be no doubt as to what he had said in that letter!

SEVEN-DAY LAWMAN

I
The Hobo Arrives

Just outside the shack, Pier Morgan lay beneath the pine tree. It was his first day outdoors. The boy had carried him by the head, and Anna, the old Mexican woman, had carried him by the feet. There had been some pain, just enough to make him taste the first pleasure longer and deeper as he lay now, looking up through the deep green heaven of the pine tree boughs.

Juan, the half-breed, his hair tumbling down over his eyes, his arms filled with branches of dead shrubbery that he was bringing in for the cooking, paused beside Pier Morgan and looked down with smiling eyes, his white teeth brightly flashing.

"Pretty good, eh?" said Juan.

"Pretty good," Pier whispered. He could speak out loud now. But the habit of whispering held over strongly from the days when he was supposed to die, when all the facts of flesh and failing spirit indicated that he was going to die, when he himself knew that he was to die, and when only the grim face of Speedy beside him forced him to live.

"Yellow dog, quitter, now turn up your toes and cash

189

in," Speedy would say. "You're only scratched, you're not hurt. But you're a quitter. You're going to die because you're afraid."

"I'm Welsh," Pier Morgan had said one day. "Welshmen, they don't quit. They fight till they die."

"Then keep on fighting," Speedy had said. "You're only quitting, and I want to tell you why I'm staying on here. It's not that I give a damn about you. It's only because I want to see a dirty Welshman quit like a yellow dog and die because he's scared."

Pier had gritted his teeth and rolled his eyes aslant with fury. He had not strength to turn his head. "If I get well, I'm gonna wring your neck," he had said.

Now, as he lay beneath the tree, he smiled a little, remembering this. He could see with a perfect clarity that Speedy had tormented him merely to keep some hot spark of life in his breast—had roused his anger to make that take the place of life, as it were. For Welshmen are bulldogs. They put in their teeth, they hardly care where, and then they hold on, and hold on, and hold on. Pier Morgan had held on because of the savage hatred he felt for his tormentor. He used to whisper his curses against Speedy until he fell into a deep sleep. Every time, when he awoke, there was a slightly brighter spark of life in him. But he understood now.

Juan and old Anna, his mother, had helped him to a right understanding of Speedy. For they worshipped the careless tramp. He was their hero.

"Speedy found you in Sunday Slough. That's all what I know," said Juan. "He brung you out here."

"Yeah, Sunday Slough. That was the place, all right," said Pier Morgan. "I wouldn't forget that. I thought I was gonna live to kill Speedy. Instead, I gotta live long enough to get Buck Masters and One-Eyed Mike and Sid Levine. That's what I gotta live for."

"Maybe better you go on and get well for your own sake," said Juan, shaking his head. "My mother Anna, she say you got no right to live, anyhow. She say you been no more'n dead. That's what she say. Juan, he don't know, very good."

He went off to the house. Pier Morgan could hear the wood falling with a crash, and his eyes returned to the consideration of the green heaven of branches above his head. Golden glints of sunshine broke through from the side. A woodpecker was hammering somewhere along the trunk of the upper branches. Now and then chips of wood came downward. The sweetness of the air made breathing easier, made him taste every breath to the bottom of his lungs. It was very true. He had no right to live. He wondered how Speedy had managed to find him, how he had managed to bring him out here. Juan and Anna said that the shack was three whole miles from Sunday Slough.

Then he returned to his first memory of Speedy, the singing tramp. He had met him in a jungle near Denver, where the thunder of a railroad bridge was shaken out over a forested ravine. There, the hobos used to rest and refresh themselves, eating stolen mulligan stew, boiling their clothes, drinking black coffee, telling tales of all the world, from Shanghai to New Orleans.

It was in that jungle that he had grown sick of the life of a tramp. It was there that he had resolved that he must go back to the world of honest, hard-working people. He had never been afraid of the sweat and the agony of labor. Only chance had thrown him out on the road. It was while he listened to Speedy, singing sentimental ballads to the accompaniment of his guitar, that he realized that he

191

did not belong to the world of the drifting idle. He had a place, somewhere, in the working world.

Before he turned in that night, he went over and shook hands with Speedy. "Thanks, kid," he had said.

"Yeah. You go straight, boy," Speedy had said sleepily.

He had been surprised by that remark. It was as though Speedy, all the evenings, had been singing straight at him and understanding him.

The next day he talked again. He was going West, going to join the gold rush to Sunday Slough.

"Don't go there," Speedy had said. "Any other place, but not a mining camp. You believe in your hands, but a mining camp believes in knives and guns."

Morgan had laughed. "I can always take care of myself," he had said.

So he had, at first. And he had found his claim, and dug out ten thousand dollars in a few weeks, and he had taken his gold dust into town for a little party, and then a big investment that would enable him to open up the claim and work it to good purpose.

Then everything crashed. His claim was jumped. He had appealed for justice. The kind of justice that emanates from a crooked judge had been done him. Bertram Daly had sentenced him for vagrancy, and, while he was in jail, fury had boiled up and overmastered him. They were looting his claim in the meantime.

So he had tried to break out of jail, and, as a result, Sheriff Buck Masters and One-Eyed Mike, his hanger-on, had managed to shoot him to bits. Oh, how well he could remember it all. No, it was Speedy who had saved him, shining into his life again like a lucky star.

Only the day before he had said to Juan: "Who is Speedy, anyway?" Juan had laid a dirty forefinger beside his nose and grinned down at him. "Ha, you don't know who Speedy is?" he had asked. "I know. A lotta people don't, but I do." That was all he had said. He had spoken like one who has had a secret view of the king's treasure.

So the thoughts of Pier Morgan dipped into the past, and then into the present until, down the mountain trail, he heard a clear, familiar voice singing a Spanish song in the distance. It was the voice, he finally realized, of Speedy himself, and the words of the song might be translated into English somewhat as follows:

> *Like a golden apple in a golden snood,*
> *Oh, lovely Anna, fair and good!*

He knew that the words and the song were meant for the ears of that withered, bent, half-toothless old dame, Anna. A golden apple, indeed. And here she came, running out of the house.

"Juan," she screamed, "Juan, Juan! He has come. *Señor* Speedy is here!"

She was like a tired old bird with a cracked voice, hailing the rising of the sun. Pier Morgan turned his head, and presently, down the trail, he saw Speedy coming. He was riding an old, slow, wise-footed gray mule. His guitar was slung by a strap across his shoulders, and he was singing in a clear tenor voice. He was in no haste. Sometimes the mule paused to crop the mountain grass. A worm's way was the way of that mule, it appeared, and yet Speedy was not troubled by this slow procedure. Time did not seem to exist for him. For that matter, it never had appeared to exist. It was as though he had an eternity of youth before him.

Well, Pier Morgan thought to himself, *he don't have to worry. He's not the kind that could worry.*

Speedy came nearer. The sun gleamed on the golden

brown of his tanned face, glistened on his dark hair and eyes. He looked hardly more than twenty—slender youth, too handsome to be right, it seemed, slightly too feminine in appearance. His clothes were rags. There seemed nothing admirable about him except that rich, lilting voice. He was smiling as he sang. Yet, this was the lad who had, in the first place, set the feet of Pier Morgan on the way toward decency. This was the youth who had also dropped from a cloud and brought him out from Sunday Slough, when others had left him for dead. Gratitude and wonder blended in the stern heart of Pier Morgan as he looked at Speedy.

He saw the gray mule stop in front of the shack. There Anna and Juan were pulling the rider from the saddle. One of them was taking his guitar, and the other was holding his hat, and then Juan was leading away the recalcitrant mule toward the hay shed, while Anna, holding the guitar with one hand, with the other urged her guest forward, half embracing him, laughing, crying out, with tears of happiness in her voice.

They were gone some minutes inside the house, and at last Speedy came out, still eating. He had tasted the hospitality of Anna before he hurried to see the sick man. And Pier Morgan grinned. The nurse must be flattered before the patient was seen. That was the scheming way of Speedy, the hobo. Yes, he was finishing a mouthful and also puffing away at a long-stemmed pipe, a household treasure of the Mexican woman. Perhaps Speedy had done for some member of her family what he had recently done for Pier Morgan.

II
A Friend

Speedy came up the path and paused beneath the pine tree, looking down and smiling at the boy stretched out in the hammock. Then he said: "Well, Pier, I see you're up, kicking the world in the face this morning, eh?"

"Not this morning, but it won't be long now," said the wounded man, his voice beginning in a whisper and strengthening toward the end. He held out his hand. His arm was so weak that his hand shook.

Speedy took the hand and held it a moment, looking him over with a critical eye. "You're a good nurse, Anna," he said. "You could make extra legs grow on grasshoppers. I thought that he'd never be able to handle a soupspoon with that arm. I tell you, Anna, you're wonderful. Go back to the house and lie down and take a rest. I'll look after him for a while."

She went back, chuckling with pleasure, like a child, and wagging her head from side to side, as though to say that she knew very well that there was talent in those old hands of hers.

Speedy sat down on a stump nearby, a high one, from which he could easily look down on the patient.

"What have you been doing, Speedy?" asked Pier Morgan.

"Looking things over in Sunday Slough," answered the youth.

The brow of Morgan wrinkled with sudden pain.

"I looked the mine over, too . . . your mine," said Speedy.

"They've looted it," said Morgan.

"It was only a pocket, but it was a deep pocket," said Speedy. "Before it punched out, they took away ninety-five thousand dollars."

A bitter exclamation burst from Morgan. Speedy said nothing, and presently, opening the eyes that he had winked shut, Morgan said: "With the ten grand that they picked out of my pockets before, that makes over a hundred thousand that I've been done out of, Speedy."

Still Speedy said nothing, and presently Morgan grinned. "Yeah, I know," he said. "I'm still alive, and that's something, thanks to you."

"I'll thank you a lot more for something else," said Speedy.

"What's that, partner?"

"For getting well enough to do some practicing with a gun. I'm going to need help."

"Where?"

"In Sunday Slough, of course."

"What's happened there? What's wrong there . . . except everything?"

"I'm in the middle of everything," Speedy said, yawning widely and stretching. He relaxed from the stretching and smiled sleepily at Pier Morgan. "I'm the town hero, my son," he said.

"That's a good job, but generally there's no salary attached," said Morgan.

"I'm the deputy sheriff. I'm a hired hero," Speedy explained.

"Deputy sheriff?" muttered Morgan.

"Yes. I'm working under your friend, Buck Masters."

"I'll eat his heart one day," Morgan said thoughtfully.

"I'll cook it and put on the salt. It's sure to be peppery enough," said Speedy.

"What's this all about?" asked the sick man.

"It was a three-headed monster that put its teeth in you, Pier," said the tramp. "The main head was Sid Levine of the Grand Palace. The number two is Buck Masters. Number three is important, too. One-Eyed Mike, I mean. I went down to Sunday Slough to look things over, but I soon saw that nut would have to be cracked from the inside."

"Whatcha mean by that?" asked Morgan.

"I'd have to be inside the ring to do them up," Speedy said calmly. "So I decided to get in with the thugs. Not as a real friend, you understand, but force myself into a position where they'd have to accept me on my own terms. I mean I wanted to make myself important in the town's eyes. So first, there was a little roulette play, where I had so much luck that they decided to roll me for my wad, just as they did you, Pier. But One-Eyed Mike and Buck Masters were too casual, and I managed to get their guns, and left them in the window of a gunsmith to be claimed by the owners. Pretty soon the town was talking a bit about the thing. A Greek never left his shield on the battlefield. A Westerner doesn't leave his gun. In the middle of the chatter, I dropped around to the sheriff's office and applied for a job as deputy. You know."

"I know they call the deputies in that town the seven-day men, because that's the average length of their lives after they become deputies," said the wounded man. "Why did you want that job?"

"To get on the inside. The sheriff gave me the job and the price of a horse, and then assigned me the little job of capturing Cliff Derrick. . . ."

"Derrick eats a tiger a day," said Morgan.

"He slipped this time," said Speedy. "I had him almost back to town when Mike and the sheriff jumped me and took him away. They made a deal with him and took him away, but I'd been expecting that and slipped back up the trail to wait. When Derrick came by, I dropped a rope over him and brought him back to Sunday Slough just as a handy little mob was getting ready to lynch Levine and Mike and Masters for letting Derrick go. If I had known what was happening, I would have come in slower. As it was, they were turned loose, and I handed Derrick over to Marshal Tom Gray. Derrick's in prison, now . . . he'll hang before long, I suppose.

"So there I am like a cat walking a fence, with public opinion holding me up and the sheriff and Levine's gang trying to pull me down. But everything's polite and good feeling, if you know what I mean. The Sunday Slough *News* makes a feature of me. When I go to bed, when I get up, what I eat for dinner. You know. A lot of bunk. But it makes Levine's thugs go slow. They know that the crowd in Sunday Slough has teeth now. And they're rather afraid to tackle me. When they do, it will be at about the same time that they loot Sunday Slough of everything down to gold fillings in the eyeteeth. That's the picture for you to look at, Pier."

The latter considered. "You're in hot water," he said.

"Boiling," said Speedy.

"And you like it, I guess?"

"It's interesting. I like thugs. I like to see the way they jump," confessed Speedy. "Levine is as smooth as oil with me now. Oh, he's a bright boy, is Levine. He wants to cook me. He wants to roast me in butter and serve me with capers."

"He'll do it, too," said Morgan, "someday when you're not looking."

"Anyway," said Speedy, "as I was saying before, it's rather lonely down there in Sunday Slough . . . what with being the town hero on the one hand and the deputy sheriff on the other."

"I know," said Morgan, nodding. "I suppose every time a tough mug comes to town, Masters sends you down to pinch him and throw him in the hoosegow."

"It's that way." Speedy sighed. "I don't mind excitement. But some of the thugs that drop into the camp are bristling with knives and guns, and such small deer. But Masters has always said . . . 'The boys know you, Speedy. You go down to such-and-such a joint, and you can clear everything up in ten seconds.' So I have to go down. But before long, I'm likely to use up my welcome, and then I'll be needing a friend at my back. A friend like you, Pier."

"I'm getting better every day," said Morgan. "I'm hurrying to get well, because I remember the way you used to abuse me, when I was lying flat on my back in the shack, here. I have to lick you for that, one day."

Speedy considered him; they smiled at one another.

"You're a hardy lad, Pier," said the tramp. "But you have to learn to use a gun. You'll need a gun before you're through with Sunday Slough."

"I'm sitting up tomorrow," said the other. "And every day after that, I intend to do a little shooting at a mark . . . until I peg out. I'll get my hand in before long. I have a pretty good eye."

"Good," said Speedy.

"But, look here, Speedy," Pier went on, "you talk about me learning to shoot, and you never will use a gun yourself."

"Last thing my old mother asked me," Speedy said, yawning again. "Never to drink more than a quart at a time, and never to use a Colt. She preferred Smith and Wessons. But, talking about getting well, I expect to see you in the saddle inside of ten days."

"In five days," said Pier Morgan. "I've been lying here daydreamin' about the time when I'd get my teeth into that gang in Sunday Slough. And there you are on the spot, breaking the ground and getting ready for the harvest." He wriggled a little. "I'd crawl a hundred miles on my hands and knees just to get at Sid Levine," he said.

"All right," said Speedy. "I've just come up to see that your appetite is good. Now that I know it is, I feel better. I'm going to need you, Pier. I'm going to need you pretty badly. Don't hurry too fast. Don't take chances. But the sooner you can manage to get on your feet, the better it will be for me. I need you."

"Then why not use me?" said a voice half deep and half nasal.

"Don't move," whispered Pier Morgan to his friend.

Over the shoulder of Speedy, he saw a young man of not more than twenty years with broad shoulders and long arms—a youth whose face would have been handsome, had it not been so muscular. Besides, it was marked in three places with large red scars that looked as though they were the result of burns. Most interesting of all, however, was the .45-caliber Colt that he balanced with familiar and affectionate ease, just above the level of his hip. The muzzle pointed at Speedy.

The latter, without turning, caught a glimpse of the

youth out of the corner of his eye. "Hello," he said. "Pier, this is a friend of mine, Joe Dale."

"Derrick's man?" Morgan asked in a whisper, his face covered with prickling goose-flesh.

"What makes you think that I'm your friend?" asked the voice of Joe Dale, pitched higher and in a more nasal strain than before.

"That was just my little joke," said Speedy. "Have you come to drill me, Joe?"

"I've come to learn Japanese wrestling or whatever the heathenish tricks are that you use," said Joe Dale. "I've brought Betsy along to thank you for sending her back to me. Come here, Betsy. Come here, you old fool, and thank the gentleman."

III
Murder for Hire

From behind a big, weather-grayed rock, stepped the loveliest bay mare that Pier Morgan had ever seen. With her ears pricked and a red forelock blowing across the white star on her forehead, she stepped daintily down the hillside. Once, on the way, a sound or sight disturbed her, and she paused with one hoof lifted, her head turned, to study the danger. When she was satisfied, she came on up to her master.

"Maybe I can stow this cannon away?" said Dale.

"It's the only one on deck, just now," said Speedy.

"Well," muttered Joe, "I didn't hardly know how things would be around here. I had to sort of take a care, d'ya see?" He was rather shamefaced as he put up his weapon. "Betsy, here," said Joe Dale, "she said that she wanted to come back and say hello to you, if you know what I mean. Betsy, go and say howdy to the gent."

He waved his hand, and Betsy, approaching Speedy, swayed her head up and down three times. The last time, she bent her knees a little, with the effect of a curtsey.

Pier Morgan laughed at the pleasant sight, and Betsy,

having finished her trick, advanced her velvety muzzle and nibbled at the shoulder of Speedy's coat. Mischief flared out to the sides like the ears of an over-wise mule.

"Come here, Betsy, you ornery old gal," said Joe Dale, filled with pride. "You look out, Speedy. She's likely to pinch you black and blue, when she gets to fooling around. She's an imp, is what she is. Come here, Betsy."

She shook her head angrily and went back to her master with a sudden gallop. The turf flew up from her flying hoofs. Now she threatened Joe Dale with her teeth, now with her hoofs.

"Aw, go on and shut up and lie down, will you?" he said, pretending to be bored. She stood still, attentive. "You hear what I said?" exclaimed Dale. "Ain't you got no manners at all? Can't you sit down when you're told to?" Betsy sank down on quivering haunches and watched her master's face. "A gent would think," Dale stated seriously, "that you never had no bringing up, the way you act around. Now go on and lie down, will you?" She laid down at his feet. He took her head on his knee and ran his fingers through the bright flowing of her mane. "You see the kind of a nuisance she is," said Joe Dale. "Just kind of always flying around and making trouble and never keeping still, if you don't lay an eye on her. Go on and get out of here, then, you rattle-head." Betsy sprang to her feet, as though released from a prison, and made a furious run, around and around the pine tree, throwing up her heels, flashing like red metal in the sunshine. "Aw, quit it, will yuh?" Joe said. She stood still and looked at him expectantly, and Dale, rather sheepishly, took from his pocket a piece of lump sugar. "You take a fool of a thing like Betsy," he said, "and she'll never leave you alone. She'll just keep nagging until you give her what she wants. She's spoiled, is what she is. And I'm damned tired of it. I'm gonna send her to school, one of these days. That's what I'm going to do. I'm gonna hire her out to work in a freighting team. They'll blacksnake her into some kind of order and good sense."

"She's wonderful," broke out Pier Morgan. "I never seen a horse like her. She's the finest thing that I ever laid eyes on."

"Yeah," said Joe Dale. "That's what gents say that ain't been at the raising of her. Some mighty damned mean times she's give me, and a lot of worry and trouble, too. She got a cold once, that pretty near turned into pneumonia. I was up with her for eight nights in a row. I had to go and sleep right under her feet, you might say, and hear the groanin' of her breathing. Them was bad days. I thought that she was a goner.

"Always playing fool tricks, too. Take one time she got into a fight with a coupla hosses in a corral, and they give her a run, and she starts to jump a barbed-wire fence that was standin' there, fencin' off a truck garden from the rest of the corral. She takes and slips and tangles her legs up in the barbed wires. They were wrapped around each leg. If she struggled, she'd 'a' cut her four feet right off, like a saw. But a lucky thing was, I seen her, and yelled, and, when she heard my voice, she goes and lays still as a mouse, in spite of the pain, and I go and cut the wire away from her. Nothin' but trouble is what she gives me, I tell you."

He looked at her with a fond eye, and Speedy smiled at him.

"Look here, Joe," he said, "how would you sell that mare?"

"Sell her?" said Joe Dale. "I dunno that I'd sell her."

"You don't like her much. What's the price on her?"

"I'm kind of used to her, I don't guess that I'd sell her,"

Joe Dale answered. "I'm kind of used to her, like to a scolding wife, or my pipe, or something like that. You know it ain't much use, but it's a habit that you can't get along without."

"I know," said Speedy. "Well, Joe, there are some *fríjoles* and *tortillas* over there in the shack. Want to eat?"

"I've eaten for today," said Dale. He fixed his keen eye upon the face of Speedy, then he said: "Speedy, I reckon that you're kind of a bright fellow."

"Thanks," said the youth.

"But you ain't a bird that flies through the air. You can't move without leavin' some kind of a trail behind you, I guess?"

"I suppose not," said Speedy.

"The kind of a trail that I could follow up here to the shack, for instance," argued Dale.

"That's true."

"Now, suppose that I'd been as mean as I might've been, why shouldn't I have laid low and socked a bullet into you, from there behind them rocks?"

"I knew that you'd been trailing me up here," said Speedy.

"Hold on! You knew it after I showed up with a gun."

"No, I knew it long ago. Three days ago when I came up this way, you were trailing me. You know, I'd ridden Betsy. I knew her. I know the sign of her hoofs and the length of her step. Going back, I looked the trail over, and I knew that you'd been up here."

"And you didn't keep no better look-out, in spite of that?" asked Dale.

"No, I wasn't afraid of you. That is, I knew that you'd play in the open, partly because I might still be riding Betsy. Besides, I took a liking to you. I trusted you to be white, Joe."

The boy listened with wide-spread eyes. "You took me to be white, did you?" he asked huskily. He cleared his throat, then he said to Pier Morgan: "This gent stands up to fight me and he paralyzes me with a lot of his. . . ."

"I know," said Morgan. "He's a *jujitsu* fiend, is what he is."

"He ain't nothing but," replied Joe Dale. "And he takes and throws me a burning fire at the wind-up, and I get burned fifty places. That's what he done to me." His eyes narrowed at the recollection.

Pier Morgan said: "I recollect a big half-ton truck of a no-good, slab-jaws Canuck, is what I recollect. And this here lumberjack, he decides to bust up Speedy smaller . . . kindling wood size. And he crowded the kid here. The kid had to defend himself. But the way he defended himself, it was a terrible thing. Because he took hold of that Canuck and handled him like he was putty. He just took and greased up the bunkhouse with him. It took four men, pulling different ways, to straighten the kinks out of the Canuck after that fight. Then he laid down in a corner and cried for a whole day and a night. He left camp and never was seen no more. That was what happened to the Canuck. You was lucky that he didn't throw you into the fire and hold you there."

Some of the hardness left the eyes of Joe Dale. He actually heaved a sigh of relief, and then he said: "Well, I'm glad it's that way. I was kind of afraid that maybe I was just a cheap fool and didn't amount to nothing. I'm glad to find out that he's kind of a champeen." He added, to Speedy: "What I wanted to tell you was something that maybe you'd like to know."

"Go on," said Speedy. "I'd be glad to hear it."

"You wouldn't believe it, what a skunk a man can be,"

said Joe Dale. "And him laying himself out to be a friend of yours, too, and always patting you on the back, and sending pretty stories about you to the newspaper. I mean that greasy-faced, pig-eyed lump of a no-good Levine . . . and the sheriff, too. Your own sheriff, what you're the deputy under! Your own sheriff, that got himself so damned famous because you caught Cliff Derrick."

"What's the matter?" asked Speedy.

"They're out for you."

"They're out to get me. Yes, I knew that, Joe."

"You . . . knew . . . that? Then, why have you been herding with 'em?" asked Joe Dale, wide-eyed with amazement.

"Because," Speedy said calmly, "I'm out to get them."

"Hold on," said Joe. "I don't follow this very clear."

Speedy hooked a thumb at Pier Morgan. "They did that to him," he said.

"I see," murmured Dale. "And him a friend of yours, eh? So you're gonna trim the whole bunch of 'em. Is that it?"

"That's the main idea," declared Speedy. "I want to stick one hook through that whole row of three faces, including One-Eyed Mike. Catching one at a time wouldn't make the same pretty picture. I want to fry them all in one pan afterwards."

"Well," said Dale, "it's a bright idea. But lemme tell you something. They're likely to fry you before you fry them. That's what I come up here to tell you."

"Thanks," said Speedy. "Have they got some plans?"

"Yeah. Murder is their plan. Murder that you hire. That's the way they're thinking."

"That's bad," Speedy agreed. "It's bad, because it's so simple, and murder is so extremely cheap in Sunday Slough."

"They ain't trying to make it cheap, though," said the other. "Will you listen?"

"I'm listening, Joe."

"If I'd pulled the trigger a minute ago and clipped your backbone into two parts, I could've collected ten thousand bucks from Sid Levine." He took a breath. "I ain't flush," he said. "But that kind of a skunk I ain't."

IV
A Price on His Head

Speedy, when he heard this, began to whistle softly to the green heaven of the pine tree above. The woodpecker stopped those rapid, accurate strokes, and the last chips floated softly down to the ground and lay unseen in the grass.

"Well," said Pier Morgan, "nobody in the world is alive when there's ten thousand dollars on his head. That's all I know about it."

"You know enough," answered Joe Dale. "That's the price they offered me. I went and I seen One-Eyed Mike. No, I mean he come and he seen me. That's the price he offered. Ten thousand bucks flat, and no lying about it. They're plumb loose with money. He wanted me to take five thousand down."

"Why didn't you take the five thousand?" asked Pier Morgan curiously.

"Well," Joe Dale said with a singular honesty, "I thought maybe that I would knock you off, Speedy. And then, ag'in, I thought maybe that I wouldn't. So I didn't go and take the five thousand. You know. I didn't wanna be tempted too damned much. That's why. Five thousand is all right to talk about, but it's a lot of money to have in the hand. It's a ticket to the Solomon Isles and soft days the rest of your life, is what five thousand dollars is. You know what I mean, Speedy."

"Yeah, I know what you mean," said Speedy. He stood up and stretched himself.

"Something had oughta be done about this," said Pier Morgan with a frown.

"Look at how he likes to walk a tight wire," suggested Joe Dale. "He wouldn't be happy, if he wasn't walking a tight wire like that. Naw, he wouldn't be happy. Life is too dull, is what it is for him. Say, Speedy, you little woolly, asbestos lamb, you, what are you gonna do about this here job?"

"I've got to get somebody," Speedy answered. "Maybe I've got to get all three of them, and get them quick. I wonder what makes them so anxious to have my scalp, Joe?"

"I dunno," said Joe. "It makes Levine nervous the way that you're always around, and ain't dead yet. He wants to see the last of you. That's all I know. You're spoiling the landscape for him and old Buck Masters. They got some big jobs on hand. You see, after I've bumped you off, I'm to go and take a whack at some of the easy money here in the town. I'm to crack things wide open. You know what I mean. They're gonna loot Sunday Slough. They're gonna clean it like a fish, is what they're gonna do."

"I suppose they are," said Speedy. "I'm a lazy beast, and I've taken too much time. Now I need to jump like a cat on a hot stove, and I've no ideas. Say, Pier, you hurry up and get well, will you?"

"You bet. I'll hurry," Pier Morgan answered softly.

"Oh, how I wish that I was riding down along the trail to Sunday Slough with you right now."

"You've got enough to worry about," said Joe Dale. "I tell you what, Morgan, I wouldn't cry about not having nothing to think about, if I was you. Because they know, now, why Speedy rides up this way. And they wanna get you plenty. They got some money out of you, and they want you dead. They don't like you alive and getting well up here. They would rather a lot have toasted young chicken that eats easy, than roasted old chicken that don't eat at all. They want you, Morgan. Not like they want Speedy, but they want you."

"I'd better be moving, then, Speedy," said Morgan.

"Old Anna and Juan will take care of that," said Speedy. "They know how to fade you out of the picture. Don't worry about that."

"I heard them talking about Juan and Anna," said Joe Dale. "They couldn't make out how you had 'em both under your thumb. Ain't old Anna the girl that's wanted in Mexico for poisoning, and ain't Juan the fellow that knifed a coupla gents in the back in Chihuahua?"

"I don't know anything about that," Speedy said with iron suddenly in his back. "I don't think that you know anything about it, either."

Joe Dale blinked. "Sure I don't know anything about it, at all," he said. "I didn't know that you always played that close with fire, though."

"Speedy," said Pier Morgan, "are they . . . ?"

But Speedy interrupted him to say pleasantly enough to Joe Dale: "I didn't know that you were such a merry little chatterbox, Joe. I say, Pier, that Anna and Juan will take care of you and keep on taking care of you until the sky falls down and drowns them with blue. D'you believe me?"

211

"I'd be a fool not to believe you," said the sick man.

"I say," went on Speedy softly, but thoughtfully, like a man who strives not to be inaccurate, "that either or both of them would walk a thousand miles up a glass cliff to keep you from losing a hair from your head."

"Man," said Pier Morgan, "what did you do for them, then?"

"One wet day I asked them in out of the rain, and they came," Speedy said more gently than ever. "Joe, are you playing this game with me?"

"To the limit," said Joe Dale. "I'm young enough to stay in school for a while. I used to think that Cliff Derrick was the whole show as a teacher, but he's all in the rough compared with you, Speedy."

"You come down and see me at the hotel," said Speedy. "See me today. When you come to my room, knock twice, count twice, and knock again. That's all."

"You know, Speedy," said the outlaw, "that, if I show my face around, I'm gonna get rapped over the head. Likely with a half-inch slug of lead that will go right through the brain. That's what I mean, son."

"I mean after dark," Speedy stated.

Joe Dale rose. He shook hands solemnly with Speedy, and with Pier Morgan. "I'm supposed to be on my way, I guess," he said. "I'm glad to know you, boys. You're gonna see me play up, Speedy." He called his mare. "Come home, Betsy. You can't eat all the grass in the world every day. Come home and sit down." She came to him and sank on her haunches. He stepped into the stirrups and said: "All right, beautiful." She came up gently, seating him comfortably in the saddle. "Terrible lot of trouble, she is," said Joe Dale. "Always gotta be watched all the time. Look at the way she stood up crooked. I never

212

seen such a horse." He waved his hand. "This evening, Speedy," he said. Instantly the mare, although she had received no visible sign, floated away up the trail at a gallop like the blowing of a cloud on the wind.

"The neatest thing I ever saw on four legs," said Pier Morgan.

Speedy was looking after the outlaw with a squint, as of one seeing distant mountains. "That cost blood," he said.

"The horse?" asked Morgan.

"No, the coming here of Joe Dale. He's not such a woolly lamb, Pier. He's as mean as they make 'em. He'd murder, that lad."

"He eats out of your hand," said Pier.

"Just now, perhaps," Speedy said. "But it worries me."

"What does?"

"Seeing him so good . . . so like a lamb."

"Look, Speedy," said Morgan. "He was all in position. He could have split your wishbone from behind, and then mine, and nobody would have known anything about it."

"Oh, yes, they would," said Speedy. "He wasn't all alone, and perhaps he knew it."

"How do you mean?" asked Pier Morgan.

"Look up there toward the berry patch," Speedy said.

"I'm looking. There's nothing there."

"Nothing but Juan and his rifle," said Speedy. "And maybe Dale got the idea just as he started to drill me. I don't know. I'm only supposing."

Just then, Pier Morgan saw Juan, the half-breed, walk out from the berry patch and saunter slowly down the hillside, half carrying, half dragging a rifle behind him. Everyday Juan spent a full hour with that rifle, shooting at targets, and no targets under five hundred yards were of interest to Juan. Scores under nine out of ten were to him a deadly sin. Pier Morgan stared, remembering these things. He began to feel that Speedy was more and more complicated. The world was more complicated, too.

"Did you tell Juan to go up there and look things over?" Pier asked.

"Yes," said Speedy. "I told you that I saw Betsy's trail the other day. I like Joe Dale. Still, one can never tell. A good rifle at hand is never wasted in a country like this. But you stick to the revolver, when you begin to practice. I know your nature, Pier. You're going to be close to trouble before you open up. It takes a lot of cast steel to do your killing at half a mile."

He went back to the shack and stood before the door, softly thrumming on his guitar. Old Anna, scrubbing wet cornmeal to a mash on a roughened stone, continued her motion, but looked up at him with a half toothless smile.

Continuing to thrum, he said: "They're after my friend, Anna. So take him away. Fade out, into the mountains, you and him, and open your eyes and keep them open, night and day. How is Juan?"

"Juan will be good for another week, perhaps," Anna stated without emotion. "Life is just a little quiet for him." The thrumming ended.

Speedy, speaking in the same purring Spanish, said: "That may be enough. Get my friend to his feet every day, and let him walk a few steps, leaning on you. A helpless man makes crooks go straight."

"Father," said the old woman, "your wisdom is out of the central blue of the sky. I shall do as you say. Is there much danger?"

"Yes," said Speedy. "There's throat-cutting in the air you breathe, all around here."

"The good mountain air," the old woman said contentedly scrubbing away at the stone, "it is much better than the mosquitoes of the river bottom."

"For thick skins," said Speedy.

Then he went to the gray mule, climbed onto the rickety saddle, and, having waved a good-bye, steered the old animal back up the trail, singing cheerfully to his guitar as he went.

V
The Lion's Den

The swinging gallop of the bay mare had carried Joe Dale up the slope, over the crest of the divide, and down the slope from which he saw the long ravine of Sunday Slough, with its ragged cliffs gleaming on either side and the sun weltering upon the water that was pooled and extended in the marshy bottom lands. Now bare rocks cropped up on either side, and he scanned them with a rapid eye. Now a grove of pines on one side and of poplars, beside swiftly running water, on the other screened him. As he galloped by this double screen on either hand, suddenly he pulled the mare to a halt and brought a heavy revolver into either hand.

At the same time, a heavy bass voice exclaimed: "Aw, quit it, kid! If I'd wanted your scalp, wouldn't I'ave gone and got it before you seen me?" One-Eyed Mike Doloroso, adjusting the patch upon his face, rode out of the screen of the poplars into the trail.

The muzzle of the gun in Joe Dale's right hand slowly tipped down. "What's all this about, anyway?" he asked in none too pleasant a voice.

"What's all that about, yonder?" asked Mike Doloroso with a scowl. "You go out to get Speedy and ten grand, and you come back without doin' nothin'. I seen you down there behind his back, with a gun in your hand."

"Yeah, and you wondered why I didn't do anything?" asked Joe Dale, as they rode their horses side by side down the trail.

"That's what I was asking myself," said Mike.

"Because there was somebody behind me," said Dale.

"Like what?"

"Like a yellow-faced, no-good half-breed, sitting in a berry patch with a rifle glued to his shoulder, and me for a target. A hound of a low half-breed that splits your head at five hundred yards and don't ask no questions who his name might be."

"That Juan, maybe," said Mike.

"Maybe it was," said Joe Dale.

"That was a bad pinch," said Mike. "I know that greaser. He can shoot till the cows come home, too."

"He can't miss," said Joe Dale. "I know about him, too. He shoots a man as slick as a deer. He don't get no buck fever when there's a man in front of his rifle sights. He gets a dead center, and away you go."

"I recollect something like that," said One-Eyed Mike, nodding his massive head. "Yeah, that was a bad break."

A rattlesnake coiled in the path. The mustang that carried Mike leaned to one side. Mike Doloroso drew a revolver with uncanny smoothness and ease and blew off the head of the reptile. As he sheathed the weapon, he said: "You never can tell about them greasers. Some are poison, and some are nothin' at all."

"You're right," said Joe Dale. "You never can tell, not till you get digestion pains from what you've set out to eat. Did Sid Levine send you out to police me?"

"You know," remarked Mike Doloroso, "when a job like this has to be done, it's better to have a man on hand to check up. I mean, what with a slick talker like Speedy on deck."

"Yeah, he can talk," said Joe Dale.

"And how was we to know that you wouldn't play double-cross as well as the next man?" asked Mike.

"Look at my face," said Joe Dale.

"Your face is pretty enough, Handsome," said Mike. "What about it?"

"Look at them scars."

"I can see 'em."

"That's where he rolled me in a living fire. How would you feel about a gent that had rolled you in a fire? The rest of me is a match for my face. I'm all over scars."

"The way I heard the story," said Mike, "you didn't let nobody roll you."

Growing redder than his scars, so that they disappeared, Joe Dale said: "You know how it is. This here Speedy, he's a streak of greased lightning with his hands and he can talk seven languages with them. Plain boxing, plain catch-as-catch-can wrestling, that's all right with me. I take 'em on, big or small. I don't much care. I handle myself pretty good, and I've had some experience even if I ain't Methuselah. But you know. He starts a lot of stuff that I never heard of. By the way, how come that he got the guns of yourself and Buck Masters, all in one day? Was that an accident?"

"The way it happened . . . ," began One-Eyed Mike. Then he paused and looked dourly at his companion.

"Yeah, I can guess how it happened," said Joe Dale.

"All right, you guess and maybe you won't be so far wrong," admitted Mike Doloroso. "He kind of has an extra set of brains in each hand, I guess."

"That's what he kind of has," agreed Joe Dale. "We both been stung, and so that makes us even with him, so far as that goes."

"Yeah, maybe it does, all right," said Mike, and added: "You seemed to part pretty good friends. I seen Betsy doing her tricks down there."

"Sure you did," said Joe Dale. "We got to an agreement."

"Like what?"

"I'm gonna double-cross you boys," said Joe Dale.

"Hold on!" said Mike.

"That's what I mean."

"You told him that you was playing with us, you fool?"

"Aw, he knew that already," said Dale.

"Did he?"

"Yeah. And now I like him so good that I'm gonna double-cross you, all three. You and Levine and Masters."

"How?"

"The details, they ain't fixed. I'm gonna see him later on."

"When?"

"That ain't settled, either, but if that hound of a greaser half-breed hadn't been sitting in the berry patch, I would've settled Mister Speedy today."

"There's been a lot of guys," Mike said, "that would've settled Speedy if things had been different."

"Yeah. Guys like you, maybe?" said Dale.

Mike suddenly laughed. "I guess that you're all right," he said. "Come on. Let's get down to town. Levine, he'll wanna know what's been happening. He'll be pretty hot to know."

"How can I get into Sunday Slough in the daylight?" asked Joe Dale. "There's too much money on my scalp, dead or alive."

"I'll show you the back way in," Mike answered. "Don't you worry about that."

It was midday, heavy with sunshine, thick with sleep, when they came in, rounding behind Sunday Slough, and One-Eyed Mike Doloroso showed the way through the rocks, through the trees and tall shrubbery, until they were close to the Grand Palace. In a patch of tall bushes, they dismounted.

"I don't like this, much," Joe Dale said. "I tell you this, sucker. If there's a bad break, my first bullet is for you, Mike, and no questions asked."

"Aw, I know that," said Mike. "But there ain't gonna be no trouble. When the boys in the Grand Palace see me, they stop looking. You pull your hat down over your eyes. That's all that you gotta do. The boys don't try to look through the shadows, when they see me. They know a friend, and a friend's friend."

They came in through the back door. A double-barreled, sawed-off shotgun confronted them, along with a burly man who looked like a pirate behind the gun. "Who you got there, Mike?" he asked.

"Your mother-in-law," said One-Eyed Mike.

The guard laughed. "That's all right, too," he said. "Come in, brother."

They passed on to an inside room. Mike banged on the door, according to a certain well-memorized rhythm.

It opened before him, and a voice issued. "Who are you, friend?"

"Mike."

"Wait a minute."

The door closed. Presently it opened again. Buck Masters, the sheriff, big, powerful, magnificent, in a new checkered, flannel shirt, stood before them. "All right,

220

Mike," he said. "Come in. Bring your kid friend in with you, if you want."

"If I'm a kid, you're a goat," was all that Joe Dale could think to say. He felt under the sneer of the sheriff that he had talked like a fool. He regretted that outpouring.

"Come on in, anyway. We all gotta be young, sometime," said the sheriff. "Only some of us don't have to be so awful young as all of that."

They passed into an inner chamber, and Joe Dale was uneasily aware that he was walking first and that Mike Doloroso and the sheriff were behind him. He was aware, through the back of his head, that they were exchanging looks, or whispers, or signs, or all three. In fact, he was distinctly uncomfortable.

In the inner room, he saw the small, bald head and the bulging red cheeks of Sid Levine, bent over a large ledger, in which the boss of Sunday Slough was writing slowly, with a most delicate and clerkly hand, finishing off each word with a little flourish. He wrote with one pen; he held another between his teeth. They were not fountain pens, but the plain holder and nib, affected by all true penmen. He said thickly, his tongue rubbing against the pen between his teeth: "What's the matter, boys?"

No one answered.

Sid Levine blotted the last words he had written, raised the page in his thick fingers, and squinted at it as an artist at a good drawing. Then he lowered the page, put down pens number one and two, and raised his head to look at the trio. He nodded, took a cigar from a silver box before him, examined it, laid it aside, chose another, turned it, approved of it, bit off the end, and lighted it.

221

"Now what's anybody got on anybody else?" he asked through a cloud of thick, rich smoke.

Mike Doloroso said: "I dunno. I reckon that Joe Dale here has double-crossed us, but I ain't so sure. I leave it to you brainy guys to find out. I can only tell you what I seen."

VI
Double-Crosser

Joe Dale grew uneasy. He had not expected a reception exactly like this. Then Mike Doloroso spoke again: "This bird may be all right. I dunno."

"We ain't asking you for your brains," said Sid Levine. "We know what kind of brains you got. All we want to ask you is . . . what did you see and hear? What about our young friend, here?"

Joe Dale did not turn his head. He did not have to, to understand that the sheriff had shifted a revolver to a coat pocket, and that through the cloth he was leveling the revolver at the guest.

A thrill passed through the outlaw, not of fear, but like the touch of cold steel that gores the side of the Thoroughbred and makes it put forth the ultimate effort in the homestretch. He grew calm, clear-minded, clear-eyed, ready for a death struggle.

"I trailed him up there to the place where Pier Morgan is hanging out," said One-Eyed Mike, "and there was our friend, Speedy, all right, just as bright as ever, and setting out under a tree talking to his sick partner. And I seen Joe

Dale go and soft foot it down and come up behind the tree, then pull his gun and have the game in his hands."

"You plugged him, Joe?" Levine asked comfortably.

"No, that's what he didn't do," said One-Eyed Mike.

Levine removed the cigar from the pale purple of his lips. His mouth remained open. He brushed away a fleck of tobacco leaf. *"Uh!"* he said. "Go on, Mike." He looked not at Mike, but at the accused man.

Mike continued: "Instead of pluggin' Speedy, he got to talkin' to him. They talked real cheerful. He called Betsy over, and the mare done some tricks. Then he rode away, and I met him on the road. He said that he hadn't shot Speedy because the half-breed son of Anna . . . that greaser, Juan . . . was setting out in a brush patch up the hill, with a rifle ready." He finished his narrative with a shrug of his heavy shoulders. "I got nothin' against Joe," he said. "I like him, in fact. But I like my boss better. That's all."

"Thanks, Mike," said Levine. "You know what it is . . . I got friends, and I got a lot of people workin' for me, but I appreciate what you just said. Enough things like that ain't said in the world. Guys get too hard. They ain't got any sentiment left about them."

"That's right," said the sheriff. He added, to Joe Dale: "What about it, Joe?"

"The greaser was up there in the berry patch," Joe Dale confirmed. "That boy can crack nuts with his rifle at five hundred yards. I wasn't gonna go and make a fool out of myself."

"Can that dago shoot like that?" Levine asked of the sheriff.

"He's pretty good," said the sheriff.

"He's pretty good," One-Eyed Mike agreed. "He's too good, if you ask me."

"How big was that tree?" he said.

"A whopper. Biggest pine that you ever seen outside of a picture," said One-Eyed Mike quite seriously.

"Speedy was setting under a tree, was he?" asked Levine.

"Yeah."

"And the kid, here, got up close to the tree?"

"Yeah, right beside it."

"You could've shot Mister Speedy and hopped around the tree away from the greaser," said Levine.

"How would I 'ave got away, though?" asked Joe Dale.

"What I mean," said Levine, spitting another shred of tobacco toward the ceiling, "is that a real go-getter like you, he don't waste no time. He just steps out and takes his chance. You wasn't taking no chances. Why not?"

"I told you why not. Mike saw why I didn't, if he had an eye in his head," said Joe Dale. But he felt that he was being cornered.

"Ten thousand dollars is a lot of money," said Levine.

"Yeah. Sure it is," Joe Dale said. "And a lump of lead to fit a rifle barrel ain't such a load, either. But it's pretty heavy when it sits in the brain."

Levine shook his head. "We oughta be reasonable," he said.

"I'm reasonable," said Joe Dale.

"You cooked us with Speedy," said Levine.

"Who says I did?" asked Joe.

"I'm telling you. You cooked us with Speedy."

"I dunno what you mean."

"You went up there to kill Speedy. But the price didn't look good. He bid over us. You're playing with him right now."

"You're crazy," said Joe Dale.

"I ain't as crazy as you'd wish," said Levine. "I'm smart, Joe. You can't pull the wool over my eyes."

"You can't make a fool of Mister Levine, Joe," said One-Eyed Mike.

"Oh, shut up, Mike, will you?" Levine ordered gently. He put the cigar back into his mouth and puffed it carefully, until the coal glowed in a bright circle again. He said around the tobacco: "You went and double-crossed us, Joe."

"Speedy chucked me in a fire," said Joe Dale. "He made a fool of me. Why should I double-cross you boys for him?"

"He sent back your horse to you," said Levine. "Not that a horse is much. It's only so much money on the hoof. But he sent *your* horse back. I know how it is. I know what sentiment is, all right. I wouldn't wanna see a gent without no sentiment in his make-up. Would I?"

"You was always kind of soft," said One-Eyed Mike.

"Shut up, Mike," Levine ordered again. "What I mean is . . . ten thousand wasn't enough for you, Joe."

"I didn't say that," said Dale. "You're stringin' your own story together out of this here."

"Ten thousand ain't so much, either," said Levine. "Maybe you could use more."

"Say, what are you driving at, Sid?" asked Buck Masters.

"I like this kid," Levine said. "I could use him. He could use me, too, only he don't know it. I could be a friend to you, Joe, know that?"

"Thanks," Joe Dale said.

Levine went on: "You want enough coin to do something big, something pretty. When you left home, you was never coming back till you could buy the farm next to the place where your old man lives. You were gonna show him that you're as big a man as he is. Ain't that so?"

The mouth of Joe Dale fell open. "Who told you that?" he asked.

"A little bird," said Levine. "I got a lot of little birds working for me. I know the language." He winked, without smiling.

"Well, what about it?" Dale asked.

"How much is that ranch worth?"

"Twenty, thirty thousand," said Dale. "What about it?"

"Suppose," said Levine, "that you ride home, one night, and rap on the front door. The old man comes and opens it. 'Who's there?' says he. 'It's Joe,' says you. 'Maybe you think you're good news?' says he. 'I don't think nothin',' says you. 'Here's twenty-five thousand bucks. Take this here coin and buy the Smith place, and run it for me till I can run it myself. Just now, I'm too busy doin' things more important than that.' Well, suppose that you could talk to the old man like that, Joe?"

Joe Dale considered. His eyes began to burn. "They always called me a worthless bum," he said through his teeth.

"That was because they didn't know a man when they see one," said Levine. "But I'm different. I know what I'm talkin' about. I know a man when I see one. I know a man's price, too, usually. I thought that ten thousand was your price . . . I was wrong. Twenty-five thousand dollars is your price. Wait a minute."

He went to a safe in the corner of the room. Most of the paint and gilding was battered from the face of it. He unlocked the doors, spinning the combination deftly in his big, soft fingers. Then he groaned as he leaned over and pulled out a drawer. He took out three packages wrapped in brown paper. These he brought back and gave into the hands of Joe Dale.

"What's this?" asked Joe Dale. He was gray-green and trembling a little.

"That's twenty-five thousand, paid in advance," said Levine. "You can count it over, if you want to."

Joe Dale closed his eyes. He felt helpless and hemmed in on every side by stronger wills and superior brain power. If he avoided this lure, he would be taken in another way. Or, else, very likely the revolver in the pocket of Buck Masters would drive a bullet through his back. But, as he closed his eyes, what he chiefly saw with his mind's eye was the picture that had been so skillfully painted for him by Sid Levine.

Levine knew everything, or else he could not have known this much. It was exactly what would happen. Afterward, he could see his bearded father slap the money down on the kitchen table and hear him say: "Ma, you was right all along. The kid had something in him." For some reason, that seemed to Joe Dale the greatest reward that he could ever hope to find upon this earth. He gripped the three brown paper packets. He thrust them into an inside pocket. It made the breast of his coat bulge.

"It's twenty-five thousand, eh?" he said dreamily.

"Count it. Be business-like," said Sid Levine.

Joe Dale shook his head. "You're right," he said. "I was gonna double-cross you. Speedy, he kind of hypnotizes me."

"Yeah, he's a fox," Sid Levine affirmed.

"That's what he is, a fox," said One-Eyed Mike.

"I was gonna rig up a play with Speedy tonight," said the boy.

The other three exchanged looks.

"What sort of a play?" asked Levine.

"I dunno. I was to meet him at his room in the hotel," said Joe Dale.

"I see," said Levine. "No real plans laid out yet?"

"No. And I see what the real plans are gonna be," said the boy. "You have some men waiting in the hall outside the door. When the right time comes, I'll see that they get in. We'll all work together to finish off Speedy!"

VII
Levine at Work

Later, when the boy had left the place, One-Eyed Mike said: "You never threw twenty-five thousand at my head like that, did you, Levine?"

"You wouldn't want it," said Levine.

"No? I wouldn't want it?" exclaimed Mike.

"What would you want with twenty-five thousand of the queer?" asked Levine.

"Hey! Was that queer?" asked Mike.

"Sure it was. What kind of a fish d'you think I am?"

"He'll spot it," said Buck Masters. "The kid has an eye in his head."

"He won't spot it, not for a long time," said Levine. "The point is that he's outlawed. He don't dare come close enough to a place where he can spend money. Besides, Speedy's to die tonight. I'm thinking that it's worth twenty-five thousand to have him out of the way."

"Yeah, or a hundred thousand," said the sheriff, "if you come right down to that."

"Yeah, if we can get him out of the way. I'm sorry about Speedy, though."

"I'll bet you're sorry," said Buck Masters. Then he began to laugh. "The way you done it was pretty slick, Sid. I mean, that way you handed him that package like it was diamonds."

"Yeah, it's the way you do things that counts," said One-Eyed Mike, leering with admiration. "It ain't the words. It's the way you speak 'em."

Sid Levine let his tongue loll, then licked the cigar into his mouth, and stowed it comfortably. There was plenty of mouth left for smiling, and he smiled.

"It's good stuff," he declared. "Those green goods are worth twenty percent of anybody's money, if they're handled right. The kid ain't beat so bad, if he uses his brains. But his brains ain't much good, except for handling a gun."

"You're the brain, Sid," said Buck Masters. "You always know what to do when the pinch comes."

"I got some ideas, that's all," said Sid Levine. "This brat of a Speedy, he's been getting on my nerves, what I mean. I got tired of him. Tonight I'm gonna have him out of the way. Who'll we send to the hotel tonight? Mike, you'll go along?"

"I wouldn't be nowhere else," said Mike. "How about you, Buck?"

"Don't be a fool," said the great Levine. "Sometimes you ain't got any sense, Mike. We gotta have the sheriff safe. He's the front of the store. He's half the business. We can't mix him into gun plays. Not before the final clean-up starts anyway. We gotta be careful of each other."

"Sure," Mike said. "Careful of everybody except me. I don't count."

"Aw, shut up, Mike. I'm thinkin' about you all the time," said Levine. "You're proud . . . that's the trouble with you. You're proud and you're always afraid that people ain't paying enough attention to you. I tell you what . . . I'm paying attention and I'm paying you cash, too. Something better'n cash. You see this here diamond in this scarf?"

"I can see a headlight on a train, too," said One-Eyed Mike, "if the night's dark enough."

"This is gonna be yours," said Levine. "If it ain't worth five grand, I'm a sucker. It's gonna be yours, the minute I read in the papers about how poor Speedy was shot up and laid out. I'd give you money, instead, but I wouldn't wanna pass money between friends like you and me are. Not on a deal like this here. There's too much sentiment about it. It means too much to me, is what it means. I got an affection for you, Mike. I wanna see you get on. I want you to have something of mine. Now you go out and rustle up three more good boys. You'll know where to find 'em. Boys that wear a padlock on their jaws and that know how to shoot. Sunday Slough is full of 'em now. They may not all be Joe Dales, but they're tough enough to finish the job if he breaks the ice."

One-Eyed Mike left the room.

"You done that pretty good, too," said the sheriff.

"Aw, Mike's easy," said Levine. "You gotta give him both sides of your tongue, is all. The rough side and then the smooth side. You know how it is. Like stropping a razor."

"Is there a flaw in that rock?" said the sheriff.

"Yeah, there's a flaw, all right," said Sid Levine, grinning so that a high wave of flesh stood out in front of each ear. "There's a flaw, but the setting covers it up pretty good. And Mike, he won't never look at it except to admire it."

"Except when he's broke and goes to pawn it," said the sheriff.

"He won't be broke while he's with me," Levine contradicted, "and, when he ain't with me, what do I care?" He then leaned over toward Buck Masters.

"You know how it is, Buck. A man has gotta have tools to work with. And you can't always choose. You gotta take the handiest thing. Ain't I right?"

"You ain't never very far wrong, maybe," said Buck Masters. "That's why you get along in the world, partner."

"But now and then," went on Sid Levine, "I find a man after my own heart, a man that I can talk to . . . a man that I can break down the wall and show him what's inside of my mind. I mean, a coupla times in my life I've found a man like you, Buck!"

"Aw, that's all right," said the sheriff lamely.

"I ain't a man that talk comes to easy," said Sid Levine. "Not when I wanna say what's in my heart. I never was that way. I'm a gent that has some sentiment about him. I got something deep down in me that don't come up easy. Only, I had to say a coupla words to you, Buck. That's all. Just between you and me. I wouldn't let the rest of the world in on it. I wouldn't let Mike know. Mike's all right, but he's small-time. You know what I mean?"

"Well, he's small-time," said the sheriff, clearing his throat. "Yeah, he's useful, though."

"He's paid for being useful, too," said Levine. "But when it comes to cutting the big melon . . . you know what I mean . . . you and me, we sit right here and split everything fifty-fifty. When we're through doing that, we pay off the small fry. Am I right?"

"It sounds like you're right," said the sheriff.

He felt enlarged with importance. He was glad that Levine had been able to look through the roughness of his exterior and find in him qualities that he was conscious that he possessed—judgment, tact, real weight of mind. He stood up and helped himself to one of Levine's cigars. He lighted it, dropped the match thoughtfully upon the floor, and watched it burn out, leaving a straight, black mark.

"Yeah," said the sheriff, "you and me could do some big business together, Sid. No mistake about that. We could get along very well together, because we know one another."

"We know one another, all right," Sid Levine echoed, his glance resting upon the plundered cigar box.

"I gotta buzz along," said Buck Masters. "So long, Sid. I got an idea about Chambers's place across the street. They're pulling in too much trade, and I got an idea for queering that joint. I got an idea for a raid or something. So long, Sid."

He went out, and Sid Levine, gloomily, for a moment eyed the cigar box. Then he jerked the lid shut with a snap. He took the half-consumed cigar from his own mouth, looked at it, and sighed. Then he went to the corner cupboard and poured himself a small glass, half full. He returned to his desk and began to drink the liquor in small sips, getting the full flavor, letting the smoke mount slowly to his brain.

It was a day, he felt, that might lead to big things, perhaps the greatest day in his crowded life. He was not counting the chickens before they were hatched, however. He was too practical a man for that. But he was beginning to wonder how he could skid Buck Masters out of the way when the moment for the cutting of the big melon finally arrived. Time would take care of that. He always found, when the pinch of the crisis came, ideas leaped, full-armed, from his Jove-like brain. He put down the glass, at last, with a final swallow remaining in it, and resumed the smoking of the cigar.

It was an odd world, he reflected, and one of the greatest of oddities in it was the manner in which the nameless, worthless tramp, Speedy, had grown large upon the horizon of Sunday Slough and his own mind. However, the last day of Speedy had apparently come.

Gradually Sid Levine began to smile. His face softened and grew younger. For he was, as he himself confessed, a man who had some deep sentiments.

VIII
The Frame-Up

Speedy lingered on the way into town, not because of the slow pace of the gray mule particularly, but because he disliked towns of all kinds and preferred to have the blue of the sky over his head in an open sweep, not narrow alleys fenced in by a ragged bordering of roof lines and eaves. Of all the places he knew, Sunday Slough was the town most peculiarly distasteful to him. However, it held a certain amount of excitement. For he told himself that he was approaching the end of the trail leading to the downfall of the great Levine and his cohorts.

He had needed, from the beginning, a man in whom he could trust, a man to guard his back, as it were. Pier Morgan would have done, but Pier was long in recuperating. Now, however, chance had put a more valuable ally in his way, young Joe Dale. Joe was exactly the fellow for him. In the first place, the opposition would not be likely to guess that he had recruited as a friend a man who had so many reasons for hating him. In the second place, Joe Dale was a man without fear, a man, too, who wielded a most accurate revolver. He would be ideal for almost any situation that could arise. Before the end, Speedy was sure that guns would start barking and smoking.

His piece of mind was almost perfect, therefore, as he finally rode into Sunday Slough that evening. A galloping party of cowpunchers from the range land beyond the valley overtook him at the edge of the town, recognized him, and swept him into Sunday Slough in the midst of cheers and the shooting off of guns.

When he came near the sheriff's office, he saw big Buck Masters in the act of locking the front door and reined in the stumbling, trotting mule. He waved the cowpunchers ahead, and they went, still roaring like a great wave on a rocky beach. Such uproars were a familiar thing in Sunday Slough.

Speedy waited until the sheriff stepped onto the wooden sidewalk. Then he said: "What's doing, Buck?"

"Nothing much," said the sheriff, looking at him with a calm and considering eye. "You oughta go home and rest yourself, Speedy. You're always on the move."

"It's hard to shoot a bird on the wing," Speedy said carelessly.

"Yeah, that's true, too," said the sheriff. "It's better to wait till they're sitting down, if you're shooting for the pot. It's better to wait till they're on their own roost and going to sleep for the night, as a matter of fact." He nodded his head. He seemed to attach a good deal of importance to his own words and the thought behind them. Again he eyed the boy.

"You won't be needing me this evening, then?" Speedy said.

"You might make an eight o'clock round, maybe," said the sheriff. "That's when things begin to warm up a little. Look in on Chambers's joint. He's a bum, that Chambers. I don't like him. He's running crooked games, I guess. You might take a look in there. Gonna be trouble in that place, one of these days."

Speedy agreed, and so turned off toward the hotel. When he reached it, he said: "Anything for me to do, Sammy?"

The clerk shook his head. "We're pretty peaceful today, Speedy," he said. "Been some boys here looking for you, and Bill Turner of the *News* was here, wanting to get some new copy for his paper."

"You tell him that I'm tired of being copy," said Speedy.

A group came into the lobby of the ramshackle little hotel, as he turned from the desk. He heard a ripple of voices, very subdued: "That's him. That's Speedy. That's the man that caught Cliff Derrick."

A picturesque figure stalked forward. He was a frontiersman of the old type. He wore his hair flowing long to his shoulders, and his trousers were tight enough to show the bow of his legs. His coat was old and patched. His hat was older and more battered still. But he carried his inches and wore his beard with the dignity of an emperor.

He came up and said: "My name's Robinson. Tell me, are you Speedy?"

"Yes," said the tramp.

"You're the man who caught Cliff Derrick?" asked Robinson.

"Yes," said Speedy.

"No good ever come out of Derrick," said Robinson. "Part of the bad that he done was the killing of my boy. He was only seventeen. If he'd lived to grow up, he would've ate a hound like that murdering Derrick. But Derrick caught him young, and I never was able to find Derrick afterward. That's why I've rode more'n a hundred miles to see you and thank you, Speedy."

He shook hands vigorously, his eyes resting on the eyes

of the boy. Then he drew a long-bladed hunting knife. "I been casting around for what I could give you as a present," he said. "And I thought of this. This here carving on the handle is Injun work. But the reason that I like it ain't that it's pretty, but because I had to fight to get it. You put a value on a thing that you've spilled your blood on. Ain't that so?" To this, Speedy agreed.

The other said: "I'm gonna go out and hunt around until I get a sheath that fits this here, and that's worthy of it. When I find the sheath, I'm gonna come back and give it to you, Speedy. It's a mighty great pleasure to meet a man, sir. I'm gonna call on you later on, if I might."

He went out of the hotel, as Bill Turner, editor, reporter, and printer, and most other things to the Sunday Slough *News,* came running in. He wanted a new story. He insisted on one. He had no good leader for the *News* that day, and he knew that Speedy could furnish him with one.

Speedy, on second thought, took him up to his room. It was a corner room, with two windows. The hotel refused to charge a price for it to the benefactor of the town.

In the room, he said: "Bill, I have no news for you. Nothing that I can give out today. Suppose that you give me some news?"

"Me? Why, Speedy, I'm a reporter. I go around and collect what I hear, and. . . ."

"Tell me what you hear," said Speedy.

"About what?" asked Turner, gaping.

"I'm a seven-day man," said Speedy. "That's as long as a deputy sheriff is supposed to last in Sunday Slough. I've lasted longer than that already. Tell me how much farther I'll run before I'm snagged?"

"You'll last forever in Sunday Slough," Turner said. "The boys would burn 'em alive . . . any hounds that tried to rook you, Speedy."

239

"I know," said Speedy. "I know about the good feeling. Now you tell me about the bad feeling."

"How would I know?" asked Turner, embarrassed.

"You know everything about this town," insisted Speedy. "Now open up and tell me something, like a good fellow. What gangs are after my scalp?"

"Levine is the main gang, and you're in with him," said Turner. "You ain't got anything to worry about."

Speedy shook his head. "Come clean for me, Bill," he urged.

Turner began to sweat. He went to a window, looked out on the street, and then turned suddenly around with his jaw set. "This town don't like law and order, Speedy," he began. "It's always been wide open. It's been closed up a little since you came to town. There's a lot of boys that like to turn loose with their guns and settle their troubles offhand. But Boot Hill Cemetery hasn't been growing very fast since you started in Sunday Slough."

"They're tired of me, are they?" asked Speedy.

"You know," explained the reporter feverishly, "the minute that there's any trouble anywhere, in a bar or a dance hall or a gambling house, there's a hurry call for you, and you always get there in time. Well, maybe if you was to be late a couple of times, it would be just as well. The boys like elbow room. You know how it is. Maybe you've been crowding them a little. Look at the number of fellows you've thrown into jail since you came to town. It makes the nights quieter, but it kind of takes away some of the life. About the only way I can find a story, nowadays," he finished plaintively, "is to go and ask you what you've been doing lately. Sunday Slough isn't satisfied with a one-ring circus. It wants three rings, and all of them filled all the time!" He mopped his brow.

"You wanted to know, and I had to tell you," he said.

"You know how it is. A lot of the workers in town, the miners and such, they'd pay you your weight in gold to keep you on here. But a lot of the other boys want more elbow room. That's all I can say, except. . . ." He paused.

"Go on," said Speedy.

"If I was you, I'd move on," said Bill Turner softly. "Don't say that I said so. But if I was you, I'd move on. You've lived several times seven days here in Sunday Slough, but seven times seven, you ain't gonna live. That's the fact."

Now that he had spoken, he turned and hurried from the room, and Speedy saw a shudder go through the body of the reporter as he opened the door and looked up and down the hall. Then Bill Turner closed the door behind him and was gone.

Left alone, Speedy sat quietly in a corner of his room, and for a moment he added up the facts. It was true that he was each day nearer to a gun play that might be his life. On the one hand, he had built up a reputation that was a fortress. On the other hand, his very reputation was a lure to the gunmen. Any lad on the loose, desiring to make a reputation for himself, could establish a very great reputation, even though it led to outlawry, by putting a bullet through the heart of the deputy sheriff of Sunday Slough. And he, Speedy, went unarmed. He shivered at the thought. He felt naked in a winter wind. However, now that he had Joe Dale on his side, it was worth lingering out his time and spending a few more days to settle the hash of Levine and company before slipping away from Sunday Slough forever.

He went down to supper. There was a general squeaking of chair feet on the floor, as the men turned in the dining room to stare at him. In the corner next to the wall, there was a comfortable armchair placed at the table, with plenty of space left on either side of it. That chair was his chair. It was always reserved for him. It was his chair from the day when he captured Cliff Derrick and paraded him down the main street of Sunday Slough at the end of a rope. Everybody was aware of these facts.

Now, as he approached it, a tall, big-boned young fellow as brown as a nut stepped in before him, dragged back the chair, and slipped into the vacant place. He stretched forth a great hand toward the bread plate and took off a stack of slices. He hurriedly began to devour one of them, without butter.

Speedy stood still. He was not deceived. The intentness of the youth on the bread was a mask to cover his real interest—which was the result that would follow his usurpation of the privileged chair.

The very thing that Bill Turner had warned Speedy about was to happen here, perhaps in the hotel dining room. For his own part, however, he would by no means fight about so trivial a matter as a seat at a table.

But a rough voice beside the stranger exclaimed: "Kid, you're in the wrong place!"

"Am I?" said the big lad. "Where ought I to be, then?"

"I dunno. In the street, maybe," said the unshaven miner who had made the remark. "That chair belongs to Speedy, and you had oughta know it."

"If I belong in the street, you can put me there," said the stranger.

"You're askin' the right man for a free ride as far as the street," said the miner. Half rising, he lashed with his fist at the head of the big fellow. The latter put the blow aside with ease, blocking it with an arm that seemed as strong as iron. Then, from the thin air, he produced a gun and laid the muzzle against the breast of the other.

"Back up, brother," he said.

IX
The Fight

The flash of that gun scattered people from the table. Speedy came as fast as he could, now that he saw a friend in mortal danger, but, with all of his speed, he knew that he would never be in time to save the miner of the unshaven face from a bullet wound. Moreover, people got in his way. In their haste to get out of the probable path of flying bullets, they dived here and there. A sudden roar of voices exploded in the room, and set nerves shivering like glassware on a table. A big fellow tripped backward, in rising from his chair, and rolled headlong before Speedy. The boy stumbled over him and ran on in. He saw what was happening as he came.

"It's Dick Cleveland!" somebody yelled. "Gimme room! It's Crazy Dick Cleveland!"

The name definitely registered upon the ear of Speedy, but he could not place it in his memory, which had filed so accurately the titles of many formidable people. However, it was plain that this youth was formidable. The big miner was a strong man, well developed by manual labor, and apparently familiar with rough-house fighting. He merely snarled at the sight of the revolver, and, clubbing a fist, he smashed it into the face of the big boy.

The head of Crazy Dick bobbed. But he was not stunned. It was rather as if his head were set on strong wires and supple springs. It flicked back and immediately bobbed forward again. He was a giant of strength, it appeared at once. With his left hand, he took the left fist of the miner, a left-handed man. With a jerk, he turned him halfway around. Then he slammed the length of cold gun barrel along the skull of Speedy's champion, and the latter slipped in a loose heap to the floor, completely out.

Speedy was glad, as he came darting in, that it had been a blow rather than a bullet that had ended that preliminary fray. In the split second that remained, he estimated his foe more carefully and intelligently.

The lad was older, perhaps, than he had at first appeared. He was twenty-one or two, in the first strength of manhood, when strength is most dangerously supple. He looked long-drawn out, but, as a matter of fact, he was rounded all over. A section of him would weigh like a telegraph pole. It was a solid substance. His three or four inches over six feet might weigh two hundred and twenty pounds—yes, even a shade more than that. He was all of a piece, in spite of his inches.

Speedy came in like a flash. He was not wasting time, no matter how many judgments he was summing up. His friend, the unknown miner, was already disposed of and lying limply upon the floor. That was something to charge against the supposedly invulnerable Speedy at the start.

Coming in with a final leap, he saw that he would not have time to reach the man, only the gun hand of Crazy Dick. That hand he reached with his best weapon—the edge of his palm with which he gave the cleaver stroke of his hand, the edge serving as the cleaver's rim. He aimed with accuracy and smote the wrist of the big fellow just across the tendons, where they stood out like whipcord. His own hand rebounded. It was as if his own flesh were frangible and had been brought into sharp contact with wrought iron. At the same time he saw the gun hand of the other relax slowly, and the heavy Colt slid to the floor. It exploded as it struck. The bullet skidded across the flooring, raising a great furrow of splinters. Somebody with high-strung nerves seemed to think that he had been hit, and yelled in terror.

The loss of the gun did not seem to dishearten the big youth. He turned on Speedy with a flaring sneer on his mouth and the wild delight of battle in his pale blue eyes. He had a tuft of hair that grew well down toward the center of his forehead; it thrust out in front, like the plume of a helmet. His eyebrows angled up and were tufted at the upper corners. He had the face of a frantic animal, an animal just then in seventh heaven because it was about to perform the work for which it was intended. He flung himself at Speedy. It was no blind rush, either. Neither rage nor hate blinded him. He had the open eyes of an artist at work.

Speedy was suddenly swallowed in a powerful embrace. By sheer luck he managed to have his right arm free. The palm of it was bruised from the first blow. But he nerved himself to deliver another. The arms of the other were around him like two tightening coils of steel cable, cables tightened by the pull of mighty engines.

The breath went out of him with one husky gasp. Then, deliberately, he smote with the cleaver-like edge of his palm, high up on the deltoid muscle just where it sprang from the shoulder, just where the tendons took hold of the bone. He had used that same blow twenty times before in actual combat, and it always succeeded. It unstrung the entire arm and left it dangling, paralyzed. But this time his bruised hand simply rebounded as though he had struck down on a tangled mass of India rubber.

He could feel a roar and hear it in his ears. It was partly his own blood and partly the thunder of the crowd. From the corners of his blurring eyes, he could see men standing on chairs, on the table, yelling and whooping, some in delight, some in sheer amazement. For here was an almost nameless man literally swallowing the firebrand of Sunday Slough. Here was the conqueror of Cliff Derrick being treated like a novice.

Speedy tried his cleaver stroke again, this time lower down, where the deltoid muscle sloped away, close to the bone of the upper arm and almost halfway down to the elbow. It was a cruel stroke. It made a leaping pain run up his own arm to the heart, but it brought a grunt from big Dick. His left arm was suddenly, for the moment, almost helpless. A twisting whirl brought Speedy into the clear.

A great thunder of applause greeted him. He saw men slapping each other on the shoulders. He heard them fairly screaming with pleasure. But he could feel the effects of that bear hug still. Altogether, he had been in that terrific embrace not more than a second or two, but if it got him again, he felt that he was fairly beaten.

Then Crazy Dick, with flaring, dancing eyes that lived up to his name, was after him as a hound is after a rabbit. Speedy tried out his man with plain fists. He had his doubts, but, after all, he had felled men of much greater bulk than Crazy Dick with simple fisticuffs.

Under the big paws of Cleveland, he ducked, and, rising, he struck four times without a return. Every blow had all his might behind it, and every blow was on the jaw of Crazy Dick, close to the bottom.

The tall youth paused, stood flat-footed; and the yell of

delight nearly burst the rafters as the spectators waited for the cowpuncher to fall. But Dick did not fall. Instead, he made a long, gliding pace forward, feinted with his left hand for the face, and then drove a steam-piston right, full at the body of Speedy.

Speedy was taken by surprise. Nevertheless, he blocked the blow. He blocked it and felt as though he had put his arm in front of the stroke of a walking beam. The punch was thrown a little out of line. It merely grazed the ribs of Speedy, but he thought the flesh had been ripped away. The glancing force of that stroke spun him around like a top and sent him staggering backward. He had seen blows delivered. He had stood before ring-trained pugilists, but this seemed to be an entirely new engine of destruction. The lights blurred before him. The room dropped into silence. He could fairly feel the sinking pulse of those who had felt that he was the sure master of any contest.

Then a snaky arm of iron, clad in a rubber-hosing of hard muscles, caught him around the neck. That strangle hold shut off his wind, crushed his windpipe, and sent red-hot splinterings of metal shooting up through his brain. He was lifted from the floor and swept about as a hammer thrower lifts the hammer and spins before he hurls it. Where would he be hurled? How hard would he hit the wall? Or would his neck break before he was flung away? Then the support that held him up staggered, went down.

Crazy Dick, in the excess of his joy at getting this unfair but certainly victorious hold, had overdone the thing and lost his balance.

Speedy was flung away, to be sure, and spun over and over along the boards of the floor, but Crazy Dick had dropped at the same time, and given the back of his head a promising thump against the same flooring. He was still rolling as Speedy scrambled to his hands and feet. He was sick, very sick. The sparks were still shooting in diminished showers across his eyes. His knees were weak. His jaws seemed to lack hinges, but, as the formidable length of Crazy Dick rose from the floor, Speedy hurled himself to run in toward the other. He knew that, as fighting tactics, this was wrong. He merely hoped that his charge might break the morale of the other. But he saw at once that this was a mistake, for Crazy Dick did not even wait to receive the charge. He rushed forward with immense strides to meet the attack.

They were yelling for Speedy again. In the jumble of their voices, he could hear them call him a "bundle of wild cats," "a chunk of India rubber," "a human black snake," "a demon on wheels." But he felt very differently about himself. One fairly landed punch from the hands of the other would be sufficient to fell him, he knew. And if he ventured into the terrible embrace of those arms, he was even more surely crushed. His cleaver stroke with his right hand was now little better than useless, so badly bruised was the palm. How could he handle his man, then?

Crazy Dick came in with the same clear, wide-open eyes of one who knows what he is about, whose wits are just as active as his hands and feet. As he came, he made only one trifling mistake. He drew his right hand back as a fist, halfway to his shoulder. It was not a big mistake. It was merely telegraphing a punch. But Speedy needed only a chance, even though that chance was a small one.

Now, at the very moment of impact, he checked his own rush short and stood to receive that of the tall man. Sure enough, the terrible right hand launched forth, straight and swift as a piston stroke, a piston whose head was finished off with knuckles of brass and steel. As it came, Speedy swerved and spun. It was a very good trick.

It could only be used against a big man, a confident man. Crazy Dick was both of those things.

So he thrust the whole length of his right arm into space over Speedy's shoulder and found that the smaller man had actually whipped around and stood with his back to Dick's breast. At the same time, he reached up and caught the arm of the tall fellow and bent forward. It was really very little of his own strength that completed the trick, which is fairly old in rough-and-tumble fighting. It was the rush of Crazy Dick himself that caused the mischief. The well-braced body of Speedy was merely a hurdle, so to speak, over which Dick flung his weight, and the downward tug on his arm was merely what flicked the feet of Dick high into the air. He sailed forward over the hurdle. He landed on head and shoulders where the floor joined the wall, and with such force that he knocked up a thin cloud of dust.

Almost more than the fall, the suddenly bursting uproar stunned his ears. Yet, he was not knocked out. To the utter amazement of Speedy, he saw the tall man leap to his feet, turn, and stretch out his long, sinewy arms on guard. Yes, that was the picture that Speedy saw. But a fury of incredulity suddenly overwhelmed him completely.

He told himself that his eyes saw no more than a lie. It was the mere seeming, the mere hollow shell of a man that stood there. No human being could withstand such a shock with impunity. Therefore, he ventured straight in, with the danger of those ape-like arms.

A fist shot at his head, and the blow seemed as strong as ever. He dropped his head to one side and let the punch hiss against his cheek. Then he stepped in, rose on his toes as he hit over the high shoulder of Crazy Dick, and dropped upon his heels as his fist flashed home with a thud, dropping upon the point of Cleveland's jaw.

Crazy Dick shook his head. He did not fall, but a troubled look came in his eyes. He lifted an uppercut from the height of his knee and strove to knock Speedy's head free from his body. But a shade of the former speed was gone from that blow, and Speedy found it fairly simple to avoid. To be sure, he felt that he was sparring with a grizzly bear, and that the first tap that landed would crush him like an eggshell. But in the range of the danger he stood.

He tried the same right hand, the same punch, the same target, aiming a little back of the point, and to the side, where the shock of a blow is more readily telegraphed against the base of the brain. This time, as he struck the mark, there was a change in the attitude of Crazy Dick. His body slumped back. His shoulders were now braced against the wall. The light went out of his eyes. His knees were still straight, and his guard was professionally high. But Speedy knew what that blank, animal look in the eyes meant. He stepped back and lowered his own aching arms. He controlled his voice and made it as casual as ever.

"Some of you boys take care of him, will you?" said Speedy. "He'll start falling to pieces in a minute, and he's a good, game lad. Will some of you give him a hand?"

"He don't look like he needs a hand, except on the jaw again," said a cowpuncher nearby. "The strangle hold blankety-blank! But I'll take care of him if he needs care."

He approached, and, at the same time, Crazy Dick began to slip along the wall and lean more to one side. His guard was still up, his knees were still stiff, but his whole body was falling.

The cowpuncher caught him. The whole mass of Crazy Dick collapsed and slid like water through the detaining hands, and so down to the floor.

X
A Sore Champion

In the armchair that was set aside for that purpose, Speedy sat and ate his supper. He felt that his color was not good. Gripping pains clutched at his throat. The whole side where Dick's punch had clipped his ribs was sore and swollen. But he knew that he had to sit there and smile and chat, and be amiable as though that battle had been a mere nothing to him. They had seen him slung about in the air like a thong in the hand of a mischievous boy. He must wipe that impression out of their minds. So he sat there and yarned with them, while the broken chairs and crockery were removed, and while the men settled down to their dinner again.

He did not want to eat. The pain had taken all his appetite, but he had to force down the stuff. He had to praise the thin, gray, greasy beefsteak and take a second helping. And he had to talk. This was what it meant to be the hero of the town.

The others could hardly eat for another reason. They could not shift their eyes from the face of this slender youth who broke up big men as children break brittle kindling wood across the knee. With shining eyes, they worshipped him. With gaping mouths, they wondered at him. All the time, his hurts were stiffening his body.

A boy came hurrying into the room. "Where's Speedy?" he cried.

"Here I am, son," said Speedy.

"There's a terrible ruction over at Chambers's place. Will you come on the run, Mister Speedy?" cried the boy.

"Oh, I'll go on over," said Speedy. He stood up, finished his cup of black coffee on his feet. Then, amazed, as he put down the cup, he saw that every man at the long table was on his feet, also.

"Here's to the most double-barreled, gun-cotton, distilled dynamite, boiled-down wildcat that ever walked!" yelled the miner, the lump on whose head was evidence that he had fought for the good name of Speedy.

The whole table roared out a cheer and made it three times three. They picked Speedy up on their shoulders. They carried him with a rush across the street and down to Chambers's place where the sounds of a near riot were beginning.

No man was at the door. They walked on into the gambling house like a river in flood, and there, behold! A longhaired monster from the hills, with a gun in either hand, was trying to eat Chambers's place like a flaming dragon.

"I want that horned toad," he was shouting, "that calls himself the boss of Sunday Slough! I wanna have a look at Speedy. I'm gonna look at his insides! I'm gonna. . . ." Then he saw Speedy, dumped down before him from the shadows of wild-eyed men, and all about him, silently, the rough men of Sunday Slough pouring in. His shouting stopped. He stood aghast.

Speedy stepped up to him and laid a hand upon his

arm. "If you'll let me take care of those guns of yours for tonight, partner," said Speedy, "I'll take you where you'll have a good, quiet sleep. In the morning, if you can settle up with Chambers for the damage that you've done, perhaps you'll get out of Sunday Slough all in one piece."

The wild man gave up his guns without a murmur. He had in his eyes the same stunned look that had appeared in the eyes of Crazy Dick, after the latter had been done in by the punches of Speedy. The mental effect seemed to be the same in both cases. So Speedy took the wrecker to jail.

After this the enthusiasm in Sunday Slough knew no bounds. The whole place began to celebrate, not its own virtues, but those of its deputy sheriff. The house of Chambers, out of gratitude for destruction stopped, rolled three barrels of whiskey out into the middle of the street, and three bartenders ladled to all who would have that liquid fire, free of charge.

It was a fine sight, a large night, a grand night. The sky rang till it cracked with whoopings and the joy that floated up to it and banged against its blue-black face from the streets of Sunday Slough. The out-dwellers in the ravine came in, hearing the noise, as of a continual explosion. Money didn't matter.

They cheered Speedy in several languages. They praised his name and soul and origin with a profound affection. They even went to the house of the sheriff and wailed and serenaded him, because he had had the brains to appoint such a corrector of crime. The sheriff came out and made a speech to them, but his own words tasted like ashes in his throat. For he saw that he was shining entirely by reflected light.

The theme of all the celebration, the original tamer of wild men, the flame eater, the one and only Speedy, lay flat on his back in his bedroom, his arms thrown out wide, his eyes half closed, trying to forget the bitter aching of his hurts and wondering when he could escape from the teeth of this mad town.

While he lay there, in pain of body, in the barn behind the hotel, on the floor of the saddle room, Joe Dale kneeled at the side of a huge and unstrung body, the body of Crazy Dick Cleveland. Dick could lift his head from the floor, and that was about all. Joe Dale thrust a soft sack of bran under his huge shoulders and propped the loose head of the big man against the board wall of the barn.

From a pint bottle, he poured a dram of whiskey down the throat of the helpless man. Cleveland looked at him with lusterless eyes. When he finished coughing from the fire that had burned his throat, he said: "Who are you?"

"My name don't matter," said Joe Dale. "I'm in the same boat with you."

The other closed his eyes, opened them again, then said: "I been whanged and banged silly by a kid about a quarter my size."

"I been whanged and banged silly by the same kid," said Joe Dale.

"You ain't so big," argued the other bitterly, tasting the full shame of defeat.

"I'm big enough to have a hard fall," Joe Dale said.

"There was a crowd looking on. He slammed me over his shoulder ag'in' the wall. He must've had an engine to help him. He picked me up, and he threw me away like a stick of this here bran. I slammed the wall. I got up. He stepped in and pressed the button. I went to pieces. There was a crowd there that seen it all. There was a crowd that looked on and seen me go down." His face twisted into terrible anguish. His head went back.

"Have another shot of this," Joe Dale recommended. His keen eyes flickered from point to point of the face of the tormented man. He studied the increasingly labored breathing of Crazy Dick Cleveland.

"I gotta go away," said Crazy Dick. "I wouldn't dare to let nobody see my face again. Nobody! I gotta go and black my face and live with greasers and blacks."

"Look," Joe Dale said in a ringing voice.

Dick opened his eyes.

"Do you see these here marks? He picked me up just like he done you. He didn't throw me ag'in' a wall. He chucked me into a fire. I near burned alive. That's what he's done to me."

Dick shook his head, staring. "I gotta go away," he repeated.

"You don't understand," said the smaller man. "We ain't gonna go away. But he's gonna go away. Look at me . . . I'm Joe Dale!"

"Go on," Crazy Dick protested, sitting up suddenly. "It would take two of you, twice as old, to make Joe Dale. Joe Dale is the man that I. . . ."

"I'm Joe Dale," the man repeated.

Crazy Dick swallowed the words that he was about to utter. He continued staring.

"I say," Joe went on, "that we ain't gonna get out, but Speedy is."

"Gonna get where?" asked Crazy Dick, intelligence dawning in his face.

"You know where," said the other. "You and me are gonna send him."

"When?" asked Dick Cleveland.

"Tonight. This here night. Inside of an hour. Come to life. I got something to say to you. I got the job cold. Tonight he dies."

XI
Three Small Packages

On the door of Speedy's room in the hotel sounded two raps with long pauses between raps. Speedy went to the door, unlocked it, and said: "Well?"

"It's me," murmured Joe Dale.

"Louder," said Speedy.

"It's me! It's me, I say."

"All right, come on in, Joe. I didn't get your voice at first."

Joe stepped away from the door.

"Come in," Speedy repeated.

Joe Dale stepped inside. His eyes swept around the room in a single, shifting glance, bright as the glance of a cat. Then he nodded.

"Glad to see you," Speedy explained. "I didn't recognize your voice at first, Joe. Just lock that door behind you, will you?"

Joe Dale closed the door and twisted the key so that it rattled. He did not lock the door. "There's that," he muttered, turning away from the door. "That'll be one fence for them to hurdle before they get at me."

"What's the matter, Joe. Got anything on your mind to-night?"

"Why?"

"You look worried."

"You're cast steel, Speedy," the young man said, "but it would worry even you, if you were in my boots inside of a town like Sunday Slough. How many of the boys in this town that shoot straight and quick would be glad to get together and hunt me down, if they knew that I was here?"

"Does anybody suspect it?" asked Speedy. "D'you think that you've been trailed, Joe?"

"I'm always trailed," muttered Joe Dale. "But I guess I'm all right. You wouldn't sell me, Speedy, would you?"

Speedy smiled.

"No, you wouldn't sell me, I guess," said Joe Dale. "But I dunno. I've seen some funny things happen in this here world . . . for the money."

"So have I," said Speedy.

"People will give you everything except hard cash."

"That's true, too," said Speedy. "Sit down."

"I want a drink."

"Not now."

"I need a drink. Why not now?"

"There's none in this room."

"Get some, then. Send a boy for some."

"They know I don't drink alone. You don't want them to think that you're in here with me, do you?"

Joe Dale made a face. From the water pitcher he filled a glass, swallowed a little of the liquid, and made another and more bitter grimace.

"It tastes like poison," he said. "I can remember when worse slime than this tasted like heaven to me. But tonight it tastes like poison. I need a drink."

257

"Sit down," said Speedy. "You're nervous. Sit down, because we have to use our heads."

"I oughta carry a flask," Dale muttered.

"Don't you, usually?"

"Sure I do. But tonight. . . ."

"Where is it tonight?"

"I met a friend and used it up."

"You met a friend here in town?"

"Here in town? No, no, no! On the trail coming in."

"You must have been traveling high, wide, and handsome," Speedy commented calmly. "Letting people look you over on the open trail, eh? You must be worrying about something, old son."

"Yeah, I'm always worrying," Joe Dale said. "I'm sick of this kind of a life that I been leading. I'm gonna quit it!"

"Good man," Speedy said.

"Good man? Maybe not so good. But I'm gonna quit it. I'm gonna get me a stake and settle down."

"Well, you ought to be able to make a stake. How much?"

"Oh, twenty, thirty thousand, maybe." He glanced down toward a bulge in the front of his coat.

"You're wearing your gun slung pretty far forward under your coat tonight, Joe," Speedy observed.

"That's where I keep it for a fast draw," Joe Dale explained. "And that's where I keep it tonight. Now, what about business?"

"That's what I want to talk, but about guns, first. You generally carry your gat in a spring holster under the pit of the arm, don't you?"

"Yeah. You gotta do that, if you're gonna try to be good. It beats a hip holster all hollow. Wild Bill, all the big ones used 'em. You get a better drop to your gun. It's faster, too. That's why I wear an extra size of coat."

"I see," said Speedy. He stood back by the window, his head bowed a little.

"You look sick," Joe Dale said gruffly.

"I am sick," said Speedy.

"The big gent hurt you, did he?"

"Yes, he hurt me, but that's not what makes me sick," said Speedy.

"What is it?"

"It's guns in spring holsters," Speedy said.

"Whatcha mean?"

"They're so fast and sure," said Speedy. "You understand?"

"You gonna start wearing guns, Speedy? Is that it?" asked the other curiously.

"Perhaps I ought to."

"Yeah, if it ain't too late," said Dale.

He looked down to the floor, so that the cold fire in his eye might not be seen. "Let me see your arrangement of that holster, will you, Joe?" asked Speedy.

"Well, why not?" But he drew back a little.

"Not if it's a patent arrangement with you, Joe," said the tramp.

"Well, you can have a look," said Joe Dale.

Speedy came nearer, unbuttoned the top button of the coat, and then his hand shot in as fast as a bird's beak dips to pick up a grain of wheat. The grain of wheat that came out in Speedy's hand was a man-sized Colt .45.

"Hey, what's the idea?" asked Joe Dale, frowning.

The muzzle of the gun suddenly dropped against the hollow of his throat. "Don't move, Joe," Speedy warned.

"You dirty hound," gasped Joe Dale. "You gonna

double-cross me, are you? You drag me in here to double-cross me, do you?"

"I just want to see the load in your breast pocket," Speedy said, and he took out three small packages, wrapped in brown paper.

XII
The Sinner Repents

He kept the revolver in place, the hard, cold rim of steel thrust into the hollow of Joe's throat. The tremor of Dale's cursing passed along the arm of Speedy. He managed, with a forefinger, to rip the paper covering of the parcels, then he flicked the greenbacks rapidly, reading the numbers in the corner.

"Twenty, more than twenty thousand," Speedy said finally. "You said that your price might be between twenty and thirty thousand dollars. And so you sold me, Joe, did you?"

The cursing stopped. Joe Dale, gray of face, suddenly looking many years older, narrowed his eyes, but even when they were squinted, they seemed to have lost all of their fire.

"That greasy pig, Levine, bought you, did he?" went on Speedy. "I'm sorry about that, Joe. You could go as straight as the next fellow. You have it in you. You're only a little spoiled, from finding out how well you can shoot and how well you can fight. But if you've sold out to Levine, believe me, he'll keep on using you for one job after another. Only, he'll never be able to use you for dirtier work than this . . . selling out a partner." He dropped the three packages of money back into the breast pocket of Joe Dale. He held the revolver by the barrel and offered the gun to its owner. "Here you are, Joe," Speedy said. "Go ahead with your dirty business."

Joe Dale received the weapon with a nerveless hand. "Whatcha mean, Speedy?" he asked. "It's like you were askin' me to plug you."

"I don't care what you do." Speedy turned his back, walked to the window, and stood there looking down into the thick wall of darkness as far as the streetlights. "I'm a gambler and a tramp," he said, "but people make me sick. You and the rest. You make me tired of life. You're simply rotten, Joe. You could be straight, too. But you let a fat pig buy you. You'd rather take what you call the easiest way. You make me sick."

Joe Dale reached out and caught the edge of the table. He had barely been delivered from the valley of death, as it were, and now, as consciousness of safety returned to him, he received something more than a bullet through the brain.

At last he said very thickly and softly: "Speedy, wait a minute, will you?"

"Yes, I'll wait," said Speedy. "I suppose you've got some partners ready and waiting out there in the hall. Well, go out and bring them in through that door that you pretended to lock. Oh, this has been a thin job. A five-year-old child could have seen that you were crooked."

Dale dropped the revolver into the holster within his coat. He leaned both hands on the table, swaying far forward. His head thrust out; his face was whiter than ever. "Wait a minute," he said.

"I'll wait here. I'd as soon be murdered by you and

your hired men," Speedy assured him, "as to go on living in such a rotten world where I have to know snakes like you. I wouldn't care about scum like Levine and Buck Masters. They're just what I expect. But you could go straight. I know you could, but you'd rather wallow in the muck!"

"I'm taking everything that you're saying," said Joe Dale. "You're right. I'm worse than scum. I'm a sneaking hound. I hear you say it. Go on, and say the rest. I wish you'd put a slug through my head, though. I'd rather be dead than to stand here, Speedy, and see the sort of a thing that I am."

"Now you're maudlin," Speedy said. "I see the way you're heading. You're going to tell me how much you repent, and that will last till your price is raised, but no longer."

"You can say anything you want to me," said Joe Dale. "You've earned the right to say it. Only . . . gimme time to breathe. Don't go and elbow me along toward murder, will you? I only wanna tell you, Speedy, that I know what you are, and how far you are above me. I wanna tell you that you may be a tramp and a gambler and all of that, but at the same time you're head and shoulders over anybody that I ever knew. I seen that in Pier Morgan's eyes when he lay up there in the hammock and looked at you. I seen it tonight in the way you acted to me. I ain't askin' you to gimme another chance. I'm just askin' you to wait and watch what I do. I don't say that I'm gonna go straight. But after Sid Levine's dead, and Buck Masters, and One-Eyed Mike, then maybe you'll think a little better of me."

"Are you going gunning for the whole lot of 'em?" asked Speedy.

"You smile, eh?"

"No, I don't smile."

"I'll get 'em or they'll get me."

"I believe you," said Speedy. "But that's not what want. I don't want Sid Levine dead. I simply want him laic out where the law can get at him. I want that ham sun cured and packed away to keep. Dying is too noble an en for Sid Levine. I want him packed away inside a jail."

"I know what you mean," Joe Dale said. "That fat porker would die a hundred times a day, if he had to sweat off his fat working at a rock pile. But he'd never stay in prison. He'd buy his way out."

"He'd buy his way out of an ordinary place," Speedy agreed. "But I'm not talking about ordinary prisons. I'm talking of federal stuff. Marshal Tom Gray is in town He'd like to have a big carcass like Sid Levine to take to jail and render the lard out of him."

"How'll you get Sid Levine on a federal charge?" asked Joe Dale. "I wanna help. I wanna play the game your way Speedy. I'll do my walkin' on my knees, the rest of my life what I mean, if that's the sort of going that pleases you."

"Joe," said Speedy, "you don't have to crawl to suit me I know you. I know the stuff that's in you. That's wha made me sick . . . thinking that even you could double cross a partner. But I think you'll never stumble as low a that again. You'll help me to get Levine in the way that want to get him?"

"You're right I will. Only you tell me how the federa marshals can get a call on him. Has he been doing som river work? Has he been smuggling?"

"Making the queer or passing it along," said Speedy "Counterfeiting is federal business."

"Great Scott," said Joe Dale. "Pushing the queer? Ha he been making the stuff or handling it?"

"I don't think that he's been making it," Speedy ex

plained. "But he's certainly been handling it. If I can nail that on him, he'll go up for a long stretch. The federal courts are pretty nasty about counterfeiting. It seems to rub the judges the wrong way."

"They sock 'em about fifteen years, is all," said Joe Dale. "Only, listen, Speedy. I started to double-cross you. How does it look if I turn around and double-cross Sid Levine? Yeah, and with his twenty-five grand in my pocket?"

"You didn't look twice at his money," said Speedy.

The face of the other changed. His brows twitched together into a frown. Suddenly he snatched the brown paper packages from his pocket and pulled out a bill from one. "This is all right," he said, snarling. "This is the straight goods. Wait a minute! You're right! I was selling myself for bad paper. I bump you off, then I let myself in for shoving the queer. Speedy, that's brains. Levine has brains. He made a clear fool out of me." He walked up and down the room with rapid, irregular steps. His fury turned from red to white heat.

Speedy said: "He could make a fool out of almost anyone."

Dale stopped his pacing. He stood against the wall, straight, his feet braced far apart.

"You tell me what to do," he said. "I'm only a fool. I thought that I was a wise one, but I ain't. Now I start taking orders. You tell me what to do."

"Thanks," said Speedy. "I'm trying to think it out. Where did Levine get that crooked money?"

"Out of the safe in his office."

"Seem to have plenty more?"

"He acted like he was tapping the Federal Reserve."

"Then we'll be able to get something more out of that

safe," Speedy said. "That will be the proof. I want Gray along. He can be a witness."

"I can't go along with Gray," said the boy. "He wants me. They all want me."

"He won't want you tonight," Speedy assured him. "Not after I've talked to him a while."

"What can we do in the Grand Palace?" asked Dale.

"Make Levine open his safe."

"You can't make him do that. Not legally."

"I'll do it illegally, then," Speedy said. "You and I will put on a pair of masks and stick him up. We'll make him open that safe, and, while it's open, we'll have the marshal just happen along. You see? There may be a lot of other things in that safe that the marshal will be interested in."

Joe nodded. "It looks like pretty complicated business to me," he said. "But I'm not doubting that you're right."

"It is complicated," Speedy said. "It means, at its best, I'll only be getting Mister Levine. What I really want is the sheriff and One-Eyed Mike at the same time. But if I get Levine, the rest of the show may fall like a house of cards. That's the bet I'm making."

"I'm ready to play, then," said Joe Dale.

Speedy went to the door of the room. "I'm going to see the marshal," he said. "He came back this evening. I'll go to his room here in the hotel, then we'll go right down to the street. Meet you there, say in twenty minutes. OK?"

"Anything you say is the right thing, Speedy. But let me go out there in the hall first."

"I understand," said Speedy. "You clear the hall, and then I'll start when you come back." He went to the window and stood there, hearing the soft, quick step of Joe Dale as he left the room. Speedy heard a murmur in the hall, then a snarling voice very like that of Crazy Dick. A blow was heard falling not on flesh but on bone.

After a moment, Joe Dale returned. He was panting. "It's all right," he said slowly. "Take your time when you go out, though. There's a gent around here who'd like to cut your throat. I just socked him on the bean and got his guns away from him. But he can find other guns in this here town."

XIII
A Letter

The marshal, Tom Gray, was in a sunny mood. This good humor expressed itself by a slight softening of the usually fixed, hard lines of his face. It expressed itself, also, in the rhythmical movement of his foot that swung, pendent, from the crossing of his knees. Upon his knee rested a small writing pad, and he scribbled upon it the well-chosen words of an official report. He was still writing when the knock came at the door. He lifted his iron-gray head and listened for a moment. Then he said: "Well?"

"Speedy," said the voice in the hall.

"Come in!"

The door was locked, but the marshal did not get up to turn the key. Instead, with a faint smile, he turned a bit in his chair to watch what might happen. There was no sound of a hand trying to open the doorknob. Only by staring with fixed intensity did the marshal see presently the inner knob turning. Then, following, came the softest *click*, a thing that no one would have noticed except by bending all attention toward the door. The door opened, and Speedy walked in.

"I was afraid, Speedy," said the officer, "that I had locked the door . . . I'm mighty glad to see that I was wrong." His smile was very faint.

"One gets odd ideas like that," Speedy said. He shook hands with Gray, who had risen.

"Sit down," said the marshal.

Speedy sat down on the edge of the table.

"What did you use on that door? A skeleton key?" asked the marshal.

"Skeleton key?" echoed Speedy. "I don't know what you mean, Tom. What would I be doing with a skeleton key?"

"Every time I touch that infernal door," Thomas Gray explained, "it grates and squeaks like the rusty hinge of a corral gate. Did you squirt some oil into it?"

"Why, Tom," said Speedy, "I don't carry an oil can about with me."

"No," the marshal said, "perhaps you don't, but you carry a set of fingers with individual brains in every one of 'em. They can see their way through the darkest sort of a night. I have some news for you, Speedy."

"Good," said the tramp.

"It appears that here and there a few old charges rest against you, Speedy," went on the marshal, "just little things."

"I know," Speedy said, nodding.

"They're all rubbed away now. They don't exist," said the marshal.

"You rubbed them out of the records?" Speedy asked curiously.

"The government rubbed them out," said the marshal. "This government of ours appears pretty stiff in the joints and rheumatic, now and then. As a matter of fact, it can be fast and supple, when it gets started. A good many people, high up, were interested in the fellow who caught Cliff Derrick."

"Ah?" said Speedy, with little apparent interest.

"They were particularly interested when they found out that you were not using the money of the reward for yourself. I still don't quite understand that, Speedy."

"Why not?" he asked.

"Well, it was a comfortable fortune, that total reward."

"It wouldn't be comfortable for me," said Speedy. "I've never had blood money, and I never want to have any."

"But to give that money to Derrick's parents . . . isn't that almost rewarding vice?"

"There was no vice in the old people," Speedy contradicted. "The one good thing about poor Derrick, with all his murders and other crimes, was that he supported his old folks. They never knew what sort of a rascal their son was. Well, it would be a pity to undo the only good that Derrick had ever accomplished. So I took the money of the reward and bought a pair of annuities. They'll be comfortable till they die, at least."

"That was a fine thing to do," said the marshal. "A mighty fine thing, Speedy."

"Do you really think so? Well, I've had my reward for it."

"What sort of a reward, Speedy?"

The tramp took a thin wallet from an inner coat pocket and out of this pulled a slip of paper. "Here's the reward," he said.

The marshal read:

Dear Speedy:
   It may be life for me, or it may be the rope. Whatever it is, I'm the only man in jail in the whole country who's grateful to the fellow who caught him. You

*were too keen for me; you beat me fairly. And now
you've taken all the sting out of my failure. I have letters from my mother and father. They don't know
who has given them the annuities, but I was able to
guess. If there's ever blood on your hands, it isn't
mine. We are quits, and the debt is all on my side.
The best of luck to you! May you never be beaten till
the finish, and may you fall fighting hard. That's the
best I can wish you, I suppose. I won't be fool
enough to suspect you of ever settling down to a
musty, rusty life on a farm.*

> *Good-bye,*
> *Cliff Derrick*

The marshal handed back the slip of paper. "That's a
good letter to have," he said.

"I'd rather have it than a diploma," Speedy declared.

"Besides," said the marshal, "it means that all of Derrick's friends have been called off your trail."

"It means that, too," agreed Speedy.

"You're a queer lad, Speedy," said the officer. "I've
given up trying to understand you. But I'd like to know
this . . . will you take a permanent job in my department?
There wouldn't be any question of taking a regular office
job, you know. Your time would be your own. I can promise you high pay. You'd have a roving commission. You
could do no end of good, and you could have what you
and I both call a good time. There would be enough excitement every week to fill a year. How does the thing
sound to you? I've talked it over with the higher-ups, and
there's plenty of money available. I think I could get five
thousand a year for you, plus all sorts of expenses . . .
from clothes to guns to horses!"

"I've given up horses and taken to mules," Speedy said.

"I'm no rider, Tom. As for the work, hunting men is all very well, but there's something still more exciting."

"What's that?"

"Being hunted!"

Tom Gray sat up straighter in his chair. "The mischief," he murmured. "Is that your viewpoint, Speedy?"

"You know," said Speedy, "that some of us are dogs and some of us are cats."

"That open locked doors and walk through walls and do little tricks like that, eh?" said the marshal, smiling. "Well, I won't argue with you, Speedy. You always know your own mind. Anything serious on it, just now?"

"Levine," Speedy answered.

"I know Levine is on your mind," said the marshal. "Anything new about him?"

"He's passing counterfeit money."

The marshal whistled. "That's interesting to me," he said.

"We couldn't get him on a better thing," said Speedy. "The murders he buys would be too hard to hang on him. Twelve or fifteen years in prison would be the same as life to him."

"It would," agreed Gray. "Do you think we can catch him with the goods?"

"He passed a lot of the stuff to Joe Dale."

"There's another young man I'd like to put my hands on," said Gray.

"I'm sorry to hear that."

"Why?"

"Dale is going straight. He'll never do another crooked piece of work."

"What makes you so sure?"

"I can't tell you the reasons, but I'm sure."

"I'll try to believe it. But he has a past behind him."

"He's only a kid," Speedy said. "He's not grown up."

"And how old are you, Speedy?" asked the marshal, with another smile.

"I was born old," replied Speedy, with a certain sad gravity in his face and voice. "I'll never change. But Dale will. He's had enough of the crooks. He'll help to grab Levine, if you'll let him help. He can be concealed so you won't know him. Masked, even, if you'll let him."

"I'd rather catch Levine than twenty boys like Dale," agreed the marshal. "How can we go about it?"

"Dale and I hold up Levine in his office, make him open his safe, and then you walk into the middle of the robbery. Instead of taking the robbers, you haul the green goods out of the safe, and there's the testimony that will slam Levine into prison for the rest of his days."

"A federal marshal, a robbery, masked men, evidence at the point of a revolver, that would make a pretty story, Speedy."

"They won't break you for a job that puts Levine in jail," argued Speedy.

"When did you plan to do the job?"

"Tonight."

The marshal shrugged his shoulders. "This may cost me my job," he said, "but I think I'll tackle it. Are you starting right away?"

"In five minutes. Dale is waiting in the street."

"I'm with you, then," said the marshal. He stood up, drew a pair of guns, looked them over with a single glance, and made them disappear again. He walked to the wall and took his sombrero from a peg.

XIV
Looks Good to Sheriff

The office of Sid Levine, on this night, was dimly awash with the noises that rose from the different sections of the Grand Palace. The uproar from the bar was a deep rumbling; from the dance-hall section came the snarling of the music and the whispering of feet. Now and again, during the intermissions in the dancing and faintly accompanying the sounds from the bar, could be heard the voices in the gambling rooms, although these were always more subdued, being generally the singsong voice of a *croupier,* the dull murmur of the men laying their new bets or collecting their winnings. It was a veritable three-ringed circus that Sid Levine ran.

All of these noises, however, became subdued as they entered the office, and any sort of conversation was sufficient to drown out the disturbance beyond the walls. To Sid Levine, reclining in his heavy armchair, nursing a cigar in his fat lips, what he heard was a music more beautiful than a symphony of many strings. It meant to him the delicious murmurings of the river of gold that continually poured out of his crooked establishment into the deep pool of his pocket.

He could sit here for hours and see visions of greater delight. The time would come when Sunday Slough was drained of all its treasure, and then he would depart to other fields. But he would go with such experience and such capital that he could afford to start on the grandest scale. He saw clearly that the way to prosperity lies over a pathway with golden pavements and with still richer promises. He could afford to pay in gold; he could afford still better to pay with hopes that would never be fulfilled. When he considered the greatness of his winnings in the town of Sunday Slough and the small percentages that he had delivered over to his great helpers, One-Eyed Mike and Sheriff Buck Masters, he felt that he was a being especially set aside from the ordinary race of men.

He was rather annoyed when someone knocked at his door, and the voice of Buck Masters sounded immediately afterward. He felt that he had seen enough of Buck that day, but he realized that it would not do to deny entrance to the sheriff at any time. So he swept in front of himself one of the big ledgers on which he had been working, picked up a pen, and dipped it in the inkstand—all this before he called out to Masters to enter.

The sheriff came in and stamped once or twice to free his polished boots of the dust that had settled over them. His face was dark. He merely nodded at Levine, then went to the corner of the room, opened the drawer that contained the whiskey, and poured himself out a large dram. He tossed it off, smacked his lips, and then threw down a second full glass before he replaced the bottle, closed the drawer, and turned toward the expectant Levine.

The latter kept his expression placid. He detested this

bohemian familiarity. He loved to surround himself with a wall of dignity. As a matter of fact, he knew very well that he dared not offend the sheriff. Therefore, he maintained the expression of calm inquiry.

Buck Masters lowered himself into a chair with a grunt and a groan. It was a cold night, with a whistling wind thrusting through the flimsy walls of the building, a wind well iced from the snows of the mountains above the town. In the office a fire burned in the stove, its openmouthed grate dancing with yellow flames. Toward this the sheriff turned himself, eyeing Sid Levine over his right shoulder.

"Things look bad," the sheriff said finally.

"Bad? What way?" asked Sid Levine.

"Bad because of Speedy," said the sheriff.

"I'd like to see him burning up," Levine admitted. "That's all I wish for him, between you and me."

"You ain't telling me any secret," answered the sheriff. "That's all I'd wish for him, too."

"What's he done now?" asked Sid Levine.

"Ain't you heard about the fight in the hotel?"

"How would I hear about fights in the hotel?" asked Levine, frowning. "I don't have an ear in every quarter of the camp, you know. What fight?"

"Aw, there was a wild buck come down from the mountains, by the name of Crazy Dick. Mean as a pair of mountain lions and strong as a pair of mules. He started in and begun to make trouble with Speedy. But the kid started his magic tricks, they say. I dunno how he does it. He picked up Crazy Dick, which is a heavy weight, throwed him into the wall, and cleaned him up. Crazy Dick was knocked out, and the town went crazy. Right on top of that, there was a riot started in Chambers's place. . . ."

"I'm glad of that," said Levine.

"So'm I," said the sheriff. "I planned the whole job. I got a long-haired idiot of a 'puncher and badman to go in there and wreck the place. He had made a pretty good start, when the word gets to Speedy, and the crowd, they carry him down on their shoulders to see what he'll do with the second brawl. My gunman, the half-breed, he goes and turns into a yellow hound and stands like a lamb while Speedy takes his guns away and throws him into jail. I just had to go up there and turn the long hair loose. He looks kind of stunned, and you'd say that somebody had shot a bullet through his brain, except that I know there ain't any brain for a bullet to strike. But now the whole of Sunday Slough is boiling and humming with the praise of Speedy. There never was a man invented before he came along and showed what a real man had oughta be."

"Yeah?" growled Levine. "We gotta do something about that pup."

"We gotta do it quick," argued Buck. "It makes me sick to hear the way that the boys are talking. You'd think that Speedy was the prince of nowhere. They worship the ground that he walks on. He's got this town so much inside of his pocket that, when we try to break his hold on it, we're gonna sprain our wrists."

"I've heard that kind of talk before," answered the great Levine, "but talk, it don't make no kind of difference to me. What I wanna see is ways of taking the great man off his throne. Got any ways in mind?"

"There's Joe Dale," the sheriff put forth. "Maybe we'll hear something from him before very long."

"Yeah," said Levine. "Joe Dale is a man that might turn the trick. He ain't exactly my kind, but he's useful, maybe. It don't take a very big snake to kill a first-rate horse. Joe Dale might sneak a bullet into Speedy's frame. But what I don't understand is that all my boys carry guns and know how to use 'em, and this sneakin' rat of a tramp, he ain't ever carrying a gun himself. How d'you make out that he manages to handle 'em?"

"He's got 'em all buffaloed," suggested the sheriff. "They dunno where he's gonna hit 'em next. That's the only answer. They turn to stone the minute they see him, and there you are, old son. I'm gonna take a whirl at him myself."

Since the head of the sheriff was well turned away toward the fire, Levine treated himself to the luxury of a broad smile at this point. It was more of a sneer than a smile.

Then, at this moment, the sheriff said: "Levine, you handed out twenty-five thousand of green goods to that kid, Joe Dale. Look here, if that money is well made, I could pass sums of it myself."

The eyebrows of the great Levine rose to points. "You want to handle the stuff?" he asked.

"What's it worth?" asked Buck Masters. "I know some fellows who understand how to shove the queer into circulation."

"I'll sell it at twenty-five dollars a hundred," said Levine. "That's how good it is. It'll go anywhere. It'll go in a bank, if you have it mixed with a little real stuff. All that most of it needs is to be a little pocket-worn, to tell you the truth. Then it'll go in a bank."

"Is that so?" asked the sheriff sarcastically. "You'd have it all deposited, if it was good enough to go to a bank."

"I mean, to most banks. But why should I step out and take a chance? Anybody could go shopping with that stuff . . . that's how good it is. I've got it in the right sizes, and the paper is as good as the real stuff. Twenty-five a hundred is what I sell it for, and it's cheap at that. But I'll tell you what, Buck. To an old friend like you, I'd make it cheaper. I'll make it twenty dollars."

"Say fifteen, and I'll take a load of it," said the sheriff.

"Fifteen? I had to pay nearly fifteen for it," Levine lied with unction. "I want to see you rich, old son, but I don't want to go to the poorhouse."

"Call it eighteen dollars a hundred," said the sheriff. "Then, if the stuff really looks good to me, I'll take on a load of it."

"All right," said the great Levine. "There's a sample. There's a real fifty and there's a fake. You tell me which is which?"

Buck Masters sat down with the two bills that the gambler had taken out of his pocket. He studied them with care. It was some time before he exclaimed. "This is the phony one!"

"Yeah, that's the phony one," Levine confirmed.

"It's slick work, all right," Masters averred, stowing both the good bill and the counterfeit in his own pocket. "How much have you got of it?"

"I've got about eighty thousand dollars," Levine responded cheerfully.

"Eighty thousand dollars is good," said Masters. "If you had eight hundred thousand of this turkey, I could use it all. Shell it out, will you?"

Levine grunted as he rose and went to the safe. He could have cursed aloud, for he had not overlooked the way in which his fifty dollars had been palmed by the sheriff's absentmindedness. He knew, however, that he could not pay any attention to mere details like this. His "friendship" with Buck Masters was established upon altogether too high a plane for that. He counted out the packets of the counterfeit, eight, neat, tightly wadded packages in brown paper wrappings. "Eight of 'em," he said. "That cleans me out, and it's eighty thousand dollars."

The sheriff shrugged his shoulders. "I'll take your word for that," he said. He picked them up and dropped them in a side pocket of his coat. "I'll push these right into the market, chief," he added, and started for the door.

XV
The Open Stove

A distinct shade of reddish purple overspread the face of Levine as he saw the broad back of the sheriff turned toward him. Then he said: "Look here, brother. Hold on a minute, will you?"

"Yeah?" murmured the sheriff. He turned, with a casual expression, as he reached the door.

"You owe me," said Levine, "a trace under fifteen thousand bucks for that wad of the green goods."

The sheriff laughed; his laughter was not exactly natural in its ring. "Oh, that's all right," he said. "You know I'm good for this stuff, Sid."

"Oh, sure," said Levine. "I know you're good for it. But you know how it is. Better to be business-like. Sloppy business methods, they don't do anything but spoil friendships, is what my old man always used to tell me."

"He's the one that went to the pen for forgery, ain't he?" asked Buck Masters, more casual than ever.

Levine's purple turned to a darker shade. At last he said: "Look here, brother . . . fifteen thousand bucks is fifteen thousand bucks, or I'm a liar!"

"Yeah," Masters agreed, "money is money. But fifteen thousand, between you and me, is just small change, Sid. You know that. Oh, I'll tell you what, I'll give you my note for it. How's that? In thirty days, eh? Here you are!"

He sat down and scribbled the I.O.U. Levine looked on with his eyes starting from his head. It was true that he had paid only eight dollars a hundred for the phony money, but still it represented a very considerable outlay. A poison ran through the blood and brain of the gambler as he watched the pen carelessly wielded in the big fingers of Buck Masters. It was a worthless scrap of paper, he knew. He would never collect a penny from the sheriff, yet he saw that his hands were tied. No matter how utterly he distrusted the sheriff, he had to pretend that all was on a basis of perfect good faith between them. If he could have handled a thunderbolt at that moment, he would have launched it at the head of Buck Masters. However, he had to take the note, nod, and push it into his pocket.

Just then the knock and the voice of Mike were heard at the door, and his henchman came in. He seemed greatly excited.

"Joe Dale is out there at the back gate," he said. "He talks like he's drunk. Chief, he says that the job's done!"

All thought of the way the sheriff had beaten him out of so much money passed from the mind of the great Levine. He leaped to his feet, light as a boy of ten. "The job's done? That means that he's bumped off Speedy and . . . the town ain't heard a word about it yet?"

"Knife work, likely," the sheriff declared with a grim satisfaction. "That Joe Dale is sure a handy boy."

"I'll go bring him in," said One-Eyed Mike. "I just wanted to find out. . . ."

"Hold on," said Sid Levine. "What would he be wanting back here, anyway? Would he maybe 'ave found out . . . ?" He paused and exchanged eloquent glances with the sheriff.

The latter said: "Well, if he comes back with anything found out, you just made a mistake, brother. If the kid's bumped off, ain't it worth a real twenty-five thousand to us?"

The teeth of Levine showed as his fat upper lip lifted. "No matter what it's worth to us," he said, "it's me that will do the paying, ain't it?"

"Why," exclaimed Buck Masters, in the tone of one who was hurt, "that's as though we wasn't all in the same boat, sinking or floating together, and . . . !"

The door sagged softly open, making only a whispering sound, and through the open doorway came Deputy Sheriff of Sunday Slough Speedy, and with him a small fellow with broad shoulders and a black mask drawn over his face.

Speedy carried no weapon. He did not need to, since his bare hands were sufficient. But young Joe Dale, his companion, carried a big Colt of the most business-like appearance in either fist.

It was he who spoke, saying: "Back up, Mike. Turn your back to me, Masters, you big ham. Levine, shove up your hands. You vile skunk, I'm gonna show you something or other. Levine, get them hands up, and stand straight. Mike, I'm watchin' you. Turn your back while you got time."

"Joe, have you gone and double-crossed me?" Levine asked. "Have you gone and done that, Joe?"

There was real sadness in his voice. But Joe Dale answered: "You green-goods bum, you dirty hound, you talk about double-crossing, do you?"

The fat man, suddenly brazen, shrugged his shoulders. "Speedy pointed it out to you, did he?"

"He pointed it out," Joe Dale affirmed. "Unbuckle your gun belts, Mike and Buck Masters! Unbuckle 'em, and let the guns fall."

"I got a pair of hair-trigger babies that may explode when they hit the floor," said the sheriff.

"I hope they do," said Joe Dale. "I hope that they blow a leg off for you."

Each of the men obeyed the command. The two heavy gun belts dropped to the floor.

Levine was saying: "Look what a gang of saps and thick-heads I've got working for me. They send you running on an errand, Mike, and then they come on marching down the hall and walk right in on us and get us off guard. What good are you, Mike Doloroso? What good are you, Masters? You're a pair of four-flushers, is all that you are. And I been wasting damned good money on you all this while. That's what I been doing." He groaned as he spoke the last words. His haunted eyes glanced toward the open face of the safe. It was as though his soul were standing naked under the eyes of enemies.

"Now, boys," went on Levine, "we'll come to an understanding. I know what you want. You wanna shake me down. That's all right. I know that the young hopes of the world, they gotta rise and grow and prosper. I don't mind a stiff one, boys. But let's get down to business. Whatcha want out of me?"

Speedy spoke now for the first time: "We want a little quiet, Sid. Keep your fat mouth shut for a while, will you?" Then he sat down on the edge of Levine's desk.

The fat man faced them. The other two stood still, with their faces turned toward the wall, and their hands well above their heads.

"My arms are droppin' off at the shoulder," said One-

Eyed Mike. "How long are you gonna keep up this crazy gag on us, Speedy?"

"I ought to feed you in chunks into that fire," Speedy said cheerfully, "but I'm holding my hand a little. There's somebody else coming in here to have a look at you boys. Don't touch that bell, Sid. If you do, I'll tear you apart. You understand?"

Levine licked his thick lips. There was no color in his face except for those lips. They were an ashen purple.

"Who's coming, Speedy," he asked, lowering his voice to a whisper.

A quick step approached down the hall.

"Federal Marshal Thomas Gray," he said.

Through the door came Tom Gray in person.

The three men wilted.

It was Levine, of course, who spoke first, gasping: "Marshal Gray, thank goodness, you've got here. The deputy sheriff of this here county and a masked blackguard . . . we think he's Joe Dale, the famous criminal . . . have held us up at the point of a gun."

"Then you'd better keep in place and stand still," said the marshal. "If somebody has you under a gun, it's better to be quiet."

"Gray," groaned Levine, "are you gonna stand by and see a hold-up, a masked man . . . ?"

"I don't see a masked man," said the marshal, turning his back upon Joe Dale. "Speedy, what are you finding?"

For Speedy was on his knees in front of the open safe, and, taking out drawer after drawer, he ran swiftly through them. Papers, account books, bundles of money, trays of silver and gold, a considerable mass of gold nuggets and dust, and finally, tied in a chamois bag, a whole mass of jewelry of all sorts, but chiefly unset stones. Many a story must have lain behind that collection of jewels. The sight of them caused sweat to pour down the face of the great Levine.

"I see what it is," he said. "It's a plot. Gray, you're gonna be busted. You're gonna be run out of the county. I'll never stop till I've got you behind the bars. You understand that?"

Speedy rose from the heap of drawers that he had taken from the safe. "What I want isn't here," he said. "I'll fan them, and see what I find."

Sheriff Buck Masters suddenly turned from the wall. "Gray," he said, "I'm the sheriff. I call on you as a sworn officer of the law. . . ." He strode forward from the wall as he spoke, and, passing the open mouth of the stove, his hand dipped into his coat pocket and cast a considerable package into the flames.

Speedy was on it instantly. A pair of tongs stood by the stove, and, reaching into it with them, he pulled out the packages, while the brown paper wrappings were still blackening and burning, but with the contents almost entirely uninjured. "These came out of Masters's pocket," he said. "Levine has passed on the rest of his stuff, I suppose. Here, Tom. Take a look at this, will you?"

The marshal received the packages, while silence deep as death fell on the room. From a brief examination, he looked up with a smile. "Good stuff, Buck," he said. "Almost good enough to be real. This will mean about fifteen years for you."

XVI
Ending in Smoke

The consternation of Buck Masters was great. He looked, however, not at Speedy or the federal officer, but straight at his business associate, the great Levine.

The massive head of the latter nodded so deeply that the heavy folds of his double chin swayed forward, as he said: "This is a plant on you, Buck. No crooked marshal and thug of a bribed deputy are gonna work any deal on you. You got friends, Buck. Don't you go and forget it."

"Joe," Speedy said to the gunman, "you've turned the trick in grand style. Now fade out of here. You know where Pier Morgan was cached away in the hills. Go up there and I'll meet you, sometime tomorrow. I think that you've cracked the whole Levine gang wide open. You'll get a reward for it."

Joe Dale answered slowly and softly: "I got my reward already, if you think that I've done this right. So long, Speedy. The next time you want me, I'll be ready and under your feet." He disappeared through the doorway, closing the door gently behind him.

287

No gun showed in the hand of the marshal. But the disarmed trio knew his reputation too well to attempt an attack upon him, to say nothing of Sunday Slough's bit of domesticated lightning, Speedy. They stood gloomily about, biting their lips, herded together, shoulder-to-shoulder, by mutual danger.

The marshal was saying to Masters: "Buck, this thing is likely to go pretty hard on you. The federal courts are pretty mean to counterfeiters, Buck. You'll spend the cream of your life in jail. Maybe all of it for this . . . partly because you've handled the stuff, and partly because you're a police officer. That makes a double count against you and a mighty black one."

"He's bluffing," Levine blurted out. "The fact is that they ain't got anything on you. They got some counterfeit dough off of you, they say. That's nothing. That's the stuff that you picked up in the execution of your duty as a sheriff of this county. What of that?"

"Yeah, that's what it was," Buck Masters announced, his great jaw thrusting forward like a bulldog's as he saw the possible line of defense opening before him. "All you got off of me is evidence that I collected myself for testimony ag'in' crooks."

"So you threw the stuff in the fire when the pinch came, was that it?" asked Thomas Gray.

The big mouth of Masters opened, but it shut again, with no more sound than the *click* of his teeth. He was silenced, utterly.

Levine put in calmly: "Don't you do no talking, Buck. Let a smart lawyer do your thinking for you from now on. I know the man for you, and I know where the money'll be had for paying him. You stop worrying, and let others worry for you. They're gonna wish that they grabbed handfuls of fire before they touched you, Buck."

The arched chest of Buck collapsed as he sighed with relief.

"You know, Tom," Speedy said, "it isn't Buck that we want so badly."

The marshal nodded and said: "You're under arrest, Masters. What you say may be used against you. But I can tell you now, that we know where you got that money. If you'll tell us who passed it to you, I can promise you an easy trial and a light sentence. I might pass it off for state's evidence and get you off scot-free. You understand?"

"I understand," said the other slowly.

"Well, then," said the marshal, "talk out, man. You have anywhere between twelve and thirty years ahead of you on the two counts."

Big Buck Masters stared at Levine for the answer.

"Listen to me, Buck . . . ," Levine began.

Speedy tapped the fat man on the arm. "The first thing you know, Levine," he said, "you'll be resisting arrest or some such thing. I wouldn't talk, if I were you."

The *purr* of his voice sent a shudder through Sid Levine. He sagged backward against the wall, and stood there stunned.

The marshal went on: "Speak out, Masters! What you say now will have double weight. We know where you got that stuff. But it has to come from you before we can make an arrest. You're not going to jail and let this big swine get away free, are you? He tells you that he'll get you off with a smart lawyer. I tell you, when the federal courts lay hands on a case like this, they go to the bottom of it. They slam a man hard. Money won't save you. But if you turn state's evidence . . ." He paused. Sheer excitement forced from the throat of One-Eyed Mike a gagging sound, like that of a man choking to death.

289

Buck Masters turned his heavy head from side to side like a bull at bay. He stared at the hard eye of the marshal—hard, but honest, the eye of a man who would do what he said. He looked at the almost femininely beautiful face of Speedy, now decorated with a faint smile of contented interest. He stared again, at the countenance of Sid Levine. Then he blinked. "Ten to thirty years, it's a lot," he muttered. "It's life, that's what it is."

Sid Levine started to speak, but the narrow forefinger of Speedy rose in caution. The fat man was silent, with no more than a gasp.

Then Buck Masters shook his head. "You birds can do what you please," he growled. "I ain't gonna give you no information. You want me to squeal on somebody. There ain't nobody to squeal on. That's final. You won't pry no more words out of me, not even with a crowbar. Not till I've talked to a lawyer."

Levine almost fainted with relief. "Buck," he muttered, "I always knew that you was a man. I knew it from the very first time that I ever laid eyes on you."

The marshal hesitated. Then, staring at Levine, he said: "Speedy, I hate to think of you remaining in this town with fat-faced Levine, the pig, still at liberty to buy the cutting of your throat. I'm sorry about it. I'm mighty sorry. But maybe we'll get our hands on Levine, too, before the case is over. Anyway, we've wrecked his gang or, rather, you have. You've cut Derrick away from his side. You've taken Buck Masters now. There's no one but a fool, in this world, who'll trust Levine or play with him any more. He's lost everything that he built up in Sunday Slough. He'll be a joke from now on. I wanted to throw him in jail. But perhaps it's better this way. He'll have to stew in his own juice. I can't wish him any worse luck. He'll have the last of the seven-day men camping on his trail. Come along, Masters. You, too, Mike. I want to question you."

He took the two from the room and, behind him, left Speedy and the great Levine, standing face-to-face.

It was Levine who moved first, and, with his eyes straining blindly from his head, with his great, bulky arms stretched out before him, he tottered across the floor with the look of a man about to die. Even the open face of the safe was disregarded, and, reaching the door, he turned slowly down the hallway.

Speedy made a cigarette and sat down before the cozy open fire to smoke it.

MAX BRAND®

JOKERS EXTRA WILD

Anyone making a living on the rough frontier took a bit of a gamble, but no Western writer knows how to up the ante like Max Brand. In "Speedy—Deputy," the title character racks up big winnings on the roulette wheel, but that won't help him when he's named deputy sheriff—a job where no one's lasted more than a week. "Satan's Gun Rider" continues the adventures of the infamous Sleeper, whose name belies his ability to bury a knife to the hilt with just a flick of his wrist. And in the title story, a professional gambler inherits a ring that lands him in a world of trouble.

MAX BRAND®

THE BRIGHT FACE OF DANGER

Through the years, James Geraldi has proven to be one of Max Brand's most exciting and enduring characters, and this volume contains three of his greatest exploits. Geraldi has been dubbed the "Frigate Bird" because of his habit of stealing from thieves, and Edgar Asprey knows just how apt the name is. Geraldi once prevented Asprey from swindling his family out of a fortune, and managed to get rich doing it. That's exactly why Asprey now wants to form an alliance with him. Asprey has his eye on a rare, invaluable treasure, and he knows no one stands a better chance of stealing it than his old enemy, the Frigate Bird.

LOUIS L'AMOUR
THE SIXTH SHOTGUN

No writer is associated more closely with the American West than Louis L'Amour. Collected here are two of his most exciting works, in their original forms. The title story, a tale of stagecoach robbery and frontier justice, is finally available in its full-length version. Similarly, the short novel included in this volume, *The Rider of the Ruby Hills*, one of L'Amour's greatest range war novels, was published first in a magazine, then expanded by the author into a longer version years later. Here is a chance to experience the novel as it appeared in its debut, as L'Amour originally wrote it.

Dorchester Publishing Co., Inc.
P.O. Box 6640
Wayne, PA 19087-8640

5580-5
$6.99 US/$8.99 CAN